Girl Jacked

A Detective Jack Stratton Novel

Christopher Greyson

Greyson Media

GIRL JACKED

Novels featuring Jack Stratton in order:
GIRL JACKED
JACK KNIFED
JACKS ARE WILD
JACK AND THE GIANT KILLER
DATA JACK
and coming soon...
JACK OF HEARTS

Copyright: Christopher Greyson
Published: August 1st 2013

Find out more about the author and upcoming books online at
www.ChristopherGreyson.com

CONTENTS

CHAPTER ONE

The Boar's Butt

"Jack?" The dispatcher's voice crackled over the radio.

"Copy."

"We got a ten-ten in progress at the Boar's Butt." The Boar's Butt was a local bar and pizza joint that mainly catered to the same crowd of rowdy guys. Jack always laughed at the name.

"Any other info?" Jack swung the car around and hit the lights.

"Bartender called it in. No other details. Backup is going to be delayed. What's your ETA?"

"Ten minutes." Jack grinned.

"Ten-four."

The smile on his face grew as the car's speed increased. Jack loved driving fast and relished this perk of law enforcement. As he raced to the opposite side of town, he looked down at the clock: 11:35 p.m. There wasn't another car on the road in Darrington County. The sleepy backwater community had little to offer in excitement and nightlife.

As he sped down the deserted streets, Jack felt alive. The leather creaked as he gripped the steering wheel and settled back into the seat. He always drove the refitted Charger when he went out on patrol; its V8 engine with 368 horsepower and 395 pounds of torque roared to life. He loved this car.

The other cops knew Jack had practically claimed it as his own. To Jack, the car did belong to him, which was why he'd almost gotten into a fistfight with Billy Murphy when someone saw Murphy doing doughnuts with it in a deserted parking lot.

Jack cut down a side road that ran straight for a mile. He pinned the gas pedal flat to the floor, and the Hemi roared with pleasure at its freedom. A rush of adrenaline surged through him as telephone poles whizzed by at the speed of light. Keeping his hands slightly loose on the steering wheel, he made minor corrections. All too soon, he neared the end of the street and had to slow down, his momentary escapism ended.

A minute later, Jack killed the lights and rolled into the bar's parking lot. Jack had a knack for getting into trouble, so he decided to angle the Charger so it pointed toward the woods and not toward the front of the bar. He was already in enough hot water with Sheriff Collins. No need for the dash cam footage to end up on his desk.

There were less than a dozen cars and trucks parked outside. He scanned them quickly. Two stood out: an old Chevy Super Sport and an enormous red Timberline work truck. Jack knew the guy who owned the Chevy had an attitude. Jack had pulled him over a couple of times. He fancied himself a tough guy and a ladies' man. Jack didn't think he was either.

The Timberline truck meant he'd find other lumberjacks inside. After three years of being a police officer—and his tour of duty in Iraq—Jack had seen some tough guys, but a lumberjack made his short list of guys he didn't *want* to fight.

He grabbed a backup set of cuffs and jumped out. Instinctively, he reached back in and snagged his hat. They taught you at the academy how to use something as simple as a hat for crowd control—from the gold shield on top, to the trick of angling your head to hide your eyes. He ran his fingers through his dark brown hair, before he pulled the hat down a little lower than usual.

It's a fight. Crowd control: investigate, intimidate, dissipate.

He climbed the steps that led to the outside deck of the bar and made sure not to touch the railing. Made out of two-inch rusted plumbing pipe screwed directly onto the porch, the thick railing turned the palm of your hand an instant rusty orange if you touched it.

Jack pushed the heavy wooden door in as a young couple hurried out. Jack noticed the door had a similar heavy pipe for a handle. He tested it as he held open the door for them.

"Thank you, Officer." The man nervously looked over his shoulder back into the bar as he prodded his girlfriend to move faster. She flashed a smile at Jack. The guy hustled her down the steps.

Jack was a good-looking guy, definitely not a pretty boy, but he never had to work too hard to attract girls.

As Jack walked through the door, he scanned the room. The entire restaurant was a large and open area with a kitchen at the back. There were booths against the wall and next to them were five large tables, each covered with a checkered red and white vinyl tablecloth. Dwight Yoakam's version of "Little Sister" played over the jukebox. The smell of pizza and beer filled the air. On the opposite wall was a long serving bar with a dozen stools. Jammed into the corners were two pinball machines and a jukebox. They had painted the brown floor so many times it was hard to tell it was wood.

Calling the Boar's Butt a restaurant was a stretch. It served a few different types of pizza. If you asked for an appetizer, the waitress pushed a bowl of popcorn closer to you. They served beer, hard liquor, and cheap wine for the rare girl who dared to ask.

Jack could see the problem the moment he walked in the door. No one could miss the three drunken lumberjacks in the back laughing.

Figures. Paul Bunyans. Wonderful.

None of the men stood less than six feet, and one was a giant of a man— three hundred pounds easy.

Jack cracked his neck and rolled his shoulders. At six one and a hundred ninety-five pounds, he could intimidate most guys, but that wouldn't work with these three.

The bartender, a big guy with a round belly, ran over to Jack. He looked pale. "I didn't serve them. They showed up stewed. They said they ain't leaving without a drink."

Jack nodded.

"These same guys were here last season. They smashed the place up when the owner kicked them out."

"Okay, thanks."

Jack looked around at the other people in the room. Some stared at him blankly. Others just peeked up. A few even smiled. The one emotion that they all seemed to share, though, was hope. Jack looked down at his badge.

They expect me to handle it. That's what cops do. We come and bring the peace.

As an uncomfortable silence settled over the bar, the three men stopped laughing and turned to look at Jack. The bartender swallowed and moved away. Jack noticed a nine-inch hunting knife in the giant's hand.

Backup is going to be delayed, Jack cautioned himself.

"Hello, Officer," the drunken goliath hollered out. "We're just playing darts." He looked at his buddies. "They didn't have any, so we had to use our own." He laughed and launched the blade across the room at the tattered dartboard. The knife hit with a thump. The three men cheered wildly.

"Are you here for a game?" mocked the tough guy who owned the Chevy.

Jack glanced at the wall and saw two other knives sticking out.

Both missed.

He scanned the hands of the lumberjacks. Empty. Jack knew he needed to get them outside, away from everyone else.

"Can I have your attention?" Jack's voice was calm as he held up his hands. He didn't have to shout. Everyone was already looking at him. "Would the owner of a red pickup truck please come to the front of the building?"

"Why?" one of the lumberjacks asked with a sneer. He put his hands behind his head and leaned back.

Jack lowered his arms. "Because their truck is on fire."

The three lumberjacks looked at one another in bewilderment and then scrambled for the front door. The smallest of the three reached it first. He yanked it open, and the giant pushed him aside. Jack let the monster pass by. Then the tough guy charged through, leaving the small guy holding the door.

Perfect.

As the last man stepped outside, Jack's hand flashed like lightning. He slapped one-half of the handcuffs over the man's wrist and the other end onto the pipe handle on the outside of the door. The lumberjack's mouth flopped open.

As the second guy started down the deck stairs, Jack yelled, "Watch your step."

In his drunken stupor, the man panicked and grabbed for the railing. While he looked down, Jack dashed up behind him, snapped one end of the handcuffs to the pipe railing and the other onto the man's thick wrist. Jack was relieved when he heard it click into place.

Two down—one to go.

The giant stopped in the middle of the parking lot. He looked at his truck. "It's not on fire." He turned to Jack. "It's fine, dammit."

His confused look quickly turned to anger when he saw that his friends were handcuffed. He crouched slightly and prepared to charge. "You stopped my dart game," he slurred. "I'm gonna stomp you." The hulking man rushed forward.

Jack stepped to the right, and his forearm crashed into the side of the man's head. He grabbed the stunned man by his collar and belt.

This is gonna hurt.

Jack pulled the guy against his leg, twisted his body, and pivoted his hip. He lifted the three hundred pounds into the air. Both men groaned. The lumberjack's feet went straight up. Jack's back strained as he supported the man's weight. As the lumberjack reached the pinnacle of the flip, Jack stepped aside. His adrenaline rush, pushed into overdrive, caused everything to slow. The man seemed to hang in the air like a basketball player whose slam-dunk had gone terribly wrong. The judo flip that Jack used could be finished in one of three ways. He could let him fall to the ground. He could try to support some of the man's weight and soften the impact. Or he could push him down and increase the force that his body would suffer as he collided against the asphalt. Jack stepped aside and let him crash to the ground. He landed flat on his back with a thud. An explosive groan burst from the man's mouth as all of the air in his lungs blasted out.

Jack flexed his shoulders and took a deep breath. The man's mouth opened and closed like a fish out of water as he gasped for air. Jack took a step forward and leaned over the man. "I'm sorry, sir. It seems you tripped. You're okay, right?" Using a little Jedi mind trick, Jack nodded his head up and down.

The lumberjack on the ground winced.

"You're going to leave now, and everything will be fine." He waved his hand like Obi-wan. "If you give me any lip, I'll take the three of you in right now."

The large man nodded his head.

Jack tried to look menacing as he walked over to the other lumberjacks still handcuffed to the porch. They'd remained silent as they watched the scene unfold. The tough guy, who no longer looked tough, held his free hand up. "We'll go. We're sorry. We'll go now," the man babbled.

A slight smirk flashed across Jack's face. *He's surrendering. Cool.*

After Jack set him free, he hurried to his friend on the ground.

Jack crossed his arms and furrowed his brow at the last one who stood cuffed to the door.

"Sorry," the man sheepishly muttered as he looked at his feet.

Take out the big guy and the little ones fall into line.

"How many drinks have you had?" Jack unlocked the cuff.

"Two, sir."

"You're the designated driver. Got it?"

"Yes. Thank you, Officer." The man kept looking back over his shoulder at Jack as he rushed to his friends.

The men helped the giant lumberjack to the truck as another police car, with lights flashing, skidded to a stop in the parking lot. All three nervously looked back at Jack. He waved them on. Jack held up his other hand and gestured to Officer Kendra Darcey as she jumped out of her cruiser.

Kendra carried her shotgun in her right hand and came over to Jack. He gave her a quick nod to let her know everything was under control. Both of them watched the red truck slowly pull out of the parking lot.

She turned and frowned at him. "I missed it?"

Jack stood on the top step and looked down at the twenty-four-year-old rookie police officer. Kendra was an all-around athlete and an adrenaline junkie; she loved the outdoors and being on the go.

He tilted his head. "If I had known you were on tonight, I'd have left one for you."

"Yeah, right." She smiled. "If you're all set, then I'll let *you* handle the paperwork." She rested the shotgun on her hip. She had her blonde hair pulled back in a ponytail and when she smiled, her blue eyes flashed. A four-inch scar ran from the corner of her chin to her eyebrow. She was beautiful in spite of the scar. Few people knew how she got it, and Jack was one of them. While she walked her enormous Labrador retriever, the dog spotted a coyote and took off after it. The retractable leash snapped and caught her in the face. The rope burn never healed quite right. The truth wasn't the kind of story that earned a rookie cop respect. When she told Jack she got it in a fight with four guys during a bust, he knew it was a lie right away. He called her on it, but he also gave her an alternative version. One guy and a broken bottle. They became good friends after that.

"I was hoping you'd volunteer to fill out the forms for the both of us?" Jack walked down the stairs and leaned in close to her.

Kendra laughed. "Don't go flashing those baby browns at me, Jack. I'm not one of your girlfriends."

Jack knew she was teasing him. They were friends, and Jack wanted to keep it that way. He also knew that *friends* could easily change into something more. He'd had enough problems with ex-girlfriends to know he didn't need one at work.

"You riding solo?" He changed the subject.

She lifted her chin. "Collins thinks I can handle things by myself now."

Jack raised an eyebrow. "Really?"

"And…Donald called in sick." She blushed.

"Don't rush solo. Maybe we can team up again soon." Jack winked and headed up the steps. "I have to go back in and talk to the bartender. Thanks for the backup."

She lingered as she watched him go. "I'll watch your backside anytime," she joked before she headed to her cruiser.

Jack wrapped up the interview in the bar as quickly as he could. It was easy, because no one wanted to press charges. After he finished, he walked back to his cruiser and made a mental note: *Buy some extra-large handcuffs.*

He muddled through the monotonous paperwork at the station. When he glanced at the clock, he grinned, glad he'd be home before two a.m. He finished his shift, thinking about the night's events, and then headed to his car with a smile still clinging to his face.

CHAPTER TWO

You Suck

Jack walked into his apartment and stopped short. His girlfriend Gina, probably just back from some bar, stood in the middle of his crappy living room with her hands on her hips. Four-inch heels, tiny miniskirt, silk top opened low to show off her cleavage, fake fur jacket hugging her waist, a mane of blonde hair—all topped off by shiny ruby-red lips. She could have been the cover girl on any hot-rod magazine, but as it was, she worked at the beauty salon two blocks down.

She threw her head back and burst into fake tears. "You suck!" She stormed off. The echoes from the slammed door blended with the shudder that rippled along the paper-thin walls. Jack tossed his keys onto the kitchen counter.

Anniversary, birthday, some promise… He ran down a list of possible screw-ups he could have made, but drew a blank. *I haven't been on a bender in a long while, so it's not that. I'd never cheat. Take that off the list. Caught in a lie? You have to talk for that to happen, and Gina wasn't much for conversation. Talking wasn't quite why they were together anyway.*

He replayed the events of the last two minutes in his head. No bags. Pocketbook, but no bags. She might be back.

Jack shrugged and walked over to the refrigerator. His reflection brought him up short. *Stupid mirror. Who puts a mirror on a refrigerator? Gina. She said it would help her lose weight. She likes to eat, but she isn't fat.*

As he looked at his reflection, his brown eyes became darker. "Way to go, Jack. Another one gone."

He was twenty-six, but he felt older. Miles, too many miles and they were hard. After he got back from Iraq, he tried a round robin of vices to kill his pain: Drinking, smoking, and he couldn't remember the last vegetable he ate. Too little sleep and too much work…it wasn't a shock that he looked rough. Gina dug that type of guy. She said it made him look dangerous.

Jack frowned. *Well, she might come back…no bags.*

She'd stormed out several times before over the last few months, but each time she'd returned. When she had, she was wild. His smile broadened into a full grin as he thought about how they'd trashed the bedroom the last time.

He opened the fridge and his smile disappeared, along with any hope for food. The only things on the top two shelves were dried spots where something long ago had spilled and an empty bottle of spiced rum. He figured there would be leftovers or something, but there were only a couple of open cans and some condiments. Gina wasn't much for keeping a well-stocked kitchen, and he wasn't much for keeping the rum bottle full.

Now he was hungry, tired, and it was the middle of the night. He debated going out to pick something up when he saw the front door was open. It wasn't the first time it had rebounded from Gina slamming it. "Stupid lock." No way was Jack going to ask the landlady to get it fixed again. She was mad enough the last time it got broken.

Jack trudged over to the door. It may have been due to the frequent slamming, but now you had to jiggle the handle for the front door to latch. He fiddled with the knob and pushed at the latch until it popped back out. He yawned, shut the door, turned around, and then—shrieked.

"You squeal like a baby." She laughed.

Jack's mouth fell open. He'd seen a lot in his life and thought he was beyond instant shock, but all of his training went out the window as he gawked at the pretty, woman who stood in his living room wearing nothing but a towel.

She moved closer. "You got nothing to eat and—"

"What the hell?" Jack grabbed the unknown woman by the arm, pushed her out the front door into the hallway and slammed the door behind her.

BANG! BANG! The walls shook. BANG!

Dammit! She must be slamming her whole body against the door.

Jack panicked when he thought about what would happen if someone found a young half-naked woman outside his apartment. When he yanked the door open, she charged headlong into the living room. She tripped and sprawled out across the floor.

Crap!

He heard loud stomping feet come down the hallway.

Oh no…just what I need.

He peeked out the door and saw his extraordinarily large landlady storm down the corridor. Dressed in her flannel nightgown, her face flushed bright red. He ducked back inside and locked the door. A few seconds later, the thuds came to an audible stop just outside.

KNOCK! KNOCK! KNOCK!

The young woman scrambled to her feet and wrapped the towel around herself. "You suck," she growled as she shoved both hands into his chest.

Caught off guard, Jack staggered back from the blow and crashed into the wall.

"Mr. Stratton, what is going on in there?" Mrs. Stevens continued to beat on the door. "Was that a girl in the hallway?"

"What's your problem?" the young woman demanded.

Jack was at a loss for words.

She shot an angry glare at him while his landlady huffed and puffed just outside the door.

"That's it, Mr. Stratton. *That is it!* You'll be evicted this time." Mrs. Stevens stomped back down the hallway.

Jack tried to keep his eyes on her face as he held his hand sideways in an attempt to block his view of everything else. Her shoulder-length dark brown hair was dripping wet, but it was her piercing eyes that grabbed his full attention: emerald green with flecks of gold.

Jack blinked and focused. "Who are you and why are you in my apartment?"

She adjusted the towel. "You don't remember me? I'm Chandler's sister." She stood defiant before him.

Jack laughed. "Michelle is his sister."

"So am I." Her hands tightened into fists.

Jack opened and then closed his mouth. There was a girl at the foster home…after Jack had been adopted, he did remember a girl who'd worn her hair in a ponytail on top of her head and was always following Chandler and him around whenever he came back for a visit. He'd moved out a few years before Aunt Haddie took the girl in. She must have been ten or eleven. That would make her at least nineteen now.

"Replacement?" He said her nickname out loud as he tried to reconcile his memories of her then with the young woman who stood before him now.

She looked at him with an expression that said, *"Yes, stupid."*

He could hear his best friend Chandler say: "Leave it to my Aunt Haddie. We're the only poor black family that goes and adopts a white kid."

His pleasant recollection of his friend faded when his memories changed. *Chandler's dead. Died in Iraq.*

Jack turned away.

Replacement stood there and glared at him.

Jack sighed. "Sorry. I forgot your name."

"Sure. Jerk," she spat.

Her tone forced him to turn around. A pair of blazing eyes ripped into him. Jack shook his head. "Wait a minute. Why are you here—"

"Hold on." She turned and went into the bedroom. "I need to get dressed." She slammed the door.

Jack's eyes narrowed. Now he had a headache.

Chandler had been his best friend since elementary school, but he could barely remember Replacement. Chandler and he were about to graduate from high school when Aunt Haddie brought her home from church one day. Jack couldn't recollect the whole story of why Chandler suggested the name or why Replacement preferred to be called that. It had something to do with her wanting to forget her abused past but Jack couldn't recall why. All he remembered was she loved it so much, the nickname stuck.

Jack was seventeen and in high school, but whenever he visited Aunt Haddie's, the girl followed him around like a lovesick puppy. He had lived with them for several years, so he always viewed Chandler and Michelle like a real brother and sister, but with Replacement it was different. To Jack, she was just one of the many other foster kids who came and went through the house after him.

He wondered why she was here or whether there was something wrong with Aunt Haddie. Haddie Williams had been Jack's foster mother for four years before he was adopted. He could never forget the big black woman's bright smile and sparkling eyes. She wasn't his or anybody's real aunt, but everybody called her that. She'd taken Jack in and loved him when he needed it most.

Jack walked to the bedroom door. Right before he was about to knock, it opened.

Replacement put her hands on her hips. She wore a green and white dress that looked familiar. It was too long for her petite, five-foot-four frame. She still looked peeved but at least she was decent.

Jack tried not to make a face. "Why are you here?"

"Aunt Haddie sent me. She needs your help."

Guilt washed over him.

Jack knew he should have gone to see her. He'd been back in the area for over six months now, but he hesitated. His memories of Chandler were still too raw.

"Aunt Haddie was your foster mother. She took care of you," Replacement continued, "and she said that you'd help." She stuck her chin out.

Jack held his hands up. "I'll try. What's she need help with, kid?"

Her knee bounced and her eyes searched the room behind him as if she was trying to figure out how to deliver the news. "Michelle is gone. She's missing."

The words were like a kick in the gut. Michelle was Jack's foster sister and friend. Chandler and Michelle, who were biological brother and sister, were at Aunt Haddie's when he had arrived. The three of them had quickly become inseparable, like the Three Musketeers. They treated him like a brother. Even after Jack had been adopted and he moved to his new parents' house, they'd stayed close.

He'd always felt guilty that he'd been adopted, but they never had been. Part of that was because they were brother and sister, and they refused to let anyone separate them. It was hard enough to place one older kid, but to place two kids into one home was nearly impossible.

He also knew that part of it was because they were black, and he was white. Jack hated that fact, but he could see it in the eyes of many of the couples who came by to adopt. Some beat around the bush, but you could tell they really wanted a little white kid.

Jack's back stiffened. "Gone? What do you mean, gone?"

He took a step closer to her. The hair on the back of his neck rose and his chest tightened.

"We haven't heard from her in over two weeks. She got accepted at White Rocks Eastern College, and then—I tried going up there, but when we went to the police—"

She was like an engine that revved too high and then sputtered out. Her eyes welled up with tears.

Jack's heart pounded. He forced himself to breathe. "Wait a second." He held up a hand as if he were directing traffic. "Michelle has to be…what, twenty-four? Why was she going to White Rocks Eastern College?"

"She always wanted to go to college, but she couldn't afford it. She got a work scholarship. It was her first year. She didn't come home and—"

"Calm down. What day was she supposed to come home?" Jack coaxed.

"Four days before Christmas."

"Okay. When you went to the police, what did they tell you?"

"They investigated it and said she transferred to Western Tech out in California and just left. She wouldn't do that. She wouldn't just—go." She threw her hands up. "She just started and had a full scholarship. Why would she leave?"

"Did she ever talk to you about transferring?"

Replacement stamped her foot. "She didn't. After Chandler died, do you think she'd just take off to the other side of the country without telling anyone?

Do you think she could do that to Aunt Haddie? Do you honestly think *Michelle* would just leave and not tell her?" Her voice trembled.

Michelle was just like Chandler and to them, family was everything. There had to be another reason. "Why do you think I can help?" Jack walked toward the kitchen.

"Who says I do?" She raised her head; her eyes blazed once more. "Aunt Haddie does. She says you're a cop. She still thinks of you as family. You were Chandler's best friend, for whatever that's worth."

He let that slight go; he knew he deserved it. "Who's handling the case?"

Jack was a third-year deputy. He'd transferred to Darrington a little over six months ago. Cops with a few years under their belt didn't get missing person cases; they were the gophers for the detectives who did.

"Aunt Haddie filed a missing persons report in the Fairfield County's sheriff's office. They said they asked someone over here to look into her last known address. They said his name's Gaven…Daven…"

"Davenport," Jack said.

Joe Davenport was an older detective in Darrington. He had a few years to go until he retired. Jack thought he was coasting to the finish line. Joe wasn't a bad guy, but he was far more interested in fishing than police work.

Still, it was a missing person case involving the college. He must have given it a solid going-over.

"If Joe—"

"I knew it. I knew it. You don't care!" She pushed him again. "You don't give a flying—"

"Shut up. Just shut up for a minute." Now it was Jack's turn to be irate. He towered over her when he stood upright. He put his face right down in hers. "Now, you listen."

"Listen to what?"

He leaned in. Normally women didn't tick Jack off, even when they were screeching at him, but this one did. Jack couldn't believe it when she stuck her head forward closer to his. Her lips quivered, not out of fear, but with fury. They stared at each other, nose to nose, like two prizefighters waiting for the bell. He closed his eyes for a second, but he could still feel her glaring at him. "I need to think. It's two in the morning, the college is closed, and I just got home. I'm taking a shower." He turned and walked to the bedroom. "We'll talk when I'm out."

Although Jack wanted to, he forced himself not to slam the door.

CHAPTER THREE

Drama Queen

Jack stood under the shower, lost in the water. The giant hot water tank was the best thing about the apartment, and it was included in the rent. After it started to run ice-cold, he shut the water off and got out. Steam filled the small bathroom and created a mini sauna. He loved to take long, hot showers and then linger in the mist.

"You suck." Gina and Replacement's words rang in his ears. Twice in short order, two girls had told him that. Problem was—they were right. Jack didn't know what he was doing.

He vainly stared into the fogged mirror, but nothing stared back. Maybe that was his reflection. Misty. Shifting. Empty.

He ran his fingers through his hair and grabbed a pair of shorts and a shirt from the hamper. He hated putting on dirty clothes, but he'd only worn them around the house yesterday, and it beat going around in a towel with a girl in the living room.

He worried about Michelle. Jack knew she wasn't the type to run off. She'd never leave Aunt Haddie. She loved her foster mother dearly. He hoped she just went out to California to check it out. She could have a boyfriend and took some time between classes. She'd be twenty-four now.

What if something had happened?

Jack hated pain and misery. He'd already had a lifetime of it, way more than his fair share. Thinking that someone else, especially Michelle, might be in danger right now tore him up inside.

Think about something else…anything else.

Mrs. Stevens was furious. She threatened to have him evicted, again. Not good. Jack would have to get an "I'm sorry" card, a box of chocolates, and a chocolate cake this time. It had been a couple of months since his last appeasement present. Jack found food worked best. The time Gina threw the phone through the window, it cost him a hundred bucks for the window, thirty for the phone, and two all-you-can-eat buffet gift cards.

For a naked chick in the hallway, I'd better get her a gigantic cake.

He shook his head.

What about Gina? She'll show up tomorrow and get all her stuff. After that…gone. Too many fights. Their relationship sucked anyway. They had nothing in common. And it wasn't as if Jack hadn't tried, but it was a little hard to make a relationship work if the other person was in love with herself. Jack wondered why he didn't kick her out and send her packing.

I never can—not with her, not with any of them. They all leave—but I never do.

He lingered at the bedroom door, not wanting to go back into the living room. He didn't want to fight anymore.

Jack exhaled and then opened the bedroom door. Replacement rushed toward him. She must have been pacing outside the door.

The second he stepped out, she was right back in his face. "What the heck were you doing in there?" The forty minutes he spent chilling out in the shower didn't seem to have calmed her down at all. If anything, it had the opposite effect. Her whole body vibrated. "I have to let Aunt Haddie know. Are you going to help or not?"

Jack hesitated.

"I knew it! I told her you didn't care. If you had cared about us, you'd have come back already." She moved forward until he could feel her breath on his face. "I saw the letters with those worthless excuses—after Iraq, you had to go straight on to college. You couldn't come for a visit? Not one holiday or summer? Yeah, right." She stood with her hands balled into fists. "You've probably never even paid your respects at Chandler's grave. And then to find out you moved an hour away months ago, and you still haven't visited or even called. That's low. Really low."

Jack would never hit a woman, but he found himself struggling to avoid making an exception. He controlled his right hand as it twitched at his side, but he couldn't control the snarl. "Kid, I'm going to help you look for Michelle, but if you say another word about Aunt Haddie or Chandler—"

Jack was cut off when the front door swung wide open. Gina sashayed in, carrying a bag and a drink from the local convenience store. She looked at Replacement and her eyes went wide. She dropped the bag and cup. Soda flew everywhere.

Her glare moved from face to face. "She's still here?"

Jack cocked an eyebrow.

Gina's disdain turned to outrage. "You...you," she stammered at Replacement. Gina took three long strides toward her.

Jack sighed. *This was gonna be good.*

"You little slut. That's my dress!" Gina's bright red fingernail shook with anger as she jabbed Replacement in the midriff.

Jack took another look at the outfit Replacement wore. He leaned back and realized why the green and white dress had looked familiar. Gina raised her hand back, poised to slap, but Replacement swung fast and hard. Jack scooped Replacement aside and into his arms just in time. The punch swished by Gina's face. Even though the blow didn't connect, Gina squealed and grabbed her cheek as if it had. She shrieked and staggered backward. Jack knew just the thought of something happening to Gina's face was enough to terrify her. "How dare you!"

Jack shook his head. Gina was a drama queen. He almost called 911 one day before he realized she'd only broken a nail. If something actually had happened to her face, she'd have needed CPR. Jack chuckled.

Gina turned her anger toward Jack. "That's it. Over," Gina declared. "I mean it. I knew it when I gave you a ride home from that crappy bar." Her red lips twisted into a sneer. "You're pathetic. Oh, poor baby. You're so sad. Poor Jack. He has mommy issues…"

Jack had enough. She was trying to hit below the belt. She'd called him every name in the book before, but he still couldn't stand when love or lust turned to hate and disgust. Gina had just turned that corner. She now looked at him with loathing. He could see she wanted to slice him to ribbons with her words, but he wasn't the type to just sit there and take it.

Replacement, wrapped up in Jack's arms, strained like a dog on a leash. It was clear she wanted another chance to pound Gina.

"You want at her, girl?" Jack looked down at her. She gave one quick, fierce nod. "Go get her then." He released Replacement from his arms.

Gina shrieked and ran for the door. Replacement nearly caught her but Gina's salvation came when Replacement slipped in the spilled soda. Replacement caught herself by grabbing the doorframe. Gina fled down the hallway. How Gina could run so fast in four-inch high heels was impressive.

"Wench!" Replacement shouted at the top of her lungs as she prepared to continue the chase after her fleeing prey.

Jack dashed over, yanked her back into the apartment, and shut the door. *For a little thing, she sure was loud.*

"What's wrong with you? Quiet down." He grabbed her by the shoulders and spun her around to look at her. "It's nearly three in the morning. My landlady is going to take my head off. First, you sneak into my apartment—"

"I didn't sneak," Replacement snapped as she tried to adjust her dress.

Jack's finely tuned BS detector went off. "Gina let you in?"

"No…but…"

"But what? Why would you break in to my apartment and take a shower?" Jack looked at her with one eyebrow raised.

"The apartment was open. It wasn't locked, and I'd waited for hours in your stupid stairwell. On the way here, I got caught in that downpour, and got soaked. I sat out there freezing. I didn't think you'd mind," she huffed.

"Mind? I don't even remember you."

Her expression was sad for a brief second. Then she shook her head and returned to glaring. "Well, thanks a lot, you friggin' jerk." She shoved him again.

He'd hurt her and felt sorry. Jack tried to backpedal. "What I meant is that you've changed so much and…you were young and—"

"Whatever." She held up her hand.

Jack continued to feel bad until he made a quick mental list: *Gina's furious and took off, my landlady blew a fat gasket, and a minute ago this girl was in my face.*

Jack waited for more, but she just stood there and stared at him.

Damn.

He looked away. On the floor, he noticed the spilled soda and bags of food. He picked up the bags and took out a loaf of bread and some sliced chicken. "Hungry?"

She just stared at him.

He shrugged, and then went to make sandwiches for both of them. He offered her one, and then went and sat on his old green couch. He looked over at the mess. *I should clean up the soda before it turns into a goo-stain. Why didn't Gina ever get bottles? She always got the paper cups.* Jack smiled. *She likes straws.*

Replacement chomped a massive bite from her sandwich as she spoke. "You're not going after her?"

He barely understood what she said. "She'll go to her friend's house. Whoever that is. I got a hunch that we're done."

"Great." Replacement moved to sit next to him. He didn't argue; he just took another bite of his sandwich. "She flipped out when she came home and found me in the shower."

Jack nodded.

"I tried to tell her who I was, but she went a little wacko."

"Well, that explains it," Jack muttered.

He watched Replacement from the corner of his eye. She acted young for a nineteen year old, but she still had the same impish grin. It had been so long since he'd last seen her, and he thought of how many things had changed since then.

They ate in silence and then stared at the wall for a few minutes. It was funny that it didn't feel awkward.

Jack got up and suppressed a groan. His back was still a little sore from flipping the lumberjack. He threw the paper plates into the trash, looked at the clock—2:57 a.m.—and then glanced out the window.

It's snowing.

"You got a ride home or do you want to crash here?" He yawned and stretched.

Replacement's face lit up as if she'd hit the lottery. "The couch is fine." She bounced up and down with her hands spread out.

"We'll go out to the college in the morning." Jack walked into his bedroom and shut the door.

He lay in bed for almost an hour, unable to sleep. Worse still, he couldn't stop thinking about Michelle.

If she isn't in California, this isn't going to be good. The police would have checked the hospitals...morgue.

He closed his eyes and breathed deeply as he tried to force those thoughts from his head.

Think about something else. Think about something good about her.

It wasn't hard for Jack to remember. He thought about that memory often.

Michelle had been twelve. While other kids were playing and having fun during summer break, she was hard at work babysitting, wiping up snot, and changing diapers. As each week passed, Chandler and Jack would guess what she was going to buy. The pile of money she had in her bureau had grown so large, the boys had gone from guessing a doll, to a dollhouse, to finally thinking that she had enough money to buy a pony.

"I'm saving it for something special," she'd said. "It's something I've always wanted."

Near the end of summer, Jack had come back for a visit to Aunt Haddie's for a sleepover. When he'd arrived, he noticed the house was dark except for a few candles lit here and there.

"What's going on?" Jack asked.

Chandler pulled Jack outside. "Aunt Haddie's work cut back on her hours this summer. They shut the electricity off and now she's worried she doesn't have enough money to pay the rent."

"Maybe we can help?" Jack suggested.

"She'd never let us." Chandler shrugged. "Anyways, I don't have any money."

While the boys discussed ideas outside, they saw Michelle with a flashlight rummaging around Aunt Haddie's bedroom closet. Jack wondered what she was doing.

The next morning, Michelle woke them up. "I had a dream last night that we should look for extra change around the house."

Chandler yawned. "A little change isn't going to pay the bills."

"Just do it." Michelle pulled him out of bed.

They started to search around the house, behind a desk, under the couch cushions—all over.

"Aunt Haddie, you should check through your old pocketbooks in the closet," Michelle suggested.

A few minutes later, they heard her yell. "Hallelujah!" She ran out of the bedroom with a large wad of cash in her hands.

Jack looked over at Michelle. She simply smiled. Jack never forgot the look on the old woman's face as she leapt around the kitchen, holding up that money. All four of them had joined in dancing in a circle with Aunt Haddie calling out, "Thank you, Lord! Thank you, Jesus!"

Jack asked Michelle about it later. "So where do you think that money came from?"

"An angel put it there."

Jack couldn't disagree.

After he tossed and turned some more, he tried to concentrate and make a to-do list in his mind, but it was no use. He lay there feeling trapped at the gates of sleep. With a groan, he pulled the covers back, grabbed his sweatpants, and headed to the kitchen for some water. When he stepped into the kitchen, he stopped short. It was spotless. Replacement must have cleaned up the spilled soda, and cleaned the whole place up.

He looked over at her curled up on the couch, asleep. She clutched the blanket tightly around herself. She looked cute. It bothered him he couldn't remember her real name. *What did Aunt Haddie call her?*

He looked back at the clean kitchen and smiled. He went into his bedroom and then returned with the comforter from his bed. He unrolled the thick comforter. Gina had thought his old army-green blanket was too scraggly, so she'd gone shopping one weekend and had picked this out for him as a present. It was super girly—purple and white with pink flowers. He shook his head. It looked utterly ridiculous, but it was *incredibly* warm.

Gently, he laid it over Replacement. Her eyes fluttered open. "Thank you," she whispered.

"You're welcome."

He watched her snuggle into its warmth. Jack started to walk away but he knew he'd never get any sleep unless he got it off his chest. "Seriously, kid, why are you so angry with me for not coming to visit?"

She slowly opened her eyes. "Do you really want to know?"

He'd regretted asking the question as soon as it left his mouth, but still he nodded.

"When you and Chandler turned eighteen and went off to Iraq, everything changed at Aunt Haddie's. Chandler was gone. I was ten. Michelle was sixteen. Before, if there was a problem, Chandler always fixed it. He was like Superman. If stuff broke or something went wrong, he was there. But if he couldn't fix it, he'd call you." Her eyes searched his face. "Do you get it?"

Jack shrugged. "He's Superman. I get that. But—"

"If something happened that Chandler couldn't handle, you'd show up and take care of it. Chandler would just pick up the phone, you'd come, and everything would be okay. To me, you were like Batman. When Chandler died, we didn't know what to do. I kept thinking you'd come back. You'd come back and fix it."

What the hell did she want me to say? She doesn't get it. Chandler really was Superman, but I'm no Batman. I was like stupid Jimmy Olson following him around.

Jack's shoulders slumped. He waited there silently, unable to defend his actions. He knew what happened in Iraq, but she didn't.

As she lay there, her eyes told the story. "You didn't come back. You didn't even try." Her voice cracked. She rolled over and buried her head in the comforter.

Jack swallowed. "I'm sorry."

The comforter moved up and down when she nodded.

Jack walked back into the bedroom, shut the door, and closed his eyes.

She thinks I'm a superhero. She doesn't understand. I'm no hero. I'm the guy who killed Superman.

CHAPTER FOUR

Fish Out of Water Dance

IRAQ
Six Years Ago

Jack adjusted his assault rifle and looked back across the dimly lit room to Chandler. Two other soldiers stood next to him. Chandler lifted the huge machine gun he carried and nodded. One of the other soldiers moved to stand behind Jack and to the left. Jack pushed the door open, and his gun snapped up. His eyes swept the room. The square interior had open cabinets against one wall and a table and chairs against the other. Rubbish littered the floor.

Empty.

In the middle of the back wall was another door. Jack held up his hand and made two quick gestures forward. He slipped silently into the room and carefully picked his way over the trash-strewn floor toward the other door.

One more room.

Jack reached the door and stood off to the side. He held up his hand and closed it into a fist. He looked back to Chandler. Chandler nodded. He pushed the door open.

Jack's eyes went wide. Canisters and gray sacks filled the room. They had all received a briefing on the possibility—phosphorus bombs.

"MOVE!"

The four soldiers sprinted back through the rooms they'd just cleared. Chandler shifted the massive gun in his arms. He knew that huge gun slowed Chandler down.

"RUN!" Jack lost sight of the other two soldiers when he dropped instantly behind his friend. "CHANDLER, RUN."

"I AM."

"LOSE THE DAMN GUN."

Chandler tossed it aside.

In under a minute, they made it to the front room where the other soldiers were frantically shoving against the now-closed door.

"It's jammed." They pounded against the thick wood.

"MOVE," Jack commanded, and even Chandler got out of the way.

Jack lowered his shoulder and hit the door as hard as he could. The door cracked, but didn't open.

Everyone started to yell.

Do something, Jack, or we're all gonna die.

Chandler called out, "MOVE!"

Jack turned to see Chandler charge across the room. He burst forward and rammed the door. The force of the impact moved the wall. The door held— but the frame didn't. The wooden frame and chunks of concrete with the door still attached fell forward and landed in the dirt.

The four soldiers scrambled out. They ran as the building behind them exploded.

Jack looked back in terrified fascination. Flames shot out where the door had been. The flames looked like dragon's breath. The fire was so hot it flicked blue and white before it wrapped together into red and yellow streams and floated skyward.

Jack looked over at Chandler. He sat on the ground and watched in awe the building burn where they'd just been. Jack walked over and sat down next to him.

"Thanks." Jack's voice was barely audible.

Chandler nodded.

Jack looked around and all of the other soldiers stared into the flames, mesmerized. They knew how close they had just come to a horrifying death.

Jack stared straight ahead, as he spoke to Chandler. "You have to get faster."

"You have to get bigger." He smiled. They laughed.

Then Chandler pushed at Jack's shoulder...

Jack looked down, puzzled. Chandler's hand had shrunk as he kept poking him in the shoulder. Slowly, Jack's dreaming ended.

Replacement pushed his shoulder again. "Are you getting up?"

Half-dazed, Jack jumped back and almost fell off the bed. He sat upright. He couldn't see clearly; he blinked and rubbed his eyes. "What's the matter with you?" he demanded.

"Me? You're the bum." She hopped onto the bed and landed on her knees. She began to talk rapidly. "It's seven o'clock. How late are you going to sleep? I thought you said you'd—"

"Shut up."

"Help me. When are we going—"

"Shut up."

"To do something about Michelle and not sleep all day. Do you always—"

"SHUT UP," he barked right in her face.

The full blast roar would have made any soldier stand at attention. It didn't seem to affect her. She just smiled. Jack shook his head.

One thing's for sure, she's Chandler's sister, all right.

"Let me clean up, and then we can go," he muttered.

"We?" Her face lit up.

He held up his hand. "Don't say another word. Not a peep or we don't go. Do you need a shower?"

She shrugged and made a twisting motion in front of her lips as if she locked them.

"Don't be a punk. I'm taking a shower, then." He headed for the bathroom.

"You took a long shower last night, and now you need another? Do you sweat a lot in your sleep?" She made a face and wrinkled her nose.

Jack stood there, blinking. This girl unquestionably could tick him off. "No," he snapped back and swore under his breath as he headed for a quick shower.

The warm water gave him the opportunity to clear his head, but he'd have loved a cup of coffee too. He doubted there was any in the house. It didn't matter anyway because he hated it black and there was zero chance of there being any milk.

Jack started to plan what he wanted to do first. He knew his first step normally would be to go to the investigator here in Darrington. He'd have been the one to check up on Michelle's last known address at the college. Nevertheless, if he went to see Davenport, Sheriff Collins would have to be informed. That would lead to the inevitable disclosure that Michelle had been his foster sister. He knew department policy. Anything involving a family member was treated as a conflict of interest, and he wouldn't be allowed anywhere near this end of the investigation. He knew the longer he stayed off the radar screen, the better. If he did get caught, he had a Get Out of Jail Free card he intended to play with by-the-book Collins. Michelle had been his foster sister, but technically, she was not a relative—even if Jack viewed her that way.

He also didn't want Sheriff Collins to think he was grandstanding. The reason Jack transferred to Darrington County Sheriff Department was partly due to Sheriff Collins. He thought he'd worked well with the former Air Force captain. Instead, Collins had written Jack up before his first month on the job and then placed him on late-night traffic detail for ninety days. That was after Jack had stuck his nose in and solved a John Doe case.

A hiker had found a partially decomposed body in the woods. Animals had eaten most of it and the John Doe's head was missing, so dental records couldn't be used in the investigation. It had been assigned to Detective Flynn, but he hadn't followed through on the only real clue they had, which was the tattoo on the guy's arm—crossed swords over a four-leaf clover. There had been nothing on it in the police database. Jack, on his own, had checked one local tattoo parlor after another until he'd come up with the name of the guy: Tommy O'Neil, a local with a drug problem.

Instead of promoting him, Collins had blasted him up and down about grandstanding. The thing Collins hadn't understood was Jack didn't care about who got the credit—he had just wanted to help.

Jack decided to start by checking at Michelle's last address. She may have a roommate or a neighbor who she told where she was going. He hoped Michelle was safe and sound, lying on some beach in California.

Because they were going to a college, he decided to dress the part. He shaved close and styled his hair. There were a few civilian shirts hanging in the closet, so he selected a navy blue casual collared pullover that was a little loose. Jack knew he was muscular and intimidating. He'd stayed in excellent shape since the Army. Still, he'd be dealing with young college girls and wanted to appear approachable. A nice pair of slacks and shoes completed the ensemble.

While he appraised his appearance in the mirror, his smile faded. *Is this what normal is?* The man in the mirror appeared normal, and normal seemed so strange to Jack.

Jack shook his head and returned to his mental checklist. It had holes.

Replacement. He still struggled to remember her real name. For some reason, he remembered she didn't like it. Every time she was called it, he could picture her as a little ten-year-old kid, looking perturbed. She was already upset enough, so he wasn't about to ask her what it was, especially if she disliked it.

Gina. If Jack was around when she came back, there would be an epic fight. She could show or not show. If she stayed away for a couple of days, there was the possibility she'd try to come back to work things out. If she showed up today, it'd be to get her stuff, and then she'd be gone, permanently. Jack hoped it would be the latter. He thought about hiding anything valuable, but he'd done that long before Gina. He'd locked the important papers in the safe, but he'd kept copies in the back of the sofa. He didn't trust anyone anymore. "Great life, Jack." He shook his head.

He thought about the gun in the safe. He didn't think he'd need it. He carried himself differently when he had his gun. It was like a tell in poker. People seemed to sense he was a cop when he carried it, and he didn't want that today. In truth, he felt prepared without it. When Jack was twelve, he confided in a friend about his birth mother. The story that his mother was a hooker burned through the school like wildfire. Jack got into three fights in one day and lost each one. The principal called his parents in for a conference. The school counselor simply chalked it up to "kids can be cruel" and Jack would have to learn to deal with it. Jack's adoptive father was far more supportive. He signed Jack up for karate. Jack took to it like breathing. Martial arts were a natural fit for him. After a few months and a few more fights, no one dared mentioned his mother again.

Now what else is there? His checklists were becoming as scattered as the pieces of his life. The soldier he was six years ago would have beaten the crap out of him for being so sloppy.

"Ready?" he called as he opened the door. He hadn't needed to ask; Replacement waited at the open front door.

As she saw him, a flood of questions burst out: "Where are we going? Where do we start? Are we—?"

"Kid, listen. This is what you do today—SHUT UP."

Her face fell. He felt bad in a weird way. "I have a job to do, and I can't have you screw it up, okay?"

She raised herself up on her toes and leaned in on him. "I won't screw it up."

"If you get in someone's face like you just got in mine, you will."

Her face scrunched up and her hands went out.

Jack took a deep breath and decided to try a different tack. "Can you do me a favor?" His voice and posture softened. "It looks like we have a truce going, right?"

She nodded her head. "Just because you said you'd help."

"Can you try to follow my lead?"

Her head rose. "Like we're in it together?" Before he could stop that train of thought, it had already left the station. "Hell, yeah. Let's go."

He rolled his eyes. This, he felt, was his first mistake of the morning. His second mistake was in taking the front steps. Mrs. Stevens sprang out of her door like a lion. Her mane of red hair stood on end, and her flabby face was blotchy. She looked as though she had waited all night at that door to spring her trap. Jack fell right into it.

"Mrs. Stevens…I wanted to stop by and offer my sincere apologies—"

She was so crazy looking that Replacement dashed behind him and he stopped talking.

Jack held his hands open and out as if he were handling a hostage situation.

Her eyes grew even larger. "You weren't stopping."

"I was going out to get you a little *something* so I could apologize *properly*." He emphasized the words, hoping that her mental image of a bribe would calm her down. Jack didn't have much furniture, but he hated moving. And right now, there was a high probability that his landlady would throw him out.

"How could you possibly apologize for all you've done?" All that was missing was the back of her hand held theatrically to her forehead. She was laying it on pretty thick, but Jack took that as a good sign. He tried to look apologetic.

"Your lease is exceedingly specific about the level of noise. Last night..."

She's quoting the lease—that's bad. Jack decided that he'd have to play on her emotions a bit. He spoke before he fully thought it through, another one of his weaknesses. "I'm just so sorry, Mrs. Stevens. You see...this girl...she's...she's the sister of my friend who has passed...his younger sister..."

Mrs. Stevens's eyes narrowed and her fat lips pursed into a puffy line, but Jack kept talking. "And she's mental and...stunted emotionally...and I just wanted to get her to a place that would take care of her—"

"What about the other one?" Mrs. Stevens tapped her foot.

"The other—"

"Girl." He didn't know how Mrs. Stevens even said the word as her lips pressed together so tightly they didn't move.

"The other girl is my, my...cousin." He regretted lying as soon as it passed his lips.

"Crap," Replacement popped.

Jack jumped as Replacement twitched and swore behind him. "Sorry, crap. Sorry, pretty lady." Her head spasmodically went back and forth as her arms and legs jerked. Even though Jack knew it was an act, it was quite unnerving. "Crap. Son-of-a—"

"There, there. It's okay." Jack wrapped an arm around her and pulled her close. He honestly wanted her to stop before he started to laugh.

Mrs. Stevens stepped back and clutched her robe to her chest. "Is she dangerous?" Her eyes were wide with fear.

"No, no. She's harmless." His voice was reassuring as he hustled Replacement down the hallway. "I just need to get her meds refilled right away."

She watched them leave through the door.

Replacement grinned from ear to ear and made a goofy face.

"What was that? Are you trying to get me kicked out?"

"You said follow your lead." She pouted.

"Shutting up would have been following my lead."

"You told her I was mental. Where did you come up with that? And your cousin? You think she was gonna believe Miss Fake Boobs is your cousin?"

"If you wanted to act, how about trying to come off harmless and not like some twitchy psycho?"

"I called her pretty." She shrugged as if that should cover everything.

Jack was speechless. He stared back at her, not knowing what to say. Movement at a second-floor window caught his eye. Mrs. Stevens pulled the curtain back to look down at them.

"Okay, act *a little* out of it—she's watching."

Replacement went back to her fish-out-of-water dance. This time, though, she toned it way down. He noticed the odd looks they received from some people on the street. He couldn't help but smile as he led her to the car.

As they drove toward the college, Replacement acted like a big puppy. Even though it was cold out, she rolled her window down and then touched all the buttons. When she went to mess with the radio, Jack swatted her hand away. "Stop touching everything."

She checked herself in the mirror and then almost climbed into the back seat. Twisting back around, she flopped down and pulled out the ashtray. Some coins fell onto the floor. "Sorry."

"Sit still. You're making me nervous," he chided. She still acted like the ten-year-old lovesick girl who chased him around.

Jack pushed the ashtray back into the dash of his semi-refurbished blue 1978 Chevy Impala. He had picked it up at a police auction for short money. It had way too many miles on it. Jack and the car were twins in that regard, but the Impala seemed to be running better right now.

Replacement made a sour expression. "This car is—"

Jack whipped his head around. His look shut her right up.

"You don't say anything about a guy's car."

She'd kept quiet a lot longer than he thought was possible.

After a few miles, she shivered, frowned, and rolled the window back up. "Where are we going?"

"White Rocks. First stop is Michelle's apartment, and then we'll go to the college."

"Why don't you go see what the cops have?"

Jack kept his eyes on the road. He knew his by-the-book boss would go crazy and tell him to follow proper channels. It was Fairfield PD and Joe Davenport's case. There was no way Jack was going to sit by and do nothing while Michelle remained missing.

"We'll start at her apartment. Do you have the address where she stayed?"

"Yeah, but I was there once already. They didn't know nothing." She tapped her knuckles against the car door in frustration.

"Didn't know anything."

"Sorry, teacher. I'm just visiting the college, not enrolling today." Replacement crossed her arms.

Jack chuckled. "Good line, kid."

She smiled, put her hands behind her head, and stretched her feet onto the dashboard. Jack made a mental note to give out more positive reinforcement.

"How are we going to start looking into this?" she asked.

"You want to start at the end of the trail—"

"Why don't we start with the cops then?"

"That's not the end of *her* trail. Besides…" He was about to go on about Detective Joe Davenport and the fact that he liked to go over case details while he was baiting a hook, but he thought better of it. "I don't want to muddy the waters. We'll start at her apartment. And I'll *quietly* call over to Fairfield's sheriff's department and see what they have."

"Do you think she's alright?"

Jack tightened his grip on the steering wheel.

When he didn't answer, she looked out the window and remained silent for the rest of the ride except for the occasional "turn left" and "turn right" when she gave him directions.

They arrived outside an upscale apartment complex, close to the college and in a great part of town.

"How could Michelle afford to live here plus school?"

"She got a full scholarship." Her voice rang with pride. "Free everything."

"Scholarship? I don't remember Michelle playing any sports."

"It was a work scholarship for computers. She had to work here, but she could take classes. She's super smart."

Jack drove past the apartment. His car would stick out wherever he parked it in this neighborhood, and he wanted to create the illusion that he was an approachable, normal guy. He swung into a parking space and shut off the engine.

"Just keep quiet, okay?"

She pantomimed a key locking her mouth again and flashed him an impish grin. Jack frowned. That smile said she was going to do what she wanted in the long run.

Jack seriously debated locking her in the car. But, he knew if he had a young girl with him, he'd appear more approachable to the college students.

"Does she have a roommate or a boyfriend? Was she in a sorority? Did she talk about friends?" He fired off questions as they walked toward the apartment, angry he hadn't asked them on the car ride over.

"Yes, she has a roommate. No boyfriend. No sorority. And no, she didn't talk about friends." She fired the answers back. "Missy Lorton." Her smile widened as she guessed his next question before he asked.

He ran his fingers through his hair and scanned the buzzers. He hesitated when he noticed that Missy's was the only apartment with one name, LORTON, typed on a fancy tan paper that was slightly darker than the others.

The paper is newer; the paper from the other apartments has faded. Someone doesn't think Michelle is coming back.

"You're sure this is Michelle's apartment?"

"It said LORTON and CAMPBELL when I came out before." Replacement jabbed the paper with each word.

Jack pressed the buzzer.

"We'll talk to Missy first and then to the neighbors, okay?"

Someone buzzed them in without asking who they were.

They jogged up the stairs. Jack's foot hadn't hit the top step when the door to apartment 328 swung open. A short, extremely plump girl stepped out of the doorway.

"I thought I was going to meet…" Her whiny voice trailed off, and she took a step back.

"Miss Lorton?" Jack put on his most dashing smile.

It didn't work. Missy tried to slam the door shut. Jack stuck his foot out and it paid the price of acting as a doorstop. "Miss, I'm just here to ask you a few quick questions." He tried to hold his smile and not clench his teeth from the pain.

"A salesman?" Her pudgy face relaxed, and the fear on it changed to barely hidden disgust. "No solicitors."

She pulled the door back and then slammed it again. This time Jack caught the door with his hands and his foot.

"We're looking for Michelle Campbell." He now had to force a smile because it was surprisingly difficult to keep the door open with the heavy girl pressing against it.

"He said she transferred to a different school." Missy stepped back from the door.

Jack grabbed Replacement with his left hand and encouraged her forward so Missy could see he was with a girl, hoping that might soften her up.

"I already told the police everything I know." Missy shrugged.

"Missy, I'm sorry. Can we start again?" Jack poured on the charm. "We're old family friends, and we just came by to get Michelle's things."

Missy's face was expressionless. "She took it all."

Jack examined her posture: hands turned out, shoulders relaxed, back stiff, and she looked straight in his eyes.

She's lying.

"That's fine." He lowered his head and his voice. "The college informed us she transferred. When did she tell you she was transferring?"

She hesitated for a moment too long. Missy stood, blinking. Her lie would reveal something. Jack waited for it.

"Tell me where Michelle's stuff is, or I'll kick your fat—" Jack caught Replacement as she lunged at the portly girl.

Missy fell backward and rolled, squealing, into the kitchen.

While Replacement hurled a string of obscenities that would make a mafia hit man blush, Missy shrieked as she struggled to sit up. "Get out!"

"Thank you very much, Miss Lorton. We'll be going now." Jack retreated.

He lifted Replacement bodily from the floor and stormed out of the apartment and down the stairs. She stopped struggling by the second floor, but he didn't let go as he carried her outside. He was beyond mad. As they got to the car, he dropped her. She had to grab the car to avoid falling on the ground.

"IN." He yanked her door open.

She lowered her head and sat down.

Jack marched over to his side and slammed his door shut. The tires screeched as he hit the gas and pulled out.

"I could have gotten her to tell us where Michelle's stuff is," Replacement began.

"What's the matter with you? You can't just take potshots at people who tick you off. What would Aunt Haddie say?"

He didn't like swearing at a woman, but he was so mad he couldn't stop himself from making some sound. His low growl made Replacement back off. She moved as far away from him as the large seats in the Impala would allow.

"Of all the stupid things to do. With a girl like that, you let them lie."

He veered to the side of the road, slammed on the brakes and glared at her. Jack's anger burned hot, but his skin went cold. "Something *is* wrong. That girl was lying. It was obvious."

"And her stuff? Michelle didn't go anywhere, so someone took her stuff." Her voice was small now.

"Missy said *he* told her. Not *Michelle*, or *she*."

He had followed enough missing person cases. Simple ones sometimes had happy endings. Missy didn't want to talk. She was lying about something. Jack quickly ran down the most probable scenarios. He had a bad feeling this wasn't a simple missing person case.

He looked at Replacement. She looked devastated. He sighed. "Maybe we can use that meltdown."

She nodded.

"Who knows? If I need to talk to her again, I can always say if she doesn't tell me what I want to know, I'll bring you back to have a chat with her."

Replacement smiled slightly, but her eyes were gray. They rode in silence. She propped her head up on her hand and leaned up against the window. Jack noticed she kept her eyes closed.

What did she think? Once I started looking, then Michelle would suddenly appear? I show up and everything is fixed because I'm the superhero?

This is reality, kid, and reality sucks.

CHAPTER FIVE

You Will Know Pain

They headed to the White Rocks campus police station. He'd been there for various calls in the last six months. Usually it was for noise complaints and the odd drunk. Sometimes he'd earned overtime with traffic duty for events.

They called it campus police, but it was only a couple of rungs up the ladder from the official high school hall monitor's office. The "force" consisted of less than ten guys and two gals who were either just out of high school or already retired. They were a nice quiet group—for a nice quiet college.

White Rocks Eastern College was an old, private institution with less than two thousand students. Although small, it was the source of a very large portion of the county's tax base, a fact that Sheriff Collins never let anyone forget. With this in mind, and his constant desire to stay under Collins's radar, Jack was getting ready to lock Replacement in the car.

"I won't say anything." She must have read his mind because she was still looking out the window. The fight had gone out of her, and she appeared even more downcast.

"I'd be very appreciative if you didn't say anything." He parked the car. "Unless, of course, you want to wait here?"

"No. I'd like to come in."

The security office was a small building, consisting of a few rooms. They walked up the cement ramp and could see a large main desk through the windows. A woman with an immense hairdo greeted them before the little bell over the door even finished ringing.

"Why, good morning to the both of you," she squealed. "How may I be of help today?" It was hard to tell how old she was, considering all the layers of makeup she had on, but her smile was genuine.

"Good morning to you, too." Jack found that when he greeted someone, trying to match their tone was best. "I'm looking for the..." He searched for the right title but drew a blank.

Sometimes security people try to match police titles and get their feelings hurt when you use the wrong one. At the mall in town, the security referred to each other as Officer, and they loved it when he did too.

"Registration office?" she added, trying to help him out.

"Oh, no. I'm looking for the person covering right now." Jack figured the generic phrase would pay off, and it did.

"Certainly." She pushed back in her chair and wheeled it over to the phone.

She dialed, and after a short pause, a phone rang. Jack looked over, hearing ringing coming from an open door ten feet away.

"Neil Waters, security," the man answered, and they could hear him from the office.

Replacement and Jack exchanged a quick wide-eyed look and even faster turned away so they wouldn't laugh.

"Neil, a nice couple is here to see you."

"Sure, send them in."

"Okay. I'm going to run and get a bite," the woman announced as she waved Jack and Replacement toward Waters's office door. "Do you want anything?"

"Where are you going?" Neil asked.

"I'm just getting a coffee and muffin at Debbie Sue's. Want your usual?"

"Sure." A second later, an older man, in one of the whitest shirts Jack had ever seen, stuck his head out of the office. "You kids all set or can May pick you up something?"

"Thanks, but we're all set, Neil," Jack reassured him as he walked over and shook his hand. He was hungry, but he didn't want to complicate things by placing an order with May. "I just have a couple questions, and we'll be out of your way."

Neil laughed and ran his fingers through hair almost as white as his shirt. "Okay. See you, May." He waved. "Come on in, folks."

"Do you mind if I wait out here?" Replacement's sad face was back.

Neil checked with Jack via a quick look, and then with all the compassion of a grandfather, nodded. "Sure you can, sweetie. Just come in if you need to."

His office was as clean as his shirt. *A place for everything; everything in its place.*

Neil gestured to a comfortable chair as he moved behind the desk. "How can I help you?"

"Jack. Jack Stratton."

"Now I remember. You helped with the alumni benefit." Neil folded his hands, leaned back in his chair, and smiled.

Great…he remembers that I'm a cop. Nod. Look happy.

"I'm here because I'm a family friend of Michelle Campbell."

"Oh, uh…you're aware that the police were here and did a safety check on her whereabouts?"

"I am. I had a couple of additional questions. What do *you* think happened to Michelle?"

Make him feel respected and get him talking.

"Well…" Neil straightened up in his chair and Jack could see him gather his thoughts. "We talked to her roommate, and she told us that Michelle transferred to Western Technical University out in California. I called myself and spoke to the registrar out there, nice group. They're way up the coast. Get a lot of rain. They said that everything looked good on their end too."

"Did they say she'd been out there?"

"They couldn't recall her specifically. Everything is electronic now anyway."

"Did they have an address for Michelle?"

"They didn't. It could be she just hasn't gotten housing yet. She hadn't started classes, but she was good to go." His expression was reassuring.

"You said she hadn't started classes *yet*. Did they say why?"

"She hasn't started yet because classes haven't started. We're both between semesters now. Maybe she just took a little time to herself, and she'll check in?" He leaned in and put his arms down on the desk.

In that moment of silence, Jack listened for Replacement but didn't hear anything.

That might not be a good thing.

"I hope so. Do you know where her belongings are?"

"The roommate said she cleared out. When we got there, the apartment was empty."

"Well…thank you, Neil. I appreciate it."

Jack shook Neil's hand, and they walked back out to where Replacement sat with her hands folded in her lap.

Too quiet. What's she been up to?

As they drove away from the college, neither of them spoke. Jack was lost in his own thoughts, grateful that Replacement was content to stare out of the window.

She finished classes and headed out West? Just took all her stuff and went? That's something I'd do. Not her. No way would Michelle run out on them like I did.

"Did Michelle own a car?" Jack's anger kicked in.

"Yeah. A blue Honda Civic. I told the brainiac detective, and he said he'd put an alert out for it."

Stupid. I should have asked her about the car first. I'll have to run it when I get home.

"When did Michelle decide to go to college? She was a lot older than your typical college freshman."

"She was—so what?" Replacement became instantly defensive. "She always wanted to go to college. She loved computers, school, and learning. She just couldn't afford it. She was saving up for it and then she heard about that scholarship." Replacement looked at her feet and shook her head. "She was so happy when she got it."

"What was Michelle doing for work before college?"

"She worked at McDermott Insurance. She did computer security. She taught me."

"What do you do for work?"

Replacement shrugged. "I have some…computer jobs. I do a little website stuff now and then. I'm sort of on call. Michelle said I should get some certification, so I took an online security class. Michelle…"

Replacement's knuckles hammered on the door panel in frustration. Out of the corner of his eye, Jack tried not to watch as she welled up. She looked up at the ceiling of the car and then the tears began to fall.

Jack pretended to concentrate on driving as Replacement quietly cried. He thought back to one of his first criminal justice classes: Psychology of the Victim. The instructor's words haunted him now.

"When a crime is committed, who is the victim?" Hands shot up all over the room, along with one brave voice.

"A person who suffers harm or death from another or from some adverse act."

"And using that definition, who is the victim in a missing person case?"

"The person missing?"

"Wrong." The teacher had brought both hands crashing down on his podium with a loud bang. "What about the mother? What about the poor little brother? The uncle, father, sister, teacher, lover?" He fired down the list; his words hung in the air, suspended on the silent response to his question.

"And…if the *victim* is a person who suffers harm or death from another or from some adverse act, what about *you*? Will you not lose sleep wondering what happened? Will you not pore over the facts and interview all of the shell-shocked people who want to know what happened? Where's their loved one, they ask, and they have turned to you for help, but you have no answer. You look at them with pity, but you look in the mirror at yourself with frustration. You turn inward and ask yourself the accusatory question: why can't you find them? In addition, what about your wife or husband who grows tired of asking, 'What are you thinking?' You remain silent and become more and more removed. What about your little child who asks, 'If I got taken, would you find me?'"

The teacher had paused, the lesson now impaled into every head in the room. They had suffered a knockout blow and silently stared at their desks.

With Replacement still forlornly gazing out the window, Jack again heard the professor's final words. "For those of you who want to wear the badge of a police officer, you must know this: *You will be a victim. You will know pain.*"

"Where are we going?" Replacement asked as the exit to downtown disappeared behind them on the highway.

"I'm taking you home."

"But I thought we were going to look."

"I will." He stressed the *I*. "I don't know if Gina will—"

"You said she won't be back," she protested as she turned in the seat to look at him.

"Look, my landlady's ticked off. My girlfriend's off-the-rails crazy. I only got a few hours sleep and I'm tired. I'm working the two-to-ten shift tonight. I'm taking you home."

"But—"

"Look, kid. My head's too overloaded to ask the right questions now. You're going home. That's it."

That ended all conversation for the remainder of the forty-five-minute ride to Fairfield.

Jack couldn't help but smile to himself as the small town came into view. It hadn't changed much since he'd last been there.

It hasn't changed since the 1900s.

Fairfield was one of the larger counties in the middle of the state, but it was also on the poor side. A large influx of artists in the 70s had rounded out the population of paper workers, loggers, retirees, and outdoors types who had earlier gravitated to the beautiful area nestled in the hills.

This was his hometown. It wasn't where he was born or where he'd spent the first seven years of his life, but it was his home. He remembered the drive into downtown where Aunt Haddie lived.

Jack didn't know whether she couldn't have kids of her own, but he did know she was married once. Alton had been his name, and the only picture she had of him was a wedding picture she kept by her bed. It was on the nightstand in an old, ornate frame.

Over her bed, she had a large portrait of Jesus. It was one Jack liked because it made Jesus look like a real guy. Frames filled with pictures of smiling kids covered the wall opposite her bed. He couldn't guess how many kids had gone through her care over the years.

Her kids. That's what she always called us.

He remembered the first time he headed down this road. He'd been numb. His birth mother was a whore. If he ever talked about her, he used that word— whore. There was no other way to describe her. He tried to use prostitute but felt it covered her sins and sounded too kind. It wasn't just that she sold her body for money. No, it was because of what she'd done to a child—done to him.

Jack hadn't thought about her for a while, but as buildings and surroundings became more familiar, the thoughts slammed into his already overloaded brain.

Why?

He didn't know the answer.

Why keep a kid seven years and then give him up?

He'd shouted that question at the therapist who tried to get him to face his feelings.

My feelings? What feelings? Most of me is just numb. Dead. Then there's the other part…the dark part of me that just…hates.

"You should have taken that right. Take a right up here." Replacement pointed with a frown, upset that he missed the street.

She thinks I forgot about the town. She thinks I forgot about them. I didn't. I'm just remembering too much.

Hennessey's, the little Bait and Tackle, Bob's Coffee, and the old candy store. It was almost all the same, yet everything had changed. He turned down the familiar road.

"This is it. Right here is fine." Replacement's hand was on the door handle as he pulled over.

"Here." She handed him a folded piece of paper. "Read it when you get home." She hopped out and ran up into an apartment building without a backward glance.

Jack unfolded the note written in a delicate script on a piece of scrap paper. *CHECK THE STOVE. TY FOR HELPING.*

No signature.

He still didn't know her name, and he forgot to try to get it from her.

Check the stove? What the hell does that mean?

He floored it and broke the speed limit all the way home.

CHAPTER SIX

Perpetually Weird

Jack stood in the hallway and let the door of his apartment swing open. He was relieved that he didn't smell gas. Even so, he was glad the hallway light and windows gave him enough light to see. He wasn't going to risk switching anything on.

Damn.

Someone had turned the place over, or that's what it looked like at first. Then he noticed what was missing. The pattern of destruction meant Gina had come back.

Now she's gone for good.

Jack could see that she'd worked the place over. The worst of it was in the bedroom.

No bedding. The pillows, sheets, and the super warm comforter—gone.

She had pulled all the drawers out and strewn their contents across the floor. Jack figured there would be a message in the bathroom, and he was right. It was now past the odd stage when this had happened to him before; it had moved into the chronically weird stage. It was at least the third time a girl had left him a message scrawled across his bathroom mirror.

This one was written in massive red lipstick letters: YOU SUCK!!!

She didn't make a little smiley face out of the periods on the bottom of the exclamation marks. Erin had done that. Erin had a little more class.

His gun and important papers were in the safe, so he knew they were secure. He looked into the kitchen, across the broken plates that littered the floor.

The stove. Replacement's note. Jack swallowed. *What did she do?*

What remained of the shattered plates crunched under his feet. He approached the stove with almost same trepidation as opening a door when clearing a room with SWAT.

All of the dials on the stove were turned off. He didn't smell gas, but the black glass of the oven door seemed extra dark. He looked and could see there was something in the oven. The light had never worked so after a moment's hesitation, he yanked open the door.

Stuffed inside the oven was a large green trash bag. He pulled the bag out and set it on the counter. When he looked inside, he laughed out loud. It was the super warm comforter and his pillow. Jack smiled. He removed both items and brought them to the bedroom. He'd have to thank Replacement later.

When he remembered he had to go to work, he grumbled. All he wanted to do was have one drink…or four. Instead, he headed over to his computer and searched his email. Jack didn't keep many emails, so it was easy to find.

Victor Rodriguez. He met him four months ago at the TEVOC training, and the two got along. Victor was on the police force in Sonoma, California. It was two towns over from Western Tech, but Jack knew Victor would check it out for him. As he finished typing the email, he thought of one detail he didn't have, and he groaned as if someone had squeezed his heart. He put his head in his hands and rubbed his face.

A picture. I don't have a current picture of her. Some brother I am.

He took a quick half-hour nap.

The glamorous life of a cop.

Jack dressed and headed out the door. He had a love/hate relationship with the police station. Part of him loved going to the new, sprawling two-story building with rows of police cars parked out front. Power seemed to surge into his muscles as he walked the halls. Another part of him hated it. There were times he couldn't stand the place because of all the people whose lives seemed to be broken apart there.

Jack would walk the station hallways and stare into the face of someone just arrested. Their eyes conveyed they knew the life they'd known would never return. Some days a victim would glance up, silently communicating their pain. That anguish would sear itself into his mind.

He checked in to the station, picked up his car, and went straight out.

Today was a day when he hated it. Patrol day. Sheriff Collins had received a call from the county commissioner's office asking how often a marked cruiser patrolled the homes at the county line. One call and now every week, some lucky stiff had to drive in a gigantic circle around the whole county. Today, Jack was the lucky stiff.

Boring. Very, very boring.

Today wasn't what Jack sought when he decided to become a policeman. He figured that after the Army, he'd be a cop for two years while he finished active duty. Then he'd go for something more exciting like the FBI or the CIA, but he kept putting that off. The problem was his training.

After 9/11, money poured in for police training. At his last job, he took every class he could, but he had to fight with all the other cops for a spot.

Training was the main reason he'd transferred to Darrington. Jack had no idea how Sheriff Collins did it, but the police department's training budget was a well that never dried up. When Jack contemplated taking the job, another colleague told him no matter how many classes he signed up for, they'd all be approved. Collins initially hesitated about letting Jack take so much training. He said he wanted to give everyone a chance, but it soon became clear that the only one who wanted that chance was Jack. The other cops here were either too busy or nowhere near as ambitious. When Collins realized that those funds would go to waste, he approved almost every course Jack wanted.

When Jack had joined the Army, he had taken specialized classes in everything from terrorism to profiling, high-speed pursuit to sniper training; he just couldn't get enough. When he'd transferred to Darrington, it was even better. It made the down times bearable. Jack could learn how to wiretap, conduct electronic surveillance, survive in the wilderness, or get TEVOC driver training.

The list of classes he planned to take went on and on. He loved it. To top it all off, he was paid to do it. He felt like a thief.

Who in their right mind would pay me to learn to fly a drone?

The vehicle in front of him slowed to a crawl because a police car was behind him.

Jack caused most of the complications in his own life. He was a master artisan for creating problems via his two main vices: shameless women and too much booze. His adoptive mother always warned him to stay away from both and still chided him about it today.

He missed his mom and dad. A few years back, his adoptive father had developed a blood clot, so the doctor thought it would be beneficial to thin his blood. His parents had moved to Florida. He hadn't been down to visit in a long while, but kept planning to go soon.

Every time he saw them, they seemed to be aging faster. They'd tried and tried to have kids of their own but couldn't, so they adopted. He was fortunate that, at age eleven, a good couple like them chose him. Typically, they all went for babies. Kids his age didn't end up with the pick-of-the-litter parents.

How stupid kids can be, he thought. *How stupid I was.*

He still felt guilty about how he acted. Two of the nicest people on the planet had brought him into their home, and he acted like a jerk. They'd come to Aunt Haddie's to pick him up, and he'd run crying into the woods.

Chandler was the one who found him. Jack had grabbed his hand and tried to pull him farther away, but Chandler just stood there. Even as a kid, Chandler was a giant. Jack could have run into him, but if Chandler didn't want to move, he wasn't moving.

"We gotta run, Chandler."

Chandler slapped him in the face, and the blow knocked Jack down.

"Jack, this is *your* chance."

"But, we need to stay together," Jack pleaded.

Chandler sat down on the ground next to him. "I'm not going anywhere. Aunt Haddie will take good care of Michelle and me. You've got a chance for a mom and dad. We had them once; you should get that too." He grabbed him by the arm and helped him up.

"Chandler..."

Jack knew he was right, but it still hurt.

When he got back to Aunt Haddie's, his new parents waited by her side. This time, he asked them whether he'd be able to come back and see Aunt Haddie, Chandler, and Michelle. His new mom promised that he could.

They kept that promise...mostly Chandler, his father, and him. Fishing, baseball, and lots of other stuff—together.

His parents had gone to Chandler's funeral. Jack wasn't there. He had been on the other end—putting the coffin on the plane.

It started to lightly snow. The car in front of him slowed down even more.

This is going to be a long shift.

CHAPTER SEVEN

Mommy

Jack passed by Mrs. Stevens's door on tiptoes.

Damn, I forgot to pick up her appeasement present.

He made another mental note to pick something up and headed upstairs. As he turned the corner of the stairs, he stopped dead. A light came from under his door.

His apartment door was solid wood, but there was a good half-inch gap underneath it and light now streamed out. Gina had wanted to get him one of those door sock things because the apartment was always drafty, but he thought getting one was way too domestic for him. He was glad he hadn't because now he could see that someone was inside.

Gina? No, she was gone.

He thought about who could have a key to his apartment, and that was a long list.

He knew for security, it was beyond stupid, but girls seemed to relax if you gave them a key and Jack wanted to keep the girls happy. He shook his head at his weakness.

He unsnapped his holster and opened the door. No sound came from inside the apartment. When he looked into the kitchen, he knew something was terribly wrong. It was clean.

The list of people who'd come into his apartment and clean was short. There was only one name—Mom. She must have flown up to surprise him.

"Mom?" he called as he trudged into his living room.

"Awkward." Replacement sang the word as she walked out of the bedroom. She had a towel wrapped around her body and was drying her hair with another one. She held onto the doorframe and arched her back, striking a comically seductive pose. "I'm not your mommy." She batted her eyes.

"Don't do that." Jack took a step back and turned away. "What're you doing here? I dropped you back off at your own apartment."

He emptied the contents of his pockets onto the counter. He knew this habit drove the girls crazy.

"Hey, I just cleaned that."

"Good thing you're not my mommy," Jack shot back with a slight grin. His mouth fell open a few seconds later when he opened the refrigerator and saw the sub. "How did you get in?"

"For a cop, I'm surprised you'd keep a key under the rug." She rolled her eyes and made a face. "It's the most obvious place to look."

Gina.

Jack cursed under his breath.

"Are you ready?" Replacement asked as she walked over to his desk.

My desk.

The workspace in the corner of the living room was immaculate. Jack could now see the wooden desk. The top was empty except for his desktop computer, a laptop he didn't recognize, a photograph, a stack of papers, and a notebook.

"Do you have obsessive-compulsive disorder?"

He walked over and picked up the photo. It was of Michelle. She'd changed so much. Gone was the awkward little girl who loved to wear mismatched socks. The beautiful woman who sat on the hood of the blue Civic had the same bright smile, the same dark brown eyes, but that was where the physical similarities ended.

She seemed confident and full of life. She seemed happy.

Happy.

If Jack had to choose one word to describe Michelle, it would be happy. When they were growing up, he thought she was cheerful all the time just because she was a little kid. He stopped thinking that when she broke her leg. They were sledding, and Michelle hit a tree. Aunt Haddie was beside herself when she got to the hospital. Chandler and Jack thought they'd get it when she came in. Michelle saved them from a big spanking because she lit up as if it was the best day in her life.

"Aunt Haddie, we had a great time sledding, except for my leg, but Chandler and Jack pulled me all the way to downtown." She beamed. "I got to ride in an ambulance. I've never been in a hospital, and the nurses are *so* pretty. Maybe I could…" and on and on she went. That was what Michelle truly was…happy.

Guilt washed over him as he looked at the picture. She'd matured into a beautiful woman, and he'd missed seeing her grow up. He wanted to hug her. He wanted to ask her why she was so happy then. He wanted…

Want, wish…they were about equal. Both the words came to the same thing, though: they never happen.

"Jack." Replacement's hand was soft on his arm. He had started to grip the photo too hard, and it was crumbling in his hands. "I thought you might need a photo to show around." There was concern in her voice and in her eyes.

Smart kid.

He turned the photo over. It was printed on photo paper with a home printer. "How old is the picture and where did you print it?" he asked.

"Three months ago at the nursing home," she answered with a crisp military tone. Jack couldn't tell whether she was mocking him or trying to be serious. "Terry at Well's Meadow—that's the home Aunt Haddie is in—printed it out after Michelle emailed it to her."

"Aunt Haddie's in a home?"

Replacement paused. "Sorry, she got real old and she started forgetting things. The doctors said it's early Alzheimer's. Michelle got her into a nice treatment center."

"Why didn't—?"

"I don't want to talk about Aunt Haddie." She folded her arms across her chest.

Jack hated to admit it, but he didn't either. It hurt too much.

"Do you have an electronic copy? I want to email it to a cop I know in California."

"She didn't go there," Replacement protested.

"Humor me, okay?"

"I already scanned it and put it on your desktop."

"How?"

"There." She pointed.

"That's my printer." Jack's lip curled.

"It's a scanner too." Replacement turned, but Jack could see her smile in the monitor before it vanished. "I printed some missing person flyers and passed some out. You didn't have much paper."

Jack stopped and looked at the small stack of papers on the desk.

"Good job. We can print some more." Jack sat down and pulled up his email. "I want to get that picture out."

Replacement walked into the kitchen as he emailed the photo to Victor.

"If she went to California then fine, but if she didn't, we need to rule it out," Jack tried to explain.

"She didn't. See, I ruled it out," Replacement snapped but quickly added, "You're right, sorry."

"Can you get more paper for the flyers?"

Replacement was silent, so Jack looked back into the kitchen.

Her mouth opened and closed but she nodded. "Sure."

He turned to the computer.

Why would she be freaked out about getting paper? Paper is…expensive.

"Use this, okay?"

Replacement's jacket was on the back of the chair. Jack took the cash out of his wallet and put it in her pocket.

"Don't do that. I'm fine…I have plenty of money." She rushed back over.

"Don't argue with me about money, kid. I'm Italian. It's part of our customs."

"Really?"

"I've got no idea what I am. I'm adopted, but I sort of look Italian and it sounds cool when I say it." He shrugged. "Besides, I'm not asking, *capisce?*" He tried his best godfather impersonation.

She grinned. "I thought you knew your parents. Aunt Haddie said you came there when you were seven."

"I knew my birth mother. I have no idea about my…the…guy. She never talked about him."

"Are they alive?" she asked.

"They could be."

"They could be? Why didn't you go find them?"

Jack could tell that Replacement was trying not to make a face, but the result was an expression that looked as if she drank a straight shot of unsweetened lemonade.

"What for? What would I ask them? Why did you get rid of me? I don't want to know. I don't care."

"Not even a little?"

"Well, trying to figure out why she left me on my birthday…it made me a little crazy, so I stopped doing it."

Replacement's mouth dropped open. "It happened on your birthday?"

"Don't get so dramatic, kid. It wasn't my *real* birthday. I don't even know when that is. That's the date they wrote on the form."

"They just pick it?" She sat on the couch.

Jack nodded. "Anyway, it happened."

She walked to the side of the desk and stared at him. "What happened? I mean how did...uh...she do it?"

Jack tried to keep his eyes on the computer, but she just kept watching him. Maybe it was the innocent look on her face or because he was so worried about Michelle, but he opened up.

"We were in a bus depot. She said we were going to Vegas. I had no clue where that was. She came back with two tickets. When she started to hand me my ticket, she froze."

He looked off into the distance, detached from the story he was conveying.

"She just stared at me. She always looked at me weird anyway. It was like a mixture of love and hate. A real yin-yang thing."

Replacement leaned against the desk.

"She just straightened up and said, 'You got needs, kid. School, friends, crap like that. This is best.' Then she turned around and went to the bus."

"What did you do?"

"I flipped out. I ran after her, begging. I grabbed onto her and she just backhanded me. I didn't know about drugs then, but I knew there were times when she was just out of it. I thought that was one of those times."

He squinted as if he were trying to see a detail that was just out of sight. "She wore these super big heels, and she was wobbling." He stared down at the floor. "She just turned around and said, 'You don't know jack, kid.'"

Replacement stared at him. "Then she just up and left?"

He nodded. "That was the last thing she ever said to me."

"You were left in the middle of a bus station?" Replacement's eyes were huge.

"Not exactly the middle. I was sort of to the right—"

She smacked his shoulder. "You know what I mean. What did you do?"

"I did what every seven-year-old would do if they got dumped in a bus depot at night."

"You cried?"

"I got caught stealing a pocketbook." Jack laughed.

"Really?"

"Yeah. I stole it so I could get enough money to buy a ticket to go with her. Anyway, I got pinched and then the whirlwind into the system began. Police station, youth services, counselors, court, lawyer...I never had so much attention in my life, and I hated it. No one talks to a whore's kid, but now everyone was asking me questions. I was seven, but..." Jack raised his head. "What about you, kid?"

"I...I don't like to talk about it." She wrapped her arms around her chest and crossed her legs.

"That's fair. Here I am baring my soul and..."

Replacement's lip quivered.

"Sorry." He held both hands up. "I shouldn't have butted in." Jack moved to the window and looked into the darkness.

Replacement shuffled over and sat down.

Jack watched one lone car drive down the street. After a few minutes, he turned and nodded toward the photo. At the bottom was a printed title: *Check out my new ride!* "Who added the title?"

"I guess Michelle?" Replacement shrugged.

"Is that her car?"

"She got it when Aunt Haddie stopped driving."

A wave of guilt washed over Jack again, and he tried to forget how he had left the old woman to fend for herself.

"Okay. Then the picture is a couple of years old. How often did she call?"

"She called all the time, almost every day."

"When was the last call?"

"Look. I wrote it up." She grabbed the calendar off the desk and flipped the pages back twice. "She called Aunt Haddie but the calls stopped on the eighteenth. She was supposed to come home December 21, Saturday evening. We called her Sunday, thinking that maybe she just hadn't left yet, but she never called back. By Monday morning, we both freaked out and started calling the campus police. They got back to us and said she transferred. I knew that was garbage, so we called the police."

"When was that?" Jack made notes, too.

"December 23." She pointed to the calendar. "I went to the Fairfield Sheriff's Department that afternoon and after an hour of filling out the missing person report, they said I couldn't because I'm not her *real* sister. I said that was bull, and he sucks, and asked if I could talk to a *real* cop."

"Hold up. Which officer were you speaking with?"

"I don't know. Officer Jerk Bag. Some creep. He says I have to be blood related. I told him that she doesn't have any blood relation living so how was that going to work? He said he needed blood for the report, and I offered to show him blood, and then they asked *me* to leave!" She looked genuinely surprised.

"A nurse called and explained that Aunt Haddie was too ill to come to the police station, so another cop was sent out and took the report from her. We kept calling. The cops just kept blowing us off, telling us to wait. We didn't know what else to do. Then Aunt Haddie said to track you down." She looked up expectantly.

"Okay. What do we know?" He grabbed the notebook. He wrote the titles "DATE" and "ACTIONS" on one page. He wrote "FACTS" in large letters for a title on the next page and then pushed the notebook and pen to Replacement.

"Can we use the computer? Twenty-first century?" She made a face.

"Humor me. I like to be able to carry it around."

Replacement lifted the laptop and made it float up and down.

"Call me old-fashioned."

Replacement muttered under her breath, "Yeah, old."

Jack looked at the laptop. The case looked well-worn, and he didn't see any brand name on it. The lid was closed, but it looked powered up, and it was connected to his computer too.

"Yours?" he pointed.

"She's my baby." She patted the case.

"Just use the notebook. Write all the dates from the calendar down and what happened," he instructed her as he went back to the kitchen to get a drink.

He came back with two glasses of water and set one down in front of her. He noticed that her penmanship was beautiful, and he laughed.

"What?" Replacement looked up.

"Your handwriting is beautiful. I guess Aunt Haddie kept writing as a punishment?"

"It sure sucked," Replacement said with half a laugh. "I think I'd rather have gotten spanked than to write."

Aunt Haddie had some unique punishments she'd use to correct the children in her care. Jack remembered having to transcribe page after page of books if he misbehaved. If his handwriting didn't meet Aunt Haddie's strict standards, she'd tear it up, and he'd have to do it again. His handwriting now was almost perfect.

He looked down at Replacement's intricate script and laughed out loud. "Boy, you must have been a pretty rotten kid."

"Thanks. I heard you were an angel, too." She shot him a frown. "Don't get me wrong. Aunt Haddie really loves you, but she said if there was ever a kid who liked to do the opposite of what he was told, it was you."

"She was just trying to make you feel good. I was a choir boy."

"Michelle backed her up." Replacement gave him a knowing look.

"Okay. Let's go over the facts," Jack continued. "First: Michelle is missing." Replacement wrote that, but added *duh*. Jack let that slide. "Second: the campus police and the roommate said she transferred. Third: the roommate said *he* told her Michelle transferred to a different school. Fourth: Western Tech said she applied and was accepted, according to Neil."

"Miss Piggy said Michelle took all her stuff," Replacement growled.

Replacement turned the page, wrote the title "EVIDENCE" and stopped. She didn't look up. Her back was still stiff, and Jack knew she was smoldering over the fact that Michelle's belongings were now missing. He admired the fact that in spite of her feelings she was pressing on.

"She wouldn't leave you and Aunt Haddie," Jack offered as the first piece of evidence. It wasn't evidence that would hold up in court, but Jack didn't care. He knew that fact was as real as a smoking gun. Replacement wrote, "She wouldn't leave Aunt Haddie."

"When did she come to visit?" Jack walked over to the window and looked out at the cars below.

"She came by about twice a month."

Jack stared into the black night.

Why walk away from a full scholarship?

He walked back to the desk and traded places with Replacement in front of the computer.

"Let's back up a couple of steps." Behind him, Replacement groaned and huffed as he connected to the police's computer system. "I'll run the plate."

Jack typed with two fingers and had to go back and forth between the photo and the screen three times. Fairfield had entered a BOLO for the car so law enforcement would be on the lookout for it but other than that, nothing.

"She's never even gotten a parking ticket." Jack drummed his fingers on the desk. "Let's see if anything was going on in the area."

"I'll drive." Replacement got right in his face. "You type like an old lady."

"I know the system. It will be faster if I—"

"No. No." Replacement shook her head and started to sit in the chair beside him.

"Hey." Jack moved over and almost fell out of the chair, so he stood up.

"That's much better. Where do you want to go?"

"Start with recently reported crimes," Jack said.

With a few clicks, lines of information scrolled up the screen.

"I'll limit them to the past three months," Replacement said as she hit a couple of keys and the data scrolled again, but the list was still long.

"You said Michelle stayed around the college. Can you limit it to an area around the campus?"

A couple of clicks and a new, much smaller list appeared. Jack scanned it. One reported car theft, two break-ins, drugs, and an assault. "Check that." He pointed to the assault.

Replacement read parts of the report. "It happened right before Halloween. A girl was jogging. The suspect grabbed her around the neck and pulled her down, but the woman began screaming and the man ran away. It was an eighteen-year-old woman. She was of African-American descent. The man in this and the other incidents was described as a white male." She turned to look at Jack. "Other incidents?"

"Check the SAR."

Replacement paused and crinkled her nose as she scanned the monitor. Jack pointed to a section of the screen. Her fingers flew across the keyboard. "Suspicious Activity Reports" appeared at the top of the screen.

"SAR links different events that may or may not be related. See if there's anything that it's been paired with."

"Bingo. The reports are connected. Look at this. Serial assaults." Replacement started to read. "There are two other reports in the group. A man approached one woman while she was getting into her car. She locked the doors and the suspect tried to open them. In the other one, an African-American woman was walking home when a white male approached her. The girl ran to a house, and the man fled. She was nineteen. What a scumbag."

She clicked a link and a description appeared. In all three incidents, the description of the suspect was the same: a white male in his late twenties, five foot seven and a hundred thirty pounds. Two of the reports stated that he had a tattoo of an eagle on his right forearm. The other just mentioned a tattoo of undetermined type on his right arm.

"I just saw that database." Replacement clicked and tapped and the police tattoo database appeared.

"*Eagle—right arm.* How can there be no results?" There was more typing and more zero results. She'd type different combinations, but the outcome was always the same: nothing.

"This database blows." She pushed the mouse away.

"Calm down. We're just trying to look at all the angles now anyway."

"Well, so far this is our best angle and we got nothing."

Jack walked back over to the window.

That guy shows an escalating pattern of violence. Three attacks. If Michelle ran into him…

"Did you try entering some other type of bird or another word?"

"I tried everything. That system stinks. If I type in just *eagle* it has two matches…two. I know more than two people with an eagle tattoo. Do you know another way to try to look it up?"

Jack stared at his own reflection in the window. "I know…I know a police tattoo expert who can help." It was a lie wrapped in a truth. "They should be there tomorrow."

"Who? The people at the lab? On a Saturday?"

He ignored the question. "I can start there. You can stay here tonight."

He looked down at Replacement. She grinned from ear to ear.

"But I'm going alone."

The smile vanished.

CHAPTER EIGHT

Inking

Jack shut the door of his car and looked across the street. The huge sign on the front of the brick building read: Vitagliano's. The little store was nestled between an art gallery and a handmade jewelry store. If it wasn't for all of the people covered in tattoos, it easily could be mistaken for an upscale coffee shop. Vitagliano's was an island for the misfits of Darrington. There was a long counter with stools and a couple of tables out front. Tattooed and pierced patrons sat at the tall metal tables with the high back stools. They stared at Jack as he strolled through the door. Their heads moved as one as they watched him walk toward the back. They seemed to sense he was a cop, and the distrust was palpable.

"Hey, boss," a tall guy at the counter called out.

Jack stopped and waited. He looked toward the far wall where a thick red velvet curtain covered the entrance to the back rooms, with an Italian statue of a female gladiator on each side.

"Jack?" A woman called his name from behind the curtain and then she yanked it aside. She was a woman in her late twenties: tall—about five foot ten—with broad shoulders. Leather pants and a black tank top revealed a toned canvas covered in tattoos. Marisa Vitagliano was owner, artist, and bouncer of Vitagliano's tattoo parlor. Jack exhaled. She was drop dead gorgeous.

She was dangerous but his being here was more so. Marisa was the type of girl his mother had warned him about. The kind he should steer clear of. Jack couldn't. He was like a little kid with fire. Even though you told him it was dangerous, the blaze was so pretty he had to touch it.

They stared at each other. It had been almost five months since he last saw her; he had forced himself to stay away. Marisa had no idea how many times he'd driven by her apartment or started to dial the phone and then hung up. He didn't want to be here, but he had to come. He needed Marisa's help to look for Michelle.

"Hey, angel."

She didn't return his smile, but he noticed that her eyes widened.

"Why are you here?" She didn't move, and her words were emotionless. He looked again at the statues and realized why she'd picked them; they could have been her sisters.

"I need a favor."

"Another one?" She lowered her chin and raised an eyebrow.

She kept score.

He caught her quick sidelong glance to the audience in the room.

This is her house. I hurt her. Showing up here, unannounced, is wrong.

"I need your help…please?" He gave the slightest bow. He learned that in an interrogation class. Humble yourself and don't puff yourself up. Begging went against his instincts, but it did work. After a moment, she stepped to the side and gestured for him to follow her behind the curtain.

The backrooms consisted of a red-carpeted hallway that ran straight down to a door with four rooms along the side. There were no doors on the side rooms, and, as Jack walked back, he saw two people getting tattoos.

A man in his twenties was getting the only available spot of his skin covered with a large skull with torches for eyes. In the other room, a young teenage girl was getting a tattoo on her back, just above her bum. Tears rolled down her cheeks, but her face was set and she squeezed her boyfriend's hand as the word TOMMY'S neared completion.

How long is it going to be before she's crying at a doctor's office, asking how to have the tattoo removed?

He looked back at Marisa; she held the door open at the end of the hallway. In spite of her tight leather pants, two-inch high heels, and an even tighter black tank top that seemed vacuum-sealed to her busty frame, Jack observed everything but her.

The look on her face begged the question that seemed to haunt her—why? Their eyes met, and she shook her head with a knowing smile.

Jack stopped and stared at her. *What could I say? Sorry?* Marisa was not a vain girl, but she was hyper-observant. *Maybe it was the artist in her.* That was what brought them together. Jack grinned whenever he thought of meeting her.

Shortly after he arrived in Darrington, he was at a bar and was on a bit of a bender. She sat three seats down, with a steady stream of guys hitting on her. She ignored all of them. But Jack never looked at her because he couldn't take his eyes off what she was drawing. He watched, mesmerized, as she sketched a detailed picture of a smiling girl running in a field.

He barely remembered stumbling over to her side. He pointed to the picture as he proclaimed to the entire bar, "This is art!" Then he staggered to the front door.

She chased after him and caught up to him on the sidewalk. "Why did you say that?" She grabbed him by both shoulders and gave him a quick shake to sober him up. "About my picture, why did you say that?"

"What?" That is when he looked down and noticed her for the first time. She was beautiful. Her eyes were deep brown and matched her long auburn hair. Her dress accentuated her hourglass figure. Jack swallowed, his mouth open slightly, and then he looked back up at her eyes.

One of her eyebrows raised, but the cutest smile was on her lips as she stated, "You noticed my art before my body."

"Your artwork...you're a true artist! The way you hold that pencil." He pinched his fingers together to mimic her sketching. "It was..." Jack struggled to find the words, but he didn't have to.

Marisa grabbed him and kissed him deeply. It was the kind of kiss a guy didn't forget, ever. Just thinking about it still turned him on.

He realized later that by noticing her art instead of her body, he'd done something no other man had done before. The reward he received that night still brought a smile to his face.

The relationship had been a whirlwind, and they had both been sucked in. Jack had never gotten so close, so fast to anyone. It was as if there had always been a bond between them.

He remembered the last time he saw Marisa...

She comforted him with a long weekend locked away in a little bed and breakfast. It was just the two of them, and they never came out of the room. He remembered what she said when they were getting ready to go back to town.

"You have to decide what you want." She stared out the window.

"Decide? About what?" It was different from what other girls would have said. He was used to the "Am I the only one?" or "What're your plans for the future?" but this didn't feel like that. Marisa wasn't a typical girl.

"Me. I can't be an accessory. I know ME. Tu sei il bello mio."

He didn't speak Italian, but he knew the phrase. You're my beautiful one. She loved him. Jack stared at her. He knew he couldn't give her what she needed. He reached deep down, and he wanted to, but he couldn't.

She stood at the window with a sheet wrapped around herself. He tried to convince himself to lie. He didn't want to give her up, but he couldn't bring himself to betray her honesty. She was special to him. He looked away.

"I'll get a ride back to town," she continued as she held her head up and stared out the window. "We can't do this anymore." There was no malice in her voice; it was still rich and kind.

"Marisa..."

"Jack, if we keep going then you'll hurt me and...I'll kill you." Her voice was so smooth that he smiled at first, but he knew how true those words were.

He blinked, trying to drive those memories from his head as Marisa waited for him at the end of the hallway. He inhaled before he squared his shoulders and marched through the door into her office.

"What's the favor now?" Her words were cold, but the question was colder.

She'll help, but she wants nothing to do with me. There was no "How have you been?" or "What've you been doing?" *She is all business, and it's all my fault.*

"I need help with a tattoo." He pulled the computer-generated sketch from an envelope.

She took it without looking at him.

She'd helped him while they were together a couple of times by identifying tattoos: once for a mugging and once for the John Doe.

He noticed Marisa didn't look at the picture. Her back had tensed, so he did something that was exceedingly hard for him but came so easily when he was with her. He told the complete truth, laying bare his soul.

"I'm looking for a girl named Michelle. She's my foster sister. She's missing. I have little to go on."

He hated this. Marisa was like a siren who pulled sailors to their death. All he could think of right now was how much he wanted to hold her. Jack was opening up, but he was the type of man who couldn't open just a little. His pride was like a dam: one little crack, and he broke.

"She got what looks like a great deal, full scholarship to WRE. Everything was going great, but she's gone."

He was close to breaking, close to screaming and storming out. He didn't want her to see him like that. He didn't want anyone to see him like that.

He paused and looked into her eyes.

"I'm sorry. I need you—"

She moved so fast he wasn't able to finish his sentence. She grabbed him and pulled his body against hers; the picture fell to the table. One of her hands held the back of his head and the other pulled him closer to her. They crashed together like two dancers, a fierce impact filled with delicate grace.

She embraced and kissed him. Her hands moved behind his head.

He hesitated and then gave in. Grabbing her waist, he hoisted her onto the desk.

A deep, lush moan, better explained as a purr, escaped her lips. Jack's hands traveled over her taut muscles. He grabbed the back of her head and kissed the base of her neck.

Jack kept his eyes closed. He could smell Marisa's hair. He could feel her breath on his neck. He lay on top of her on the desk, one hand behind her head and the other on her waist. He breathed in her scent, and it stoked a growing fire within him. The rhythm of their movements quickly synchronized. Their mutual need was palpable, and their entwined bodies began to undulate as one.

"Jack." She whispered his name and softly kissed his ear.

He opened one eye, and when he looked at her, she stared at him with her big brown eyes. They were open, inviting, and enflamed with desire. Her eyes softened, and he read something else in her expression: vulnerability. She reached out to pull him close.

He leaned in to kiss her, but guilt enveloped him.

I can't do this. I can't hurt her again.

He slowly pulled back and slid off the table.

Her eyes traveled the length of his body again, and Jack swallowed hard.

"I don't…I don't want to hurt you." Jack's jaw clenched.

The heat in Marisa's eyes cooled along with her voice. "You don't want to hurt me…or Gina?"

Jack's chin lowered to his chest, and he sighed.

He shook his head. "No, Gina walked out." He looked up into her eyes. "She's not in your league. You're…*tu sei il bello mio.*"

Her eyes widened, and her mouth danced between a smile and frown. "Then why?"

"Marisa, any guy would kill to be with you, but right now…you don't need me in your life."

She slid off the desk and leaned against it. Her look turned cold. She stood up and walked over to a computer in the corner of the room. "He has an eagle on his right forearm? He got it here about a year ago."

She pressed a few keys and a page printed out.

Jack stared at her, confused.

"I knew the tat right away." She straightened her back, putting on her best face. "I just wanted to make you beg."

She flipped the page over, scribbled a quick note, and then folded the paper and placed it in an envelope. Without looking at him, she pushed the envelope to the edge of the desk and looked back to the computer.

"Marisa." He touched her shoulder, and she let her head rest against his hand. She had a new tattoo on her back, a heart with a golden lock wrapped around it.

"Go." She didn't open her eyes, but in the reflection in the computer monitor, he saw the slightest tremble in her lip.

What was I thinking, coming here?

Jack grabbed the envelope and walked out the door. He didn't look back. He wanted to, but it was wrong—what he did to her. It was wrong—what she did to him. He knew it was wrong because, for some reason, it could never be right. They both knew it. He stormed down the now deserted hallway.

As Jack walked out front, all eyes were on him. He knew someone must have said something. The men's eyes narrowed in envy and the women batted their eyes. He focused on the door and kept walking, his jacket in hand. It was freezing out, but he let the cold wash over him. *Guilt.* He hated guilt.

Never again, he vowed as he crossed to his car.

He opened the envelope and looked down at the picture inside. A rat-faced guy was posing to show off his new eagle tattoo on his right forearm. Kevin Arnold. He'd have to run him when he got home.

On the back of the picture she'd written, "I'll wait." Next to it, she'd written the number 2614 and had drawn a heart around it. He remembered the new tattoo on Marisa's back, a heart with a gold combination lock. He hadn't made the connection before, but he did now. The combination was 2614.

Jack Stratton, you suck. 2614. My badge number.

Someone laid on a car horn as Jack pulled out. He didn't care.

CHAPTER NINE

She Slimed Me

On the way home, Jack remembered to stop by the supermarket and pick up a gigantic chocolate cake, an "I'm sorry" card, and a box of chocolates for Mrs. Stevens.

As he walked back to the car, he changed direction and headed to the liquor store.

I'll just have a little. Take the edge off. Nothing more.

The bell on the door rang as he entered. Cappy, an old fat guy, sat behind the counter, barely looking up. It was a small store with three rows of hard liquor and four coolers of beer in the back. Jack headed for the rum.

He grabbed a half pint, took two steps, and then put it back. Reaching out, he picked up a pint, but then hesitated. As he returned it to the shelf, the glass clinked against the other bottles. Settling on a fifth, he headed for the front.

Cappy got off his stool as Jack approached and set the bottle down on the old worn counter.

"Hey Jack, you want anything else?"

Jack stopped cold and stared at the back of the cash register.

Cappy set his hand on the counter and leaned in a little. "Hey. You want anything else?"

Jack still didn't speak. He stared at a flyer taped to the back of the register. Replacement must have put it up. He stood there, gazing at Michelle's picture.

"You want it or not?" Cappy grumbled.

Jack turned and walked out the door empty-handed.

"Jack?" An elderly woman in a worn brown coat paused in the middle of getting into an old sedan as she called to him.

Despite being in her late 70s, Mrs. Sawyer had always been very active. Jack had met her when she was convinced her home was being robbed after finding a broken window. He felt it was from a tree branch nearby and a bit of wind. Nonetheless, he went by to check on her every day for a month to make her feel better and now he had a lifelong friend.

He went over to accept a hug. She wrapped her arms around him and rocked him back and forth. It always made him feel good.

"It's so nice to see you, Jack."

"How have you been, Mrs. Sawyer?"

"Wonderful. I just picked up some fresh apples. They're on sale. So is the haddock. I might make a chowder."

"I was going to stop by."

"You'll have to. I'll give you a warm cup of cocoa and a big slice of pie." She patted him on the arm. "I stayed out a little too late running errands, so I better head back. The General will be wondering where I've gone."

The General was her cat. Jack closed the door for her and stepped up on the curb. With a wave, the little old woman gunned the car out of the parking lot. Jack was glad there was only light traffic; she drove faster than most in town.

After he returned to his apartment, Jack stood outside Mrs. Stevens's door. He tried to balance the cake, card, and chocolates as he knocked. He took a step back when she opened it. It was obvious she'd been crying, and she looked scary.

When she saw him standing there, she let out a mournful wail and threw both arms around his neck.

"Mr. Stratton, I'm so truly sorry." He could hardly understand her through the sobs and sniffling. "You're the nicest man."

Jack's mind raced to find an excuse so he could get out from her clutches without offending her too much. He also didn't want to drop the cake. "It's okay, Mrs. Stevens."

She patted the side of his face with her wet hand and then took the cake, card, and chocolates. "God bless you, sir. You're an angel for what you've done for that poor girl." Another strange wail of a sob caused her to turn and run into her apartment. The door slammed behind her.

Jack stood there and wiped the side of his face with his jacket.

Gross. She slimed me.

He shook his head. *Replacement. I wonder what she could have told her that—*

He turned and ran up the stairs three at a time.

"What did you tell her?" he demanded to the empty living room and kitchen. *Maybe she went to get something to eat.*

He walked into the bedroom and sat down to kick off his shoes. Replacement walked out of the bathroom wearing her long nightshirt with her head down as she wrapped her hair in a towel.

Jack smile mischievously.

She doesn't see me.

"Boo."

Replacement shrieked. Jack saw her hand shoot out, and the next second she launched the candleholder on his bureau at his head. It just missed and smashed against the wall. She ran shrieking into the bathroom and slammed the door.

Jack sat there for a second and then fell over laughing.

She ripped opened the door and yelled, "Jerk. What the hell is the matter with you?"

He laughed harder.

She stormed out. He tried to stop, but he just rolled over and laughed at the ceiling.

"Seriously? Seriously?" She slapped his legs.

"Stop. Stop. I can't breathe." Jack's sides hurt.

"Do you knock? You hide in here?"

"Hide? Knock? It's my apartment." He was down to giggling now.

"You're a total JACKASS." She stomped back into the bathroom and slammed the door.

After a minute, Jack rose with a groan and went to the door. He shook his head and knocked softly. "Sorry." Jack listened and waited. "I'm sorry," he said again louder.

She opened the door a crack. "Do you mean it?"

"Yes."

"Will you announce yourself next time?"

Announce myself? It's my damn apartment.

Jack exhaled. "Okay. I'll stop. Truce?"

Replacement eyed him warily. "Truce."

"Is your shower broken?" Jack asked, trying to control his laughter. He realized every time he came home, she was getting out of his shower.

"You have unlimited hot water. You're not a save-the-water-and-conserve type of guy, are you?" She got so close to him they were inches apart. She was trying to make him a little uncomfortable while making a seductive face. "But I did hear that those save-the-water types have a slogan: Save the planet, shower with a buddy." She laughed as his mouth dropped open. "Did you want me to wait?" She raised her eyebrows up and down suggestively.

"Don't go there."

Not after this morning...too far.

Jack walked over to the computer.

"Now I'm sorry," she continued to joke as she skipped over next to him. "Forgive me?"

Jack tossed the envelope on the desk. She tore it open.

"Did you run this guy? Do you know where he lives?"

"I just got here. I was going to log in and run him."

"I thought you went to the police lab? Why didn't you run him there?" She turned the picture over, and her eyes narrowed when she saw Marisa's note. "Gee...the guys down at the lab must think you're pretty sweet." She pointed to the heart and batted her eyes.

"I said, knock it off; I'm not in the mood." He grabbed for the envelope. "Hey, what did you say to Mrs. Stevens?" he asked as the memory of the crying landlady came back.

"I bought her a pie."

Jack got out of his seat as he sensed Replacement's frustration. She sat and began typing.

"A pie?" *I should have kept the cake.*

Jack's stomach growled, and he headed for the kitchen to scrounge for food. He opened the refrigerator and there was milk and a large apple pie on the top shelf.

"Can I have some of this, please?" He sounded like a little kid as he begged at the refrigerator.

"I bought it for you," she called over her shoulder as she kept typing on her laptop.

"It had to be a lot more than pie to get her crying like that. What else did you say?" Jack poured a tall glass of milk to go with the huge hunk of pie he dished out for himself.

"I...I just...I kept in character."

Jack shook his head, dreading what she might have said, but he didn't care; the pie was delicious.

"Kevin Arnold. This guy's a piece of work," Replacement spat.

Jack choked on his pie. He rushed over to the computer.

She's logged in to the police database.

"How did you do that?"

"I've been looking through it all day looking for the car, so I just went over and ran his name. Look at the pictures. This is the same guy." She pointed at the screen and sat back in the chair.

"How did you log in?" Jack was trying to control his growing exasperation, but he was losing that fight.

"I used your log-in." She shrugged.

"How did you get it?"

"I saw you type it. Chargers, just with a dollar sign instead of the letter *S*. I pick up on stuff like that." She looked at him with a genuinely innocent smile.

His irritation evaporated. He didn't know whether it was because it was his own stupidity for letting her see his password or the fact that the look on her face showed she had no idea that she'd broken a whole string of laws.

"Okay," he mumbled as he walked back to his pie. "What's it have on him?"

He ate some more. Jack was shocked that a pie could abate his anger so quickly. He shrugged and took another bite. It was *really* good.

Replacement's fingers flew over the keyboard. "He's been arrested eight times: breaking and entering, drugs, and three assaults." She continued to type. "No jail time. There are two restraining orders out on him. Both expired. He has one outstanding warrant." The typing stopped.

"What were the assaults?"

"One domestic. Looks like a girlfriend. That's how the restraining order came up."

"What about the other assaults?"

"First one was a girl inside a bar." She scanned the page. "It doesn't look like he knew her. Relationship says none."

"Second one?"

"Oh, this is different, girl *outside* a bar. He didn't know her either."

"What's the race of the women?"

"Girlfriend is listed as white. Girls from the bars are African-American."

If this guy touched Michelle, I'm going to kill him.

"You have an address? Since he has no jail time, they'd have listed it under probation records. It should be in there."

"I'll try." Her fingers flew over the keyboard again.

Jack shook his head. He worked at the station and knew next to nothing about their computer systems. He'd have to sign up for some more classes.

"Nothing."

Jack closed his eyes, laced his fingers behind his head, and exhaled.

"Check who posted his bail."

After a minute, Replacement tilted her head and shook the mouse. "That doesn't make sense. Nancy Mulligan bailed him out, but that's the girlfriend he assaulted."

Jack frowned. "It happens all the time. I don't get it. Why would a girl stay with someone who treats them like that?"

"She lives at 303B Hillside Downs Road."

Jack was too familiar with Hillside Downs. It was an apartment complex with about a hundred units. They looked like something from a third-world country and going there was about as safe.

Gun. Taser. Vest. Mace for the dogs.

Jack grimaced as he made a list of things to take.

Jack looked at the clock. "I can't go out there now. I'll need backup. I'll go in the morning. You'll stay here."

"Great. Sure." Replacement smiled and moved to the couch.

Jack looked down at her and frowned. *I didn't mean that you'd sleep here. I meant that I'd go, and you won't go.* He wanted to say it aloud, but instead he ran his fingers through his hair. *I'm getting soft.*

CHAPTER TEN

The Downs

The next morning, Jack drove out to Hillside Downs, followed by Kendra and Donald Pugh. They stopped before the entrance, and Jack walked back to meet with them.

"Thanks for coming."

"No problem." Donald gave a curt nod.

Donald was Kendra's partner. He'd cajoled Jack once into promising to take him to the police gun range for an afternoon and he was still waiting for Jack to deliver. When it came to shooting practice, Jack went alone. Not because he was bad; quite the opposite. He was like a celebrity at the range. Jack had found out the hard way the downside of being the fastest gun hadn't changed since the Old West. The title put a mark on your head, and everyone wanted to try to take you down. He didn't know whether Donald wanted tips or to take a shot at *besting* him.

"I normally enjoy watching you get into trouble but not here." Kendra looked over, and her eyes rounded in concern.

Jack understood her meaning. He spoke in his stern military no-nonsense tone. "The guy we're looking for is Kevin Arnold. He's a skinny, little rat-faced white guy." Jack handed them a copy of Kevin's mug shot. "He has an outstanding warrant for failure to appear from Lincoln County."

Kendra passed the paperwork to Donald.

"He has no known address, but I looked up who bailed him out: Nancy Mulligan. It's her apartment. If we're lucky, Kevin Arnold won't be far behind."

The two patrol cars rolled through the front gates of Hillside Downs, four three-story buildings with all the warmth and charm of 1950s Russian architecture. They were squat, square, and appeared as if whoever had built them had asked for the cheapest model possible. The peeled paint, rusted railings, and crumbling walls added to the feeling of desolation.

As they drove to Building Three, the windows all appeared empty. There were only a couple with shades and even fewer with curtains. Most windows had a sheet or blanket that concealed the room from the outside world.

Jack, Donald, and Kendra parked at the side of the building.

A dog tied to a railing of one apartment rushed the car. It ran straight at them before it reached the end of its chain and the collar yanked its neck. The dog's whole body twisted violently, and it fell into the dirt before it scrambled to its feet and barked incessantly.

They looked up, and the windows stayed empty in spite of the dog's warning.

"Is this place deserted or what?" Kendra asked as she scanned the area.

There wasn't a soul in sight.

"It always is at eight in the morning. Everyone's still sleeping off the coke and booze from last night," Donald cracked.

"Kendra, you watch the back. This guy's assaults have all been on women, and he's jumped them. If I were going to put money on it, I'd lay four-to-one that he takes off. The balconies on the end apartments connect them. He could try to go there. Plus, there are utility closets that link the apartments. I've seen water heaters in them, but this guy may be skinny enough to slip through," Jack said.

Kendra nodded. "I'll cover them. If he bolts, I'll nail him."

"Good."

Jack gave himself a once-over and went through his list: *Gun. Taser. Vest. Mace. Cuffs. Baton.*

Donald looked over at his partner. "No unnecessary chances, okay?"

Kendra nodded.

Jack forced himself to walk slowly, and Donald followed behind.

Third floor. All of these apartments, same layout.

A pair of yellowed eyes peered out from a first-floor window and hastily disappeared.

The stench of urine hit his nose when he got to the staircase.

Front door. Square living room. Kitchen in the back. Utility closet in the kitchen. Bathroom to the left and then the bedroom.

The second floor had a couple of old lawn chairs next to the stairs and cigarette butts littered the cement. A chain held a mountain bike frame that was missing the tires, seat, and handlebars.

Third floor.

Jack flexed his shoulders. He leaned over the railing and saw Kendra. She was watching the back, and her head was in constant motion.

Head on a swivel. Good girl.

Jack reached the unit. He motioned and Donald waited near the window. As he stood to the side of the door, Jack knocked. He didn't pound on it like some cops did. He didn't want to sound like the Gestapo. A dog two apartments down started to bark, and then another. Both sounded like big dogs. He instinctively put his hand on his mace. He knocked again. The face of a little girl appeared in the corner of the window.

Damn. A little kid.

A woman in her early twenties opened the door. She was dressed in gray baggy sweatpants and a loose top. The baby in her arms pulled on the top so much that her left breast was almost exposed. She yanked her shirt out of the baby's hand while using her leg to try to hold back the little kid who'd been peering out the window.

Jack categorized them as a non-threat and scanned the background. The living room was dark, but there was enough light to see.

No one visible. Kitchen empty.

He listened intently for any sounds in the apartment.

"Yeah?" She alternated from looking at the floor to trying to look at him. Her eyes would catch his for a brief moment and then dart away.

Red mark on cheek. Bruise on arm. Distrust. Fear.

"Good morning, ma'am. I'm Officer Jack Stratton."

"Yeah?" She pulled the baby's hand from her hair.

"Sorry to disturb you but I have a few questions." He kept his tone light. "May I ask your name please?"

"Nancy Mulligan."

"And this is your apartment?" He gave an extra wide smile.

She just nodded her head.

"I'm looking for Kevin Arnold. Is he in?"

"He doesn't live here."

The little kid turned and looked into the apartment. The mother is lying.

"Ma'am." He gestured for her to step a little outside of the apartment. She stood frozen for a second, but then Jack turned his eyes to her. She faltered and stepped out.

He turned slightly and leaned in a little. "I know you want to protect him. I'm not asking you to give him up, but he needs help."

His training in domestic violence kicked in. Beaten women often turned on the authorities and protected their abuser.

"Momma?" the little girl tugged on Nancy's shirt.

Jack could tell that she was on the edge of letting him have access to the apartment.

"Nancy." Jack paused and lowered his voice to a whisper.

She looked confused for a second and then looked down at the little girl. She grabbed her daughter and pulled her closer.

"You want him to get help, right?" Jack looked down at the little girl. "Everyone needs help sometimes."

A soft cry escaped her mouth and she shook her head.

She kept her gaze down as she whispered the words, "He's in the bedroom."

That was all Jack needed to hear. He nodded to Donald and stepped into the apartment, motioning for her to leave. She scooped up her children and ran down the corridor. Jack moved into the apartment, scanning constantly. The bathroom door was open. It was empty. The bedroom door was closed.

He gestured to Donald and then pointed at the closed door. He stood to the side, out of range, and slowly attempted to turn the handle. It was locked.

He heard a door open inside the bedroom.

I knew he'd run.

"POLICE," Jack yelled before he popped the door with a short thrust from his shoulder. The cheap plywood shattered.

He caught a glimpse of someone running out to the mini balcony that connected the two apartments. Jack rushed toward the door to the balcony. He heard a woman scream from the other apartment. Jack whipped over the railing and onto the other balcony.

"Police," he warned as he went through the door, his gun at the ready.

The other apartment bedroom only had a mattress in the corner. A woman sat screaming on it and frantically pointed.

Jack raced across her kitchen to an open door that led out to the back of the building. He heard footsteps running down the stairway and sprinted after him.

The sound of barking dogs filled the air, followed by angry shouts from Kendra. On the second floor, Jack looked over the edge and saw Kendra macing an enormous dog that howled in pain but held its ground.

"Go around," Jack called as he sprinted down the stairs.

Jack saw Arnold as he ran for the other side of the building. A flash of metal in Arnold's hand caught Jack's eye.

"Knife," he yelled.

Jack watched Arnold knock over a chair as he scrambled away. Jack's legs pushed into the ground; adrenaline raged as he pursued the perp. He felt power course through his body as he flew forward.

Jack rounded the corner and saw how much ground he'd gained. Arnold was now less than twenty yards away but beyond them was an open field.

"Freeze!"

Jack grabbed his nightstick and threw it sidearm. The baton caught Arnold right behind his legs, and he became entangled. Arnold's hands went wide and he face-planted in the dirt. The knife bounced along the ground in front of him.

Kendra raced around the corner of the building and tackled Arnold.

Jack snagged his baton before he helped her cuff the guy.

"Way to go, rookie. Nice job taking this guy down," Jack congratulated her.

Kendra was short on arrests and shorter on confidence. Being a new cop was hard enough. She had two things that made it a lot harder for her. She was a woman, and she was pretty. That meant the guys hit on her, and the few women on the force were jealous. Jack didn't care who got credit for the arrest; he liked Kendra.

She pulled Arnold to his feet; a string of obscenities mixed with *don't* and *move* poured from her mouth. She was beaming as Donald ran around the corner.

Kendra's mouth was twitching between nervousness and unbridled pride. She looked up at him with a smile from ear to ear.

"I got him. I got him!"

"Nice job, Officer," Donald said.

CHAPTER ELEVEN

Try to Out Shout Me

Jack stood next to Detective Charlie Flynn behind the two-way mirror and looked into the interview room where Kevin Arnold sat chained to a table.

"I appreciate this, Jack. How did you get the guy?" Detective Flynn was fifty-two years old and completely bald but had thick bushy eyebrows. His brown suit, although pressed and neat, looked to be at least ten years old.

"I got a tip that Kevin Arnold was at his girlfriend's apartment. We picked him up this morning on an outstanding warrant. Kendra Darcey made the collar."

Flynn chuckled. "Darcey. She's the one with the...um, big um...*eyes*." He practically drooled.

"She's the one with the big shotgun. Anyway, she made the collar. This guy looks good for these cases." Jack patted the folder in his hands. "I put them all in here for you."

Flynn looked at the folder again. "Thanks. It's great. This puts him on a silver platter for me. But what do you want again?"

"I just want to know his whereabouts before Christmas. See if he was anywhere near White Rocks."

Flynn nodded. "He looks good for the other cases in here. He matches the description, right down to the tattoo. I think we may have found our guy."

Jack sighed. "Right."

Flynn walked to the door.

Jack leaned back against the wall and watched as Flynn methodically picked apart the guy's alibis for the sexual assaults. Kevin started to squirm.

"So where were you before Christmas?"

"I was in rehab."

"Rehab?"

"Court ordered."

"You know the probation office would have that in their system. There's nothing in your file here." Flynn shuffled through the folder.

"I was out-of-state in Sanderson County Rehabilitation for four weeks. Check it out with them."

"Don't worry, I will." Flynn looked over toward the two-way glass and nodded.

Jack stormed out of the room and over to his desk. He called the rehab and got them to email him the information. It was a county lockup, not a country club rehab, so there was no way he could have snuck out of it unnoticed. Still, Jack was always one for due diligence. He called and double-checked with the staff. Kevin's story checked out. Dead end.

As he sped home, Jack's leg shook. He looked at his hand; it trembled. He squeezed the steering wheel harder.

Get a grip, Jack.

In the field, adrenaline was like a drug that pumped him up. When he came home, he crashed—total withdrawal. Fear and doubt would drag him toward the pit of memories that he fought to escape. He couldn't fill the abyss. He couldn't seal it up either.

He closed his eyes for a second and pictured Donald outside the door. Jack remembered every detail. He could recall the smells and feel the sweat running down his back. It felt as if he was there again, only now, the window behind Donald shattered. Donald flew back and landed on the sand. His mouth opened and closed but no words came out. There was a huge hole in his chest. Donald reached out for Jack and gasped, "Please."

A horn blared. Jack looked up at the oncoming truck. He had drifted into the wrong lane. He yanked the wheel hard over and swerved the car back into his lane, narrowly avoiding a head-on collision with the huge truck.

Dammit!

Horns blasted, drivers swore and flipped him off as he pulled onto the side of the road. He hit his hazards and put the car in park.

Blended memories. Donald's fine. That was that kid. The one…

Jack stared straight ahead as he tried to remember the young soldier's name. He closed his eyes.

What was it?

His breathing was ragged, and his hand shook.

It was in Iraq. I was on patrol with two other soldiers. Jimmy Tanaka. Tank. He was there.

Jack remembered his friend's name. Jimmy was Japanese. He was only five foot five but he was a powerhouse. Jimmy may have been small, but he never backed down.

It was me, Tank, and the kid.

Jack could picture him. He had short red hair and freckles. He was young, at most nineteen. He was always chewing gum.

That day they had to search a building with three doors on the front. Jack, the kid, and Tank each picked a door. They let the kid go first, and he went to the left. Tank chose the right, and Jack ended up with the middle. They were all supposed to kick the doors open on three. The kid died on two. The enemy machine gun fire blew the door apart and killed him instantly.

Damn. The kid is dead, and I can't even remember his name.

Jack put his head down on the steering wheel.

Defeated, Jack walked in the door, and Replacement was instantly in his face. "You went after him without me? Without ME?"

"When did you become my partner? Back off," Jack snapped.

Replacement froze. The problem was she froze angry.

*"Argh…*I just walked in the door." Jack threw his hands up.

"You said…" she growled.

"I didn't say I'd take you." He headed into the kitchen.

"You did." Now she was shouting.

Go ahead and try to out shout me, kid.

"I didn't," he yelled louder.

"I sat around here on my ass while Michelle is out there." Her lip trembled. "You promised that you'd take me. You—"

A loud hammering on the door interrupted her.

They both stopped. Replacement marched over and opened the door.

Jack listened while he got a glass of water. He couldn't make out who was speaking with her. Mrs. Stevens marched into the apartment with Replacement at her side. His landlady's face flushed a beet red as she tried to catch her breath.

Replacement's eyes were wide, and her head twitched spastically.

Not again. Jack shut the water off.

"Mr. Stratton." Mrs. Stevens puffed her big frame up even larger as she addressed him. "While I do appreciate how stressful law enforcement can be, I cannot permit you to yell at this poor unfortunate girl."

"Mrs. Stevens…" Jack's jaw clenched as he tried to control himself.

"Jack, sorry." Replacement hopped over to him at the sink. "Jack, very sorry. Jack, are you sorry?" She put her head on his arm and looked up at him with big eyes.

Jack glared down at her. Replacement's arm went around him, and she poked him in the side. Jack had to force himself not to laugh.

"I'm sorry. Okay?" Jack smiled thinly. "Mrs. Stevens, my…apologies."

"Mr. Stratton, I'm trying to look out for her best interests."

"Well, thank you. You've been very kind to…to her."

"And you have too. Remember that. She's an angel, and when you deal with her, you need patience and love. Patience and love." Mrs. Stevens must have concluded her work here was done because she turned and waved as she headed out of the apartment.

"Patience and love. Patience and love," Replacement repeated as she followed her. She shut the door and ran back into the kitchen.

"Thank you," Jack fiercely whispered. "Now my landlady thinks I'm a jerk."

"No, she doesn't. She likes you. She thinks you make poor choices in women and drink too much, though."

Jack's mouth fell open. "Are you talking with her? Stop, okay? I'm serious." He paused. "How could she know I drink too much?"

"She goes through your trash."

"She told you that?"

"She thinks I'm slow."

"You are. I'm taking a shower," he announced and then headed into the bedroom.

"Jerk, wait. You didn't tell me what happened," she protested as she followed behind him.

"Fine. Hold on." He shut the bedroom door to close her out. "We caught the guy," Jack yelled to Replacement.

She whipped open the door. "What? Awesome."

Jack stood there in his underwear. "Get out." He tossed his shirt at her.

Replacement didn't shut the door, but she did turn around.

"Anyway, he's the sexual predator, but he didn't have anything to do with Michelle." Jack headed for the shower.

"How can you say that?" Replacement walked backward and followed him.

Jack turned on the shower to let the water heat up. "He was in a lockdown rehab for four weeks in another state. He went in three weeks before Michelle went missing and was there for a week after. He couldn't have had anything to do with it. I checked myself and confirmed it. Can you get out now?" Jack jumped behind the opaque shower curtain.

Replacement kicked the wall and half of her foot disappeared into the drywall. "Oh, crap." She knelt down and tried to pull the cracked piece back into place. "I'm so sorry. I'm sorry." Her voice trembled.

"Forget it, kid." Jack kept his back to her and twisted around. "I'm pretty good at patching walls." He stuck his face under the water.

"I'm sorry."

"I can fix it."

"Not just for that." Replacement stood up. "I've been a psycho. You're right. I'm a little…mental."

Jack laughed.

"Thanks for agreeing." She sniffled.

He peeked around the curtain, and Replacement now leaned against the sink. "Everyone is a little mental, kid. Apology accepted. Can you please get out?" Jack turned his back on her.

"I have my eyes closed."

"Get out."

"Victor wrote back. He went to Western Tech and asked around, but Michelle has never been out there."

"How can he be sure about that?" Jack splashed his face in the water.

"It was the same story that Neil Waters told us. She signed up for classes, but no one had seen her. He showed the picture around. Victor said maybe she signed up electronically."

"Well, at least we sort of ruled that out."

"Sort of? She didn't go." Replacement tossed her hands up in the air.

Jack slowly turned his head. "How do you know he emailed me?"

"You use the same password for everything." She hopped up on the sink. "That's not smart."

Jack stood there blinking.

It wasn't smart but…

"You read my email?"

"I needed to see what he wrote. I found something else, too—an entry in the error log of the police database. It's only one line."

"In the error log? How could you get to the error log? Isn't that on the backend of the system?" Jack looked back at her.

"Once you're in a system, it's easy to move around." Her shoulders popped up and down.

Jack let the hot water wash over him as he tried to think about what she'd just said. He yanked the curtain around himself and glared at her as the meaning hit him.

"Are you saying you hacked the police database?"

"No. I just gained access to the backend."

"Accessed the backend? You hacked the database."

"I don't call it that." She crossed her arms. "I just exploited a security flaw."

"That's hacking. Did you use my account?" Now his eyes were wide.

"No. I made my own account." She twisted back and forth. "Don't sweat it. They won't know. Their security sucks. I used my laptop, so they have no way to trace an IP even if they did suspect something. I mask, then go through a VPN, and then double jump high anonymity proxies. The second proxy is offshore, so don't sweat it. No one is following my butt." She grinned.

"Out. Get your butt the hell out." His voice rose.

"Shh...I'm sorry."

Jack shut the curtain and just as quickly pulled it back again.

"Damn it. What did you find out?"

She turned back around.

"Look, get on the other side of the door and tell me."

She made a face but still walked out, pulled the door almost closed and pressed her face against the opening.

"Someone started to run a site inspection on Michelle's car. I don't know—
"

"A site inspection? Are you sure?" Jack switched the water off.

"Yeah. It was only one line, two codes in an error log file. The license plate number partially matched, and the purpose field said site inspection. I think they didn't put in enough information, and it errored out."

"Turn around. I have to get dressed." Jack jumped out of the shower.

"What's a site inspection?"

"That's police speak for an abandoned vehicle in an accident. If you find an abandoned car that shows signs of being in an accident, you have to do a site inspection. You first run the plate. Someone started one. Did it have a date?"

"No. Just those two fields."

"I don't know what went wrong, but if a cop ran a site inspection, the next step is the car gets towed. There's only one impound they'd take the car to. Now, turn around."

CHAPTER TWELVE

Killer Reindeer

Jack had to keep forcing himself to slow down as they raced out to Sullivan's Auto and Salvage. Sullivan's was the main towing company the police used, and the official impound yard. The gigantic auto yard was on the west end of Darrington County. Most cars ended up as scrap, but if they towed a car, they'd take it there.

I should have checked there first.

Jack pulled down the rearview mirror and glared at himself, but his reflection glared right back. Jack's harshest critic was Jack.

Jerk.

Jack flipped the mirror up.

Replacement fit the role of his new puppy more and more. It was forty-two degrees outside, but she had her window half open and kept popping her head out. She hopped in her seat, and he had the feeling he should roll the window up, or she'd jump out.

It was starting to get dark, so once they got out of town, he punched it. His Impala's gas pedal was about as sensitive as a moody schoolgirl. The difference between going twenty and one hundred twenty miles an hour was about half an inch. He knew how she ran, and she never left him stranded: 185,768 miles and she still purred.

He decided to give Replacement the look that said, "Don't worry, I can handle driving this fast." One glance at her and he could tell she loved speed and was grateful they were getting there fast.

They towed Michelle's car. That means she didn't have the car for a while. That isn't a good sign.

It made no sense she'd go to California, but part of him wished she had. She'd be safe then. The alternative was not good.

He thought back to leaving Chandler and Michelle and going to live with his new parents. Could she have done that? Would he blame her? Didn't he do the same thing when he came back from the Army? He abandoned them.

But I was selfish; Michelle was good. He chalked his selfishness up to pain. *What a pansy I am. Michelle must have been hurting just as much as I was, more so, and I know she wouldn't have left.*

He barreled into a turn and the car strained against the chassis. *Too fast.* He was going into a slip. Everything slowed way down. His adrenaline kicked in, and the world seemed to freeze. He loved this feeling. *Cut the wheel; go with the skid.* His training was taking over, kinesthetic muscle memory. Dancers, athletes, martial artists all strive for it. If you perform a motion often enough, you teach your muscles to move; when the time comes, the muscles repeat the motion on their own, almost independently of the brain.

Jack smiled, but when he glanced at Replacement, both of her hands had grabbed the oh-crap handle on the ceiling of the car. He still accelerated into the turn. It went against instinct to speed up as the car was going into a slip, but if you didn't, you'd spin out.

As they straightened out, he relaxed his grip on the wheel but noticed Replacement hadn't settled back into her seat. Her knuckles turned white on the handle. He forced himself to slow down.

"I…I'm sorry about driving so fast. I just…I just want to find Michelle."

Replacement adjusted her grip on the handle. "Me too. Punch it."

Jack stomped on the gas. He raced the rest of the way there.

Jack stopped in front of the two large gates to the auto yard. A thick chain and padlock were in place. Replacement jumped out the second the car stopped. He gave three loud blasts on the car horn.

She ran up, grabbed the gates and peered in. "Why is he closed?"

As he walked along the ten-foot-tall, rusted, barbed wire fence, Jack inspected the cars, desperately searching for the blue Honda Civic like a mother frantically scanning faces of people as she looks for her lost child.

Found it. Jack's jaw clenched.

The roof of the car was partly smashed in.

The car must have rolled over at least once.

Replacement looked back at him and then followed his eyes to the car. Before he could stop her, she pulled the gates as far apart as the chain would allow and squeezed her slender frame through the gap.

"Replacement." He grabbed the fence. "No, no, no!" The warning burst out like a machine gun as he dashed back. His arm reached through the gate, and he tried to grab her, but she was too fast and Jack was too bulky to fit through the opening. "Stop!" He tried not to yell—it was more of a shouted whisper.

It wouldn't have mattered if he'd screamed; he knew she was fixated on Michelle's car. As she ran up to it, Jack could see the windows were both down, and the windshield was broken. The front end was damaged, and pieces of headlight and bumper were gone.

"Replacement!" Jack attempted to get her attention again, but she stared at the car.

Then he heard the jingle of the bells.

He pulled at the gates, but he couldn't break the chain, nor fit through.

"RUN!" Jack could always yell loudly, even as a little kid. Sheer panic amplified his yell. It was so loud it broke through the dark cloud that Replacement was in, and she looked up.

Jack saw the huge pack of dogs. He couldn't even count the number of animals that raced toward her. Junkyard dogs—muscular, enormous beasts that were as mean as they come. They made no noise except the ringing of the little bells around their collars. He saw her body tense for the run back to the gate. The dogs must have sensed the hunt was on because they roared and when they did, she froze, her eyes wide with fear.

She'll never make the gate.

Jack stared as the beasts drove forward, mouths open as they rushed to tear her to pieces.

"GET IN THE CAR," Jack shouted. He took one look at the barbed wire at the top of the fence and knew he couldn't climb over it in time.

"GET IN THE CAR!"

Replacement tried to open the smashed car door. It creaked, but it didn't budge. Jack could hear the dogs' claws on the frozen ground now.

"IN," he ordered.

She scrambled through the open window. Jack saw her legs vanish inside the car. He could only watch as the huge, snarling dogs chomped at the window where their prey disappeared. Their open jaws snapped, and they barked and scratched at the car. Baying and yelping in frustration, they howled and circled it.

The biggest dog Jack had ever seen put both of its front paws on the open window and rammed its giant head in. Jack heard Replacement scream and saw her kick again and again. Her feet slammed into the beast's head, but it wouldn't back away.

Jack's chest muscles strained as he pulled the gates open as far as he could. He rammed his body between the gates. His upper body went partly through before he became stuck. He struggled to pass, but the metal refused to move. He roared louder than the dogs in a fusion of desperation and fear.

The dogs stopped circling the car and looked as one to the sound of the challenge. They snarled, and their claws raked the ground. The giant alpha dog howled, and the pack turned to hunt their new prey.

The pack trotted toward Jack and broke into a run. Jack smiled. He succeeded in luring them away from Replacement. He pushed to move back through the gate, but found that he couldn't budge; he was wedged fast. His legs strained, and he pressed at the gates, but his upper body stayed where it was. He tried to plant his feet, but they slipped on the frozen dirt.

The dogs closed the distance. Jack's shoulders burned as his back muscles went into overdrive. His shirt ripped open, and the metal slashed his skin. He growled, heaved, and tore himself free just as the dogs smashed into the fence. They howled in frustration now that both their prizes seemed outside their grasp.

"Donner! Blitzen!" An old man dressed in dark blue overalls rushed into view. "Comet! Heel!" The dogs turned and raced toward the man. They nuzzled up against him, eager for praise because they had protected the junkyard.

Jack winced as he got up. All the buttons were gone off the front of his shirt, and his chest was scratched and bleeding.

"That you, Jackie?"

Why older people referred to him as Jackie he'd yet to figure out. The old man walked over and unlocked the gate. Jack darted through and headed for the Civic.

"What the hell were you thinking, boy? Heel," the old man snapped as the dogs growled. "Move slow, boy."

"Sorry, Sully." Jack had to force himself to slow down and not run to get to Replacement. "I'm here about the blue Civic, and my friend ran in to check it out."

"What? Is your friend stupid, crazy, or both? You never go past the gate at Sullivan's. Doesn't everybody know that?" Sully shook his head, and his wild white hair bobbed back and forth. "Go check to see he ain't bit. If he is, it's his own darn fault."

Jack jogged over to the car and found Replacement curled into a tight ball on the front seat. He grabbed the door and yanked it open.

"Kid," he whispered. "Are you okay?" His voice was calm and soothing.

He touched her back and her arms shot around his neck. She sobbed and buried her face in his shoulder. He lifted her from the car and cradled her in his arms, his back to Sully.

"What kind of daisy is your friend, Jack? Is he bit or not? Either way, tell him to man up."

Jack felt Replacement go rigid, and he smiled. *She still has fight in her so maybe she's okay.*

"Man up?" She wriggled her way out of Jack's grasp. "I'm a woman, you killer dog owning psycho." She wiped her nose with the back of her sleeve. Jack noticed a small cut on her chin and another on her cheek.

"A girl. I'm so sorry, honey." Sully went as white as his hair and looked as if he was about to faint when he realized his mistake. "Jack, what the hell is wrong with you?" he grumbled, and his legs wobbled. He looked as though he was having a heart attack.

"Me?"

Replacement rushed to the man's side and took him by his hands, concern for him all over her face. How she could go from one extreme to another perplexed Jack. One second he thought she'd punch the old man in the face, and now she rushed to care for him. She shot an angry glance at Jack, but as he tried to approach, the pack growled as one.

"Easy, boys. Sit, sit!" Sully pulled one hand free from Replacement and waved at the dogs.

"Let me help you back inside,"Replacement offered as she took him by the arm. "You're as pale as a ghost."

The old man grinned like a schoolboy at the attention and let her lead him into the trailer. "You got cut up. I have some bandages inside."

She led Sully back to the office as Jack followed at a slight distance, and the dogs followed him. The dogs were very well trained. He might as well have been under guard. If he got too close to Sully, the dogs would growl. If he lagged too far behind, they'd growl. He tried his best to follow at the right distance.

The office was what you'd expect for a junkyard trailer office. It smelled of a mixture of mildew, cigarette smoke, and motor oil. There was a small counter and a desk covered in greasy papers. An old TV was turned on full blast across from a worn-out chair. A little space heater provided a surprising amount of heat and Jack was grateful considering he could no longer zip his broken jacket, and, because his shirt buttons were gone, he'd been walking around bare-chested.

Sully had Replacement sit in the portly old chair while he switched off the TV. "Sorry, I'm a bit deaf," he apologized.

He's probably deaf because the TV is so loud.

"What brings you out, Jackie?" Sully asked Jack the question, but he looked at Replacement. "You want a soda?" He moved over to the small brown refrigerator in the corner.

"Sully, I'm not here officially, just yet." Jack added the last part as he noticed the old man's puzzlement. "I'm looking for my missing foster sister."

Sully's eyes went wide, and he swallowed hard. "Missing? I'm so sorry, Jackie." This latest bit of news caused him to pale even more. "How can I help?"

He handed a soda to Replacement and offered another to Jack, who mumbled a thank-you and put the soda in his coat pocket. Jack already wasn't looking forward to going back outside, but he didn't want to do it holding a cold can.

"The blue Honda Civic." Jack cocked his head in the direction of the car. "What can you tell me about it?"

Sully reached into a drawer and took out a box of bandages. He offered them to Replacement, but she waved them off.

"That one? Found her on Reservoir Road. Totaled. Bent frame. Some kids must have rolled her."

"Kids? Who found it?"

"A hunter called it in. He was out on the reservoir looking for deer and said he saw a group of kids trying to start it. He thought they were stuck, but when he went to give them a hand, they all took off. Murphy said he figured we'd get the story when she showed up stolen. I hadn't heard anything, so I was going to check back with him."

I knew it. Murphy, you stupid bastard.

Billy Murphy was half a cop. If he weren't the county commissioner's son-in-law, he wouldn't even be that. He had his own carpentry business and worked part-time as a cop for extra money. He did mostly on-call stuff, like traffic details. Sheriff Collins couldn't stand him and neither could the other police officers. The work was slow here, but the other cops took it seriously at least. Murphy working the car explained the error line in the police database.

That jackass started to run a site inspection, screwed it up, and didn't run it again.

"Did he go through the car?" Jack tried to mask his frustration.

"He gave it a once-over. We picked up some pieces of it off the road, and I brought it all back here. It sure is banged up, but she started. It was just some kids, right? They okay?" Jack could see the older man was concerned. It wasn't his fault that Murphy was lazy.

"Is it all right if I go take a look?"

Replacement jumped out of her chair and moved to the door.

"Sure, Jackie."

Sully went first and shooed the dogs away as the three of them walked back to the car.

Kids? This didn't make sense. Jack was fuming and couldn't wait for Murphy to try to explain it.

He took a deep breath and decided to start on the inside of the car. Besides little piles of broken glass, the car was clean. The keys were still in the ignition. He opened the glove compartment.

Owner's manual, a pair of sunglasses, and some tissues.

It was worthless to dust the car for prints. It had lightly snowed off and on for the last couple of weeks and the car would have gotten soaked, erasing any fingerprints. Jack walked around to the trunk and stopped.

He closed his eyes and inhaled. He could only smell the faint odor of gasoline. He looked over at Replacement, and she still peered into the inside of the car.

His hand trembled.

Please God, don't let her be in here.

Jack opened the trunk.

It was empty.

He exhaled.

Jack pulled the trunk closed. "Were you there with Murphy when he first saw the car?"

"No. I arrived a little after he got there. It wasn't real stuck. I turned her over, and she started right up. Ben Nichols." He jumped as he shouted the name. "I couldn't recall who called. It was Ben. He was bow hunting."

"Where can I find him?" Jack reached for his notebook that was normally in his uniform pocket and frowned when he realized it was in his car.

"He lives over on Juniper, big white house. You'll go past Weston on the way back to town. Turn right on Weston, go half a mile, and take a left onto Juniper. He's on the right. Got a couple canoes off to the side, you can't miss it."

"Thanks, Sully." Jack offered his hand. "Listen, can you do me one more favor?"

"Sure, Jackie." He shook his hand.

"Call Murphy and tell him the car's still here. Tell him to check that it's in the database. Just don't say I was here."

Sully gave him a questioning look.

"I don't want to embarrass him since he must have forgotten."

I don't want to embarrass him; I want to kill him, but this way Collins still won't know I'm looking into this.

Sully turned to Replacement. "Sorry about the dogs."

"Thank you for the soda, sir." Replacement's eyes stayed on the car for a moment. Her shoulders slumped, and then she turned and headed toward the Impala.

CHAPTER THIRTEEN

Anyplace Can be Dangerous

"Where's Reservoir Road?" Replacement shivered in the passenger seat.

Jack took a hard right. Replacement looked at him. "The hunter's place is on the way. We need to interview him and see what he knows first and then we'll check out where they found the car."

Jack lifted a knee against the steering wheel and breathed into his hands to warm them a bit.

He blew past a stop sign, and Replacement gave him a surprised look. He ignored it. They were running out of daylight.

The hunter said he saw kids run off, but why would they have Michelle's car? Did they steal it? Were they driving it or did they find it like that?

His knuckles on the steering wheel turned white as they sped on.

He slowed down when he saw the canoes. He pulled into Ben Nichols's driveway. "Stay here." He left no room for argument as he got out of the car. He left it running to keep her warm, but something bothered him about leaving Replacement in his car with the keys in it.

She scooted over to the driver's seat before he shut his door.

"You're not coming with me. It will look weird," Jack tried to explain.

"You could say that again," she answered. "You look like a Chippendale's dancer."

Jack looked down at his jacket and shirt, both torn open. He frowned.

Great, I look like an idiot.

Jack's hands went up, but he was too embarrassed to thank her. He popped the trunk. After going through his gym bags, he pulled off his jacket and shirt and put on a police sweater. It was so cold he had to force himself to breathe. He grabbed his notebook and pen.

It was starting to get dark.

He shot Replacement a do-not-move look as she sat smiling in the front seat. Shivering, he jogged up to the house.

The door opened as he approached. A short, bald man with thick glasses stood in the doorway. The man had a blank stare on his face and his eyes looked odd.

"Can I help you?" the man asked.

Jack froze. He forgot he was a good ways out of town, and different people lived out here. Ben Nichols's left hand was visible, but his right wasn't. Jack noticed the muscles on the right side of his neck stood out.

A little guy meeting me at the door with that face and the way he's standing? He's a hunter. Odds are there's a shotgun in his other hand.

Jack angled his body so Ben could see the word POLICE printed across his sweater. "Mr. Nichols." Jack forced himself not to move his hands. "I'm Officer Jack Stratton. Sully over at the auto yard said you called in the abandoned car report on Reservoir Road. I came out here to thank you."

"Thank me?" Ben's chest puffed up. "I'm just doing my duty, Officer."

Jack was surprised he didn't salute.

"I just left Sully's, and I have a couple of questions." Jack kept smiling but resisted any impulse to move.

"Yes sir. Won't you come in?" Ben opened the door wide, and Jack's eyes went to the double-barrel shotgun in his right hand. Ben shrugged and then grinned. "You can't be too careful."

"Certainly. Thank you." Jack followed the man inside.

It was a pleasant home, but he had a ton of lights on. Ben Nichols walked through a door to the left and into a large room with bookcases and a hefty, warm wood stove. Straightaway, Jack moved next to it. He rubbed his hands as Ben settled onto a tan couch.

"Are you making an official report?" Ben asked, thrilled about the attention.

Jack coughed. "Yes. Can you please explain in your own words the events starting just before you found the car, Mr. Nichols?" Jack took out his notebook. People loved it when you wrote down what they said and writing things down let Jack pay attention to the person. He could pore over the details later.

"I was out hunting near the Onopiquite Reservoir." Ben's voice dropped a couple of octaves, and he now sounded as if he were giving a televised report from some war zone. "I'd been out for a few hours when I first heard the kids. It was around three o'clock. There were five teens who were around a blue Honda Civic."

"Do you remember where on Reservoir Road this was?"

"No, not exactly. They were due west of the reservoir."

Jack continued to write.

"From a distance, I could see the teens were trying to start the car. I naturally assumed they'd just broken down, but as I approached to help, I could see the damage to the car. When they saw me, the perps fled the scene.

People loved to try to use police jargon and Jack tried to let it go, but the word slipped out. "Perps?"

"Perpetrators," Ben answered but continued with his narrative. "I realized afterward that the car must not have been theirs, seeing as how they ran."

"Can you tell me anything about the teens?"

"There were five of them. They were on snowmobiles. Two rode double. Umm...one had a red coat and another guy had a Roman thing on his head!"

"A Roman thing?" Jack stopped writing.

"Like a Mohawk? A gold one on his helmet." Ben's hands moved over his head. "Like a Roman soldier would wear."

"On his helmet? Like a centurion?" Jack scribbled a quick picture of a Roman soldier's helmet and turned the notebook around.

"That's it." Ben nodded.

"What about the one in the red coat? What else can you tell me about him?"

"It was a big red parka. The kid was very chunky. I think that's why he rode alone. He was stocky. Fat."

"Anything else about them? Jackets, hats..."

"Not really. They took off when I called out to them."

"Have you ever seen any of them before?" Jack continued.

"I've seen kids snowmobiling out there a lot. I think I've seen the Roman kid too."

"You ever see the car before?"

"No."

"Was there snow on the car when you first saw it?" Jack stopped writing.

Ben thought for a minute. "Yeah, the windshield was covered. It was light. A dusting. There was even snow in the car. I remember because I looked in the back and—"

"Did you touch the car?"

"No sir. That could contaminate the crime scene." Ben's head shook back and forth.

"Did you notice anything else?"

Ben shook his head.

"Well, thank you, Mr. Nichols." He closed his notebook.

"If you need anything, I'm always ready to do my part, Officer Stratton." Ben stood at attention as he held open the door.

Jack paused. "Thank you, sir. If more citizens like you took the time to help us, it would make our job a lot easier." Jack was glad Ben couldn't see the smile on his face as he walked away. What he said was the truth, but when he said it out loud it sounded a little silly.

Replacement looked out the window, waiting for him to get back. "What did you find?" The image that he'd gotten a new puppy was now complete. She sat on her haunches and looked up at him with her big emerald eyes.

"Move it," he said, trying to sound annoyed. Inwardly though, he smiled. *I like my new puppy.*

"What did he say?" Jack watched as she scooted across the seat without straightening her legs in a little reverse hop.

"When he got to the car, there were five kids who were snowmobiling around it. One had a weird helmet with a gold Mohawk on it. It should be easy enough to find out who that is."

"You don't think they're involved, do you?"

"No. He said there was already snow on the windshield and in the car, so I think the car had been there for a while."

He threw the car in reverse and then sped out to the reservoir.

The Onopiquite Reservoir was the size of a large lake. No boating, swimming, or fishing were allowed. Nevertheless, everyone overlooked the fishing ban because the fishing was so good. The reservoir sat at the bottom of a large, natural basin, shaped like a long serving dish. Reservoir Road circled the lake on the lower side of the basin, closest to the water, and Pine Ridge ran along the eastern ridge on the lip of the bowl. During foliage season, Pine Ridge saw a lot of traffic because the view of the lake down below with the reflection of the trees in its water was breathtaking. However, Reservoir Road saw very little traffic and almost none during the winter.

Jack slowed as they drove down Reservoir Road. It was now dark, and the lack of streetlights made it impossible to see anything beyond the headlights.

"Where did they find the car?"

"I don't know. Ben Nichols just had a general description."

As they drove up and down the road, nothing stood out. Jack shook his head.

"It's too dark. I'll call Sully and try to get a better description of the site the car was towed from."

"Do you think we could just go and start searching the woods on foot?" Replacement kept her eyes closed.

"Kid…" Jack kept driving. *What am I going to say? It's been two weeks. It's freezing, and you're hoping she's just out there waiting for us?* "We'll come back tomorrow. I promise."

Damn.

He tried never to promise anything.

I don't know anything. I don't know what the hell happened to Michelle. I don't know jack, so how could I promise anything to anyone?

He gripped the steering wheel tighter, and they sped back toward the highway. He shook his head. He didn't need this.

Replacement didn't seem happy when he pulled onto the highway and went past his exit.

"Where are we going?"

"I'm taking you home."

"Why? I thought—?"

"You're not staying at my place. I don't know what you told Mrs. Stevens, but she won't stay happy for long, so let's leave her that way…happy."

"She won't care."

"I do. It's my place. You're not far."

"Far enough that you never came over." She intended to hurt him, and that did.

"I'm not doing this now." His voice was so crisp the words seemed to snap. It was true. Aunt Haddie lived an hour away, and he hadn't seen her or Michelle since he came back. "I'm…"

I'm what? I'm a coward? Do I tell her I can't face it? What the hell was I supposed to say to them? Apologize? Say I'm sorry he died? I'm sorry; it was my fault…

Jack glared at Replacement and was glad she was looking out the window. "Not now," was the last thing he said for the next hour.

He pulled up in front of her apartment building, and she got out and walked away without looking back. Jack didn't wait for her to go in. He pulled away, tires screeching. He drove half a block before he pulled back over.

Damn.

He shut off the engine. His fist pounded the steering wheel.

What's she want from me? He was fuming. *She's not my sister. I'm only watching out for her because of Chandler.*

While he debated with himself about what he was going to do, he grabbed the rearview mirror to stare himself down, but as he moved it, he saw Replacement. She walked back down the steps of her complex and headed down the street away from him.

He turned and watched her go, and so did his anger. She looked small and vulnerable. His police training kicked in.

Where's she going?

Jack grabbed the keys and followed her on foot. He tried to stay far back; there were few people on the street. He hugged the side of the building and walked at a steady pace, keeping his head down, and hunching his shoulders. Replacement never looked back.

She went a couple of blocks before she turned to the left. It was a business district, but everything appeared closed. This part of the town had seen better days, but it wasn't dangerous.

Not dangerous? Anyplace can be dangerous. A girl alone at night—that was dangerous.

He saw her turn in to a doorway, and he silently rushed forward. He stopped and leaned against the building.

She cursed as she fumbled with the lock of the door. With a bit of anger, she threw it open and marched through.

Jack hesitated and then moved. He sprang forward and grabbed the door just before it locked. Holding it open an inch, he waited.

What was she doing?

After a minute, he opened the door and slipped inside the entranceway. The odor of mothballs and stale air greeted him. A hallway ran toward the back of the building, and an old worn staircase went up.

Three floors?

He tried to remember how tall the building was. He listened, and he heard a door open and then close on the floor above. On the wall leading upstairs was an old sign: STORAGE RULES, followed by a bulleted list of regulations.

A storage place? What's she getting here this late at night?

This was an old office building someone had renovated into a storage facility. They were about as secure as locking something in your car. He shook his head.

As Jack went up the stairs, he moved along the edge of the wall to try to minimize any creaks; any sound would be loud in a building this quiet. On the next level, the worn wood floor ran straight back. The last door on the right had a bit of light creeping out from underneath it.

He could feel his face contort as he struggled to think of a reason Replacement would be here this late. He couldn't come up with any plausible answer.

What's going on?

He stood outside the door and debated whether he should knock or just try to open it. He tapped on the door.

"Replacement?" He listened to the silence. "Replacement?" he whispered again, and this time he heard movement from the other side of the door.

A couple of soft footsteps and then the door slowly opened a crack. Jack wished it hadn't.

Replacement's head appeared, but she refused to look him in the face.

Her lips trembled. It wasn't from anger or fear; it was from shame. He could see it in her eyes. The same look he'd seen so many times in his own, he knew it well.

Jack put his hand on the door and gradually opened it.

A storage room. It's more like a closet.

His anger rose. He was angry with himself. He knew or at least he should have known.

She said Aunt Haddie was in a nursing home so she couldn't live with her. She didn't mention any friends and what was she, nineteen? She'd be out of the foster care system. This explains the showers every time she came over. She has no other place to take one.

Jack looked at the sleeping bag on the floor. There was a small table with a little light. Three green bags were in one corner and a couple of boxes in the other.

"The homeless shelter...you know some of the freaks who live there are weird." She looked down sheepishly. "Aunt Haddie tries to give me money when she can, but this...this is just temporary...I mean, I don't need much." She looked around.

He imagined this small nineteen-year-old girl at a homeless shelter, and he clenched his teeth.

"Things will change." She smiled at him. The smile was so forced, but there was some glint of hope. That little bit of light cut right into Jack.

A closet in a storage facility. She's living in a closet.

"Yeah." Jack cleared his throat. "It's temporary because it's over. From now on, you're staying with me."

She looked up at him.

"Hand me a couple of things and I'll go get the car."

She started to tremble. Jack stepped forward and pulled her close.

Don't cry. Please don't cry.

Her arms started to rise as if to give him a hug, but then stopped and dropped loosely to her sides. Jack hugged her tighter. Her arms shot out and wrapped around his waist. He patted her back. He held her for a minute. Then she stepped back and rubbed her eyes.

Jack reached in and grabbed the trash bags. "I'll get the car."

By the time he returned, she was already waiting for him. Everything else she owned was in the two boxes at her feet.

"Not much of a life." The shrug that accompanied her words cut Jack to his core.

"Your new one starts today, kid. Come on; let's go."

CHAPTER FOURTEEN

Oh, What a Beautiful Mornin'

Jack looked down at the table and froze.

It's a dream, Jack. Germany. Before you shipped out to Iraq. Chandler's about to come over to the table...

"Hey, Jack." Chandler's voice was happy. "You gonna have any?"

Chandler held up a plate covered with scrambled eggs as he tried to fit his large frame into the small booth.

Jack looked at his friend and couldn't bring himself to close his eyes and wake up. He remembered the day. He knew he was dreaming but he didn't want to stop replaying the memory.

"In a minute."

"The best part of this German food is breakfast." Chandler flashed a big grin.

"You're like a giant hobbit. What's this, your second breakfast?" Jack chuckled.

"I'm a growing boy." Chandler shrugged. "You know, if we were home right now, Aunt Haddie would be waking us up singing, 'Oh, what a beautiful mornin'. Oh, what—'"

"'A beautiful day. I got a beautiful feeling everything's goin' my way.'" Jack smiled. "Yeah, how could I forget?"

"Do you remember her fire drills? She'd get freaked about having so many kids in the house, she'd have those mock evacuations. All of us standing out on the sidewalk, freezing, while she did a head count." Chandler started choking a little as he laughed.

"She woulda made a hell of a drill instructor."

"Remember that one where you and I decided to go out the window and slide out over the porch? She nearly killed us." Chandler chuckled as he tried to keep his food in his mouth.

"We had to copy that entire fire safety book."

"My hand still hurts." Chandler jokingly flexed it.

"Don't forget why she did it, big man. She always said, 'Keep your eyes on the exit whenever you go someplace new and be prepared.' Guess she made us ready for this." Jack sighed and stopped laughing.

Chandler tried to change the subject. "Hey, I have it all figured out what I'm going to do when I get out."

"We haven't even left Germany. Then we have to get through Iraq, and *you* have it all figured out?"

"I'm going to be a teacher. I want to teach math."

Jack burst out laughing.

"Thanks, jerk." Chandler tossed down his fork. "I thought the plan was we both go in and get money for college."

Jack put his hands behind his head. "I just came to watch your back."

"Yeah, but it's been the other way around." Chandler grinned. "Seriously, do you think that's stupid?"

"No. My dad's a math teacher. Did he bite you or something? Made you some sort of math zombie?"

"He gave me the idea. It's a great job. Help kids. You get the whole summer off."

"It's not stupid." Jack held up a glass of orange juice as a toast. "I just don't know how any kid is going to have the guts to ask a question with you standing in the front of the room."

They both laughed.

"Seriously." Jack kicked back the last of the orange juice. "You'd make a great teacher."

"Do you like eggs?" Chandler asked with a big smile.

"Do you like eggs?" Jack heard the words again, but he struggled to try to stay dreaming.

"Up you go. Get up, sleepyhead," Replacement commanded as she pulled the blanket off him. He grabbed it, but she still caught an eyeful. "Wow, I didn't know that you slept *au naturel.* Nice butt."

"Get out—now." He was tempted to stand up and give her the full show, but from the look on her face, he didn't think she'd back down, and he'd be the one to get embarrassed. "Can't you wake me up nicely?"

"I try. I start off really gentle, but you won't wake up. So I have to escalate it. You could snore through a train wreck."

"I don't snore."

"Sure." She tilted her head at him. "I made breakfast. Get dressed now, *nudist,* or I'll eat it all." She laughed as she sprinted out of the room.

Jack wrapped the blanket around himself and went to the bathroom. He pulled on some sweatpants and then he smelled the eggs.

She made me a hot breakfast.

Jack had just about given up on ever having a hot breakfast again. When he had to work the night shift, his mornings suffered, and he frequently woke up in the afternoon. He never liked to eat breakfast later in the day, so the meal was slowly being worked out of his diet.

He yanked open the bedroom door and saw the kitchen counter set with two places. Replacement stood there grinning like the Cheshire cat with a frying pan in one hand and a spatula in the other. She wore a big old Fairfield High School shirt. Jack walked around the counter and saw that the shirt was all she was wearing.

"Knock off surprising me in my bedroom and go put on some pants." He shook his head. "That stuff is weird." Jack couldn't bring himself to frown because he was so happy about breakfast, so he settled for trying to look stern.

"You like scrambled eggs?" She pushed a large plate toward him that also had four pieces of buttered toast.

"I love them." Jack grabbed his fork but stopped with his hand halfway to his face.

Replacement had the same look Aunt Haddie would give him when he didn't say grace. He sighed, folded his hands, and bowed his head as she began.

"Thank you, Lord, for this food. Thank you for Jack's help. Please help him find my sister and have her be okay. Bless Aunt Haddie and say hi to my brother. In Jesus's name, thanks."

Jack kept his eyes closed, and his head bowed. There were times when he felt as though he didn't have anything that was core to his being. That he was missing something about being a human. Missing was the wrong word to use even. Missing meant that at one time, he had it, and it was now gone. He shook his head. He didn't think he ever had what Replacement possessed. It was as if he were defective. Something inside him was incomplete. This was one of those times. With his eyes still closed, he shook his head. Replacement understood something he didn't.

He opened his eyes and dropped his fork in surprise. Replacement's face was right next to his and staring into his eyes as if she searched for something.

"There you go again, kid. You have to give me some space," he protested but swiftly grabbed his fork and started to eat.

"What? I'm just looking at your face. Did you just think of something?" She eyed him.

"You can just ask me. Don't get right next to me, don't sneak up on me, just ask."

She walked over to the far counter and returned with two cups of coffee. "Are we off to the reservoir?"

"Coffee, yes…whatever you want. Wait, no," he added. "I'll call Sully this morning first. But I was thinking last night, we should go see if we can find one of those kids. They may know something."

"Why are we going to hunt down kids first?" Replacement didn't mask her disappointment well.

"Look, I think the kids are just that, kids. We need to know if that's where they found the car or if they drove it there. On the other hand, maybe they saw something. There's an Eddie's Sport on 54, and it has a small garage for ATVs, snowmobiles, and dirt bikes. It's on the way to the reservoir. It has to be local kids, so a short conversation might yield us a name."

Jack looked down at the empty plate, and then glanced at his watch. Five after seven. He didn't think breakfast was a bribe, but if it was, it worked. "How soon can you be ready?" By the time he finished asking, she already pulled out a pair of jeans.

"I need a minute." He grabbed his coffee and headed into the bedroom.

Between Ben Nichols's shotgun and the dogs at Sullivan's, Jack had wished he'd had his gun twice yesterday. He opened the small safe under the medicine cabinet and grabbed his pistol and holster.

CHAPTER FIFTEEN

Chicken Head

As they drove to Eddie's Sports, Replacement fidgeted in her seat. She looked up as they turned. A large sign read Ridge Hill High School, with a picture of a mountain lion in blue and white.

"The high school? What's here?" she asked.

"Kids. We're looking for the group of teenagers who were at the car. One of them has that helmet; another's a hefty, fat boy in a giant red parka. It's worth a drive-by. We might be able to see them here."

"That's great. How are we going to pick them out of that crowd?" Replacement pointed to the sea of teens arriving at the school.

Jack scanned the crowd and began to doubt the wisdom of his decision too.

"There." Replacement pointed to a heavy kid in a red parka. "Wait, over there too." She pointed again.

"I get it. Look for the Mohawk kid."

"Third red parka but sort of thin."

He scanned the sea of jackets and slowed down even more.

"Fourth fatty in red off the starboard bow," she bellowed.

A large group of students turned to glare at the car. Jack realized she'd rolled down her window and was now halfway out of the car as she yelled.

Jack pulled her back into her seat. "Keep it down, Captain Obvious."

She sprang right back up. "There he is. It's him." Replacement almost opened the door as she frantically jabbed the air with her finger.

"What did I just say?" Jack was getting ready to abort the whole thing.

"No, there he is. It's him," she yelled and gestured wildly.

"Where?" Jack scanned the crowd, milling around the buses.

"The chicken-headed kid." She grabbed his chin and turned his head. Jack saw the teen parking his motorcycle, and atop his helmet was a large gold Mohawk.

Jack double-parked right behind the bike and blocked him in. "Stay here." He jumped out of the car, and the rider, who was being greeted by a group of friends, turned back toward him.

"Excuse me," Jack called. He wanted to talk to him without the friends. "Can you come over here for a second? I need to ask you a quick question."

The kid has to be close to eighteen. Judging from his helmet and the fact he's driving a motorcycle in winter, he thinks he's a tough guy.

"You a cop?" He laughed as his friends circled a little closer around him.

"I am. I just have a question."

"Talk to my lawyer." The teen held up both middle fingers, and his friends laughed.

Replacement pulled herself up so her whole upper body was halfway out the car window.

"How about you come and talk to me? I don't bite…hard." She giggled.

The kid laughed, punched one of his friends in the arm, and sauntered forward.

"I'll talk to you, babe." His arrogance made Jack's anger rise. He didn't change expression, but his eyes grew blacker. He got right up next to the kid.

"You can talk to me, you wise-ass, and answer a couple of questions now, or I can have your bike towed, impounded, and checked by the MVD, and then I'll throw your sorry ass in a cell."

The teen gulped and the color drained from his face. Jack nodded to the other side of the car, and the boy followed him.

"I need to know about the day you were out at the reservoir and saw a blue Honda Civic." Jack spoke low.

The kid looked back at his friends, and his bravado returned. "I don't know what you're talking about." He might as well have been a peacock with how he gestured and posed.

"Okay." Jack leaned in, and his voice turned cold. "Listen up. Now I'm doing you a favor by treating you like a man in front of your friends. If you try jerking me around one more time, let me tell you what I'm going to do. I noticed you swerving when you pulled into the school, and I suspect that you're under the influence of class B drugs in a school zone. Under paragraph 95 of the DEA act, that means I can detain you until the school principal comes and the two of us will escort you down to Mrs. Kazikinski's office."

Mrs. Kazikinski was the school nurse. He knew she taught a couple self-defense courses at the local Y. She was also the wrestling coach for both the boys' and girls' teams. She was large, burly, and at almost six foot two, she had the widest frame he'd ever seen on a woman. Jack was making up the codes, but he bet the kid would know Mrs. Kazikinski and would be extremely afraid of what Jack said next.

"Under section 53 part C, any student who's viewed as being under the influence of a class B narcotic can and will be subjected to a full body cavity search by trained medical personnel. That would be Mrs. Kazikinski." Jack smiled. "So what's it going to be?"

"Teddy, Tommy, Brian, and Scott, and I were down at the reservoir."

Jack smiled again. *The kid just threw everyone under the bus.* Jack took out his notebook and wrote the details.

"And your full name?"

He swallowed hard. "Ricky Matthews." He rolled his eyes as Jack wrote it down.

"You saw the car and then what?"

"I saw the car, so we figured we'd just check it out." He shrugged.

"What did the car look like?" Jack's voice was still cold.

"I don't know. Um...it was blue. It had been there, you know. And—"

"Been there?"

"The windshield had snow on it. It snowed the night before."

"Did you get in the car?"

He looked at his feet and shuffled them awkwardly. "Yeah, but...I opened the door. There was nothing in it. The keys were still there, but...I just looked." He looked Jack straight in the eyes.

He's lying.

"Did you start the car?" Jack leaned in.

"Yeah, I was just sitting there, so I turned it over. It started right up. It was busted up already. There was glass in the front seat, and the window was broken open. "

Jack frowned. He was holding something back.

"Ricky, have you ever looked at the size of Mrs. Kazikinski's hands? She can palm a watermelon. You're leaving something out, and you have one chance to give it up."

The teen was squirming, and his eyes went wide. "There was a smart phone. It was wedged in the seat."

"Where is it?" Jack's eyes narrowed.

"I took it but…I forget." Ricky whined, and he looked like a little boy who had to go to the bathroom.

Lie.

Jack pulled out a pair of handcuffs.

"No, no," Ricky begged. "Wait a minute—I got it. I got it." He pulled off his backpack and desperately looked through it. "Here." He handed Jack the phone.

"Is there anything else?" Jack's eyes bored into him.

"No, nothing else." Ricky waved his hands back and forth.

"Thank you for your time. I'd hurry to class if I were you."

Ricky bolted, avoiding the friends who called after him. Jack laughed as he opened the door of the Impala and hopped in.

Replacement reached out and attempted to grab the phone.

"Hold on. I think there should be a plastic bag I threw into the glove box." She pulled out the bag and handed it to him.

"It's dead." He placed the phone into the bag and sealed it up.

Jack saw the excitement on her face change to disappointment. "Do you have a charger?"

"I have a normal phone, kid."

"You mean an old one."

Jack drove around the buses and headed for the exit.

Replacement stared down at the phone. "Good job getting this. I hope it works."

"Me, too." Jack nodded back toward the school. "Think Ricky will make it to the bathroom?"

"I think he peed himself next to the car." She laughed.

"The kid's angle is what I thought really happened. Three people have confirmed the car had been there a while: Sully, Nichols, and now Ricky."

Jack's eyes turned back to the road, and he smiled when he pictured that wise-ass kid running for the bathroom.

Jack's phone rang. *Ding-a-ling.* It was an old-fashioned bell, like telephones used to have.

Replacement laughed. "What kind of ringtone was that?"

"Hello?" Jack scowled at her as he answered. "Yeah, thanks for calling back, Sully. I just needed to know where on Reservoir Road you found the car."

Jack nodded his head as Replacement tried to put her ear up to the phone to listen.

"Thanks, I appreciate it." He hung up.

"What did he say?"

"Sully said he found it near the sharp curve in the road."

"Are we going out there now?"

Jack nodded, but his mood soon turned as gray as the sky as they drove to the reservoir.

CHAPTER SIXTEEN

It Was Me

Replacement looked as if she wanted him to speed up but at the same time not get there. Jack felt the same way.

The day was very warm for January, and they both cranked down the windows a little. The smell of pine trees soon filled the car.

When they turned onto Reservoir Road, they scanned up and down the area where Sully had said he found the car. That's when he noticed some marks. Jack could tell where a car became stuck on the side of the road by the turned up dirt and deep tire tracks. He pulled ahead and got out. Replacement fell in behind him.

The day had warmed considerably, and the melting snow created deep mud on the side of the road. He walked over to the tire tracks. The ruts by the side of the road told Jack just where the Civic had come to rest. The deep tracks of the tow truck sat just outside those of the small sedan. A series of thin ruts showed where the teens had parked to check out the car. The snow had melted, and he could see bits of plastic and broken glass.

Replacement walked away, following the debris trail, while he examined the tire tracks. What he was looking for, he didn't know. Sometimes it helped him think if he just stared at a crime scene.

It's a possible crime scene.

Jack forced himself to calm down.

Go over your notes: Michelle went missing. The kids found the car here. If the car—

Jack was going down the list but stopped while he watched Replacement. She was not walking down the street as she followed the debris trail but across it.

Jack walked after her, following the bits and pieces of plastic and glass like breadcrumbs. Replacement's face was puzzled as she looked up the hill. It was extremely steep for about ten feet and then it rose at an easier angle. Because of that, they couldn't see that far over the lip, but one thing was obvious to Jack. The car had come from that direction. Tire tracks came straight down the grass hill, and he could see where the front end scraped the pavement as the car came back on the road.

Could she have been driving up on Pine Ridge?

He had to pull himself over the lip of the hill, but once he stood up it was clear; the Civic had gone off the road at Pine Ridge, come down the hill and stopped on Reservoir Road. Replacement now stood beside him, covered in dirt from the climb up the slope.

"Walk slowly after me to make sure I don't miss anything," he told her, but the reason for the request was different. Something felt off. Other cops and soldiers had told him to put away gut instincts and go on facts, but his gut had saved his life more times than he could count.

He could tell that this section of the hill had been the scene of a terrible brushfire years back. Because of that, the trees were new and small. A few dead trees refused to fall over, and some twisted ones refused to give in. Jack could see the trail the car had made as it careened down the slope.

They followed the path up until the trail veered at almost a ninety-degree angle and large clumps of grass and dirt stuck out. There was a slight gulley. It wasn't very low, but it dropped off after a couple feet.

The car must have come off the granite rocks, and this was where it rolled over.

He could see some shattered glass. Jack pictured the crash. The car flipped and then landed back up on its wheels. Jack examined the original path the car traveled and then estimated its trajectory.

It was going straight toward the lake. Instead, it flipped on the rocks and went off to the road below.

Jack looked up and down again. The very straight path it had taken until that ninety-degree twist in the middle surprised him. He looked around the rocks where the car flipped over. There was a lot of glass, a soda bottle, and some trash.

They must have been tossed out when the car—

"Replacement." Jack's voice was calm, and he forced himself to adopt a neutral expression. He turned around and spoke directly to her. "I need you to go and get the camera out of the trunk of my car."

"Why?"

"It's very important, and I need it now."

She started to protest some more but instead turned and headed back down the hill. Jack watched her as she slipped and slid, cursing under her breath, back to his car.

Jack watched her for a long time because he didn't want to look anywhere else. He stared down at his hands, and they shook. He squeezed them into fists and closed his eyes.

Please God, help me.

His pleas were always the same. It didn't matter whether he was in Iraq or whether he was making a drug bust.

He opened his eyes and went to the top of the rock. He tried to picture the car. It wasn't too smashed, a surprising fact considering what had happened to it, so it couldn't have rolled more than a couple times. He looked where the car had changed direction. The tires had dug deeply into the ground in one spot. It must have landed there. He imagined the car again, and the path it took.

He walked past the spot where it had flipped, moving more toward its original path. He walked a couple feet and stopped.

No God, please. Please...

Jack's eyes involuntarily slammed shut, and his head fell forward as it felt as though someone crushed his chest. A low guttural moan exploded from him.

Michelle's body lay on the grass, partly hidden by some shrubs. Her face was turned away from him and looked toward the lake. It appeared as if she were just sleeping with her head resting on her arm, but he knew she was dead. He could smell it, that unmistakable foul odor of death.

He sank to his knees and his vision blurred. He wanted to scream. Then he thought...

Replacement.

He staggered back down the hill. She was already almost back to him. She was muttering to herself, and she was mad. "There was no camera…"

Her words trailed off when she saw his face.

"It wasn't in the trunk." Her voice went tight.

She shook her head and tears welled up in her eyes.

Jack slowly nodded. Replacement swayed, her feet slipped, and she fell onto her hands and knees. Jack rushed to her and also slipped as he came up beside her. A wretched sob twisted his body as guilt and pain washed over him. He loved Michelle like a sister. He should have watched over her when he'd come back from the Army, but he'd failed. He had two real friends, Chandler and Michelle, and they were both dead now.

Why?

Images assaulted his mind: Michelle riding her bike, Aunt Haddie holding her hand, Michelle at Christmas…

Replacement wailed and clawed her way up the hill on her hands and knees. Jack knew that he couldn't let her see Michelle's body. Not like this. He grabbed her, and her pain exploded at him in a focused rage.

Her hand attempted to smash him across his face. He grabbed her around the waist. Her punches rained down on his hands, but he held on. She kicked at his shins and clawed at his arms.

"I don't believe you. I want to see her."

Jack just gripped her tighter.

"You were supposed to come back. You were supposed to watch out for us. Why didn't you?" She continued to hit him and try to break free. Jack just held on. "Why? What did we do?" She collapsed in the mud, but he didn't let go.

Jack dug into his pocket for his phone. Cindy was working dispatch, but he couldn't seem to make out what she was saying. "Officer Jack Stratton." His voice sounded far off to him. "I'm on Reservoir Road. Send a car and the coroner." He hung up as Cindy was frantically calling out to him.

They sat in the mud; Replacement sobbed until she shook uncontrollably from the cold.

As he closed his eyes, he realized how alone he'd become.

It was me. I pushed people away. I wouldn't leave, but I made them get out of my life. I only lived an hour away, and I never went to see Michelle. I always blamed it on Chandler's death. I always made excuses.

He stared off into space, and he realized how broken he was. He had parents now, but he'd brushed them aside. Aunt Haddie was like his mother, but he'd turned his back on her. He'd said he loved Michelle yet she lay dead on this hillside for a couple of weeks, and he hadn't known.

"Jack." Replacement's voice was quiet and soft. "Jack, I'm sorry," she whispered.

Jack turned to her, and her muddy, tear-stained face was strained with fear.

"No, you got it right." His mouth twitched, and he stared down as he shook. "I'm such a rotten bastard I can't even remember your real name." He expected to see a look of disgust but instead her eyes filled with concern.

"Please tell Aunt Haddie I'm sorry." Jack felt the cold metal press against his temple as he put his gun to his head.

"Jack." Replacement held a trembling hand out toward him. "Please give me the gun."

He felt as if he was watching what was going on but was not actually there.

"No, please." She was crying. The tears cut channels through the mud on her face.

Jack could hear the sirens now. When they came, everything would be over anyway. You can't have a breakdown as a cop. "They'll know."

His chest hurt. His heart hurt. He was so tired of pain.

Replacement shut her eyes, and when she opened them, she was transformed. She spoke calmly and firmly. "If you do it, I will too." She looked straight into his eyes.

As the sirens grew louder, they stared at each other. Jack couldn't seem to think. He lowered the gun. "I'm broken," he whispered.

"Me too, Jack." Her hand came around to lie softly on his. "Don't leave me all alone."

She seemed so young and yet so old at the same time. She slid forward and placed her shaking hand over his hand that held the gun. Jack shut his eyes. When he realized how he'd just acted, a fresh wave of shame washed over him and dragged him back toward the abyss.

He turned his head to look at the approaching vehicles. He could see Cindy had pulled out all the stops. Two fire trucks, an ambulance, and three cruisers now rushed down Reservoir Road.

"Jack. Please."

He let go; she pulled the gun away and hid it in her jacket.

The fire trucks pulled up, and Replacement sat next to him and watched the men scramble up the embankment toward them. She took his hand, and Jack pulled her close. They sat in the mud, and he gently rocked her as she cried.

CHAPTER SEVENTEEN

Sometimes...We All Do

The last few hours were a blur. The cops and firefighters coming up the hill, someone covering Michelle's body, the pained looks... Now he was sitting in a hospital, a thick blanket over his shoulders, and a bunch of medicine clouding his brain.

He hated hospitals. They reeked of death. They tried to mask the smell with cleaners, perfumes, and disinfectants, but Jack could still smell it. He looked down at the bed he was on and wondered how many people died in it.

Normally he'd never allow them to take him to the hospital. They should have interviewed him at the ambulance and then allowed him to go home. Instead, the EMTs checked them both out, mentioning something about shock, and insisted they go to the emergency room. Jack had been so defeated he just climbed in the back of the ambulance and let them take him there.

He shrugged the blanket off, burning with shame. He tried to shut down his emotions as he always had in the past, but they smoldered. He felt as if something had broken inside him. The pain was too intense, and it cracked the prison within him, hidden for all these years. That pain now burned unabated.

He jumped off the bed and reached for his jacket. He heard someone clear his throat and the curtain pulled back.

"Hey."

Jack froze at the sound of the deep voice. He turned around slowly. Sheriff Ethan Collins. Collins came from Texas. He was tall and a little lanky, and even though he'd been up north for years, he always had a tan. He was nearing sixty, but he wore the years well. He was a by-the-book cop's cop, and he followed rules and procedures to the letter.

He held his hat as he looked at Jack. "My condolences for your loss, Jack." Collins was also a good man, and Jack knew he meant every word.

"Sheriff Collins." Jack straightened up. "I want to apologize, sir."

"We'll cover that later." Collins stiffened. "You need to take some time, okay?"

Jack relaxed, and he swayed like a deflating balloon. He hated drugs, but whatever they gave him had mellowed him.

Collins shifted uncomfortably. The older man cleared his throat. "I talked to the girl you were with. She seemed convinced it wasn't an accident. I read over the missing person's report, and I read that Michelle was getting ready to transfer schools. It looks like she went for a ride, but something happened."

Jack stared at the floor. "I know that something is wrong. I have no hard proof, but I know that she just didn't go for a ride and...die."

"Jack, right now you need to think about you."

"I know it wasn't an accident."

"Jack, are you looking for my answer as a sheriff, or as a man?" Collins looked at him, and Jack couldn't read him. Maybe there was nothing to read because he was so black and white.

Jack swallowed and stared back at him. Something about a Texan accent added weight to the question.

Did it matter what Collins answered? It wasn't an accident.

Jack nodded but didn't say anything.

"Jack, if it's all right with you, I can handle the notification."

Jack's legs wobbled, and he put his hand on the bed for support.

Aunt Haddie.

Jack nodded his head.

"Take your time coming in, Jack." He turned around but stopped again. Keeping his back to Jack, he added, "You need to talk. If you don't talk to me, then talk to someone, okay?"

Jack wanted more than anything not to talk—not to him, not to anyone. He thought back to the burning inside him. Some anger had burst out, and he could no longer contain it. His jaw clenched.

"I will. Thanks."

Jack and Replacement got a ride back to his apartment from Cindy Grant, the police dispatcher. Jack's call had upset Cindy so much that she came out to the reservoir herself. She was part of a cop family. The joke was even her dog was a police dog. The whole station loved her, and she doted on them all. She made cakes for every birthday and reminded every cop of their spouse's, parents', and kids' birthdays, anniversaries, and anything else.

Cindy was in her sixties but still looked young. It may have been her round, chubby face or her constant smile but Jack wondered what she must have looked like as a little girl every time he saw her. She had short, light brown hair that was cut in a bob and wore a modest dark blue skirt and a blouse with a bright green tree brooch.

The whole ride back Cindy talked. She talked nonstop about nothing in particular but Jack was grateful for the distraction. His chest still hurt. There was a dull burn due to the medicine, but the pain was raw. Replacement sat a few inches away from him. She gripped his hand. Her face was very white. She constantly watched him but tried to do so without him noticing.

He wanted to tell her he was okay, but he couldn't. He wasn't. He wanted to comfort her, but whenever he tried, he began to break down himself.

Cindy took them both to the apartment. Mrs. Stevens came out into the hallway. She took one look at Jack and Replacement's ashen faces and stopped. Mrs. Stevens bowed her head and retreated without a word.

Cindy hugged them and whispered to both of them. Jack didn't hear what she was saying, but her being there was comforting. When she shut the door, the silence was oppressive. Jack felt his chest tighten and a knot formed in his stomach.

Replacement leaned against the counter, and Jack noticed the plates from breakfast behind her.

Was it just this morning she was laughing?

The girl in front of him was a shell of the girl from the morning. He clenched and relaxed his fingers, forcing blood into his hands.

He walked over to her and gently led her to the bedroom. He tenderly lowered her down onto the bed. She lay still as he removed her shoes and pulled the comforter over her. He stood there, looking down at her. Her hand reached out for his. It looked so small as she grabbed his fingers.

She moved over and softly pulled him to sit down on the bed next to her. Jack lay back and stared at the ceiling. He turned his head, and Replacement watched him as she cried.

Jack closed his eyes and sighed.

"Alice," he whispered.

Her name was Alice. Jack finally remembered it. Chandler and he had cracked up laughing and had made jokes about rabbits and Wonderland when she first arrived. That was until Michelle told them to be nice. Michelle reminded them what it felt like when they first came into foster care. How scared they were. That's when Chandler gave her the name Replacement. Alice immediately liked it. Maybe because she just wanted a new start. He could picture her now.

When he opened his eyes, she was still searching his face. "I'm sorry. I couldn't remember your real name."

"I know." She looked hurt.

"It's nothing to do with you. Something is wrong with me. I can't remember names."

She looked at him, but his eyes drifted off as he struggled to remember. He inhaled and held his breath. He exhaled little by little and then stared at the ceiling.

"I was seven, but I still couldn't remember it."

"What couldn't you remember?"

"It's stupid." He put his hands behind his head. "My name," he whispered. "I didn't know my real name. How's that for a joke," he scoffed.

His eyes followed along the cracks in the ceiling.

"She just called me kid or brat or moron, usually with swear words attached to the front and back."

"Your mother?"

Jack cringed and then nodded.

"After she left me in the bus station, I went into the youth system. It was like a whirlwind." He glanced at her. "Everyone was asking me questions. They kept asking me my name, but it was just beyond my reach. It's such a basic question, but I couldn't grab it." He shook his head. "They brought in a woman with an armful of stuffed animals and she talked to me like I was a baby. 'This is Freddy Bunny and his friend Suzy Squirrel.' She danced the stuffed animals around. 'And they want to say hi, but they don't know what to call you.' She pretended to speak in a cartoon boy's voice. 'What should I call you, buddy?' She smiled at me and held up the bunny. I wanted to die. I was so humiliated. Who doesn't remember their own name?"

"You were seven."

"What's my excuse now? I didn't know your name, and I still don't know mine."

"I don't understand. Your name's not Jack?"

Jack shook his head. "No. That's not my birth name." He hesitated. "I just wanted to get out of there and get away from that lady with the puppets but she kept asking. All I could think of was my mother getting on that bus, and the last thing she said to me, 'You don't know jack, kid.'"

Replacement inhaled and looked at him. A tear hung off her lashes and fell onto the bed.

"I named myself. I just told her my name was Jack. To me it meant nothing. You know the expression? You don't know jack. It means you don't know anything. That's what I was…nothing."

"You're not nothing."

He looked over at her.

"That's how I feel…sometimes."

Replacement slid up next to him. "Sometimes, we all do."

CHAPTER EIGHTEEN

First Dibs

Replacement and Jack had spent the morning in silence. It wasn't the awkward silence Jack had expected nor was it the type of silence that follows a fight. This was the kind that comes between two people who have known each other for years. It was oddly comfortable. In the stillness, they seemed to console each other. The crushing pain of Michelle's death had fused them together.

As they entered the Well's Meadow Nursing Home, the woman at the front desk and an orderly smiled sad, knowing smiles. The well-dressed woman came out from behind the desk and rushed to comfort Replacement. Jack watched as she held her close and the orderly walked away.

"There, there, precious." The woman consoled her. "Sheriff Collins came out last night," she explained to Jack as she looked over Replacement's head. "He was extremely kind. He stayed with Haddie for quite some time."

As they walked down the hallway, Jack realized why the orderly had departed. He felt as if they were on a solemn funeral march as staff and nurses came out into the hallway and hugged Replacement or reached out their hands. Some hugged him too or touched his shoulder. Jack tried not to look around.

Aunt Haddie sat in the corner in a large, comfortable chair in a private room. She hadn't noticed him yet, and he was glad because he gasped. He couldn't believe how much she'd aged. She looked so vulnerable that tears burned his eyes. He remembered how hard she worked. She had two jobs, took care of a house full of kids, kept them spotless, and taught Sunday school. She was a tornado.

Now he looked at a frail old woman with thin salt-and-pepper hair and a bent back.

Sorrow and shame grabbed him, and he wanted to run for the exit. She turned and looked straight at him. Their eyes met, and she smiled the smile he so often saw in his sleep.

He started to rush forward but remembered his selfishness and guilt. Today was not about Jack. It was about Michelle. He walked forward as Replacement moved to Aunt Haddie's side and took her hand.

"Alice, honey." She looked over to Replacement and reached out her arm. She gave her a big hug.

Jack walked around, and Aunt Haddie looked up at him. He bent down, and Aunt Haddie lunged forward and pulled him close to her. After a long time, he pulled away and glanced at her. Her face was full of concern for him.

"Aunt Haddie…" Jack tried to look at her but he couldn't. "I'm so sorry about Michelle. She was such a good person; she didn't deserve this…to die so young…I just wish I could have brought her home."

"Jackie, Jackie." Her voice was still rich, and she held him close. "Michelle is home. Michelle's at home with Chandler. I knew it the first week. I knew God had taken her home."

Replacement patted Jack and Aunt Haddie.

"I knew something had happened."

It was all Jack could do, not to break down.

"She's at peace now. She's happy. You remember how happy she always was?"

Jack nodded.

"She's happy now." She squeezed Jack's hand and tried to smile, but her chin trembled.

Jack inhaled sharply and held the old woman's hands in his. He looked into her face. She was still the same wonderful woman.

He whispered to her, "I'm sorry I never came back."

"Me too, Jackie. You're one of my babies too," she looked at him, "but you remember, no matter where you are, I love you, and I know you love me. Do you think I forgot that? I didn't. Neither did Michelle." She rubbed his hands.

Jack loved Aunt Haddie's honesty and straightforwardness.

They hugged and talked as if they'd never been apart. The nurses brought them a tray of cookies and some water as they mended the gap of time.

"Alice, I need to talk to Jackie privately for a moment."

"Yes, ma'am," Replacement walked away.

Aunt Haddie leaned closer to Jack. "Alice took it very hard, Jackie. She loved Chandler like an older brother. I know Alice is not your sister but she's one of my babies, too. She can be a little hard to handle." She squeezed his hand. "Remember some people had it harder than you, and I appreciate you watching out for her."

Jack paused.

Aunt Haddie knows the hell I went through, and Replacement had it harder than me...

Jack looked across the room at Replacement. She leaned against the wall and looked out the window. She had her arms crossed. She looked even smaller, younger.

What did she go through?

"She's a little spitfire but deep down she's been wounded too." Aunt Haddie said.

Jack nodded.

"I understand how you hurt, honey," Aunt Haddie continued. "When I lost my Alton, all I wanted to do was keep running. You shouldn't have stayed away, but you have to get over that now. Michelle would have forgiven you, and so would Chandler. I'll forgive you now, too, but let me be clear, I expect you to visit from now on." She lifted up his chin so he could look at her. Her eyes were filled with concern and love for him. "I need to know something. You'll tell me straightaway, right?" She held his chin and peered into his eyes.

Now it was Jack's turn to say, "Yes, ma'am."

Aunt Haddie softly touched his arm. "Jackie, what do you think happened to Michelle?"

Jack looked at his hands and thought about what he should tell her. He chose the only way he ever spoke with her, honestly. "I think…I think someone killed her."

Aunt Haddie nodded, but her lower lip trembled. "Jackie, I want you—"

"I'll get the people who did this."

"Jackie, Jackie." She was crying now. "I want you to stay safe. God will get the people who did this. He'll punish them."

God will punish them. I just want first dibs.

CHAPTER NINETEEN

Good and Bad

The following day, Jack started the Impala and pulled out. The police station was a fifteen-minute drive, so he tried to take his time as he practiced his version of events.

Sheriff Collins, I originally was not aware this had been officially...don't lie. Damn. Collins was so by-the-book he wouldn't listen to any excuse for breaking protocol. Fall on your sword and tell it like it was. I didn't... Damn. Ben Nichols? Do I tell him that? The stupid Mohawk kid? I didn't tag the phone...

Every angle that he tried to think of to minimize damage ended the same way: with Collins ticked off. The ride went by way too fast. Driving around the block a few times wasn't an option. Jack didn't want to go in, but he didn't hesitate. He hated that. He hated indecision, so he marched straight into the station.

Cindy came out from behind the desk, her arms open wide. She was still smiling, but it was a sympathetic, comforting smile. Jack welcomed it. Cindy was the type of person you couldn't help but like.

"Just remember to apologize and let him do most of the talking," she whispered in his ear.

She gave him a reassuring pat on the back and a little push toward Sheriff Collins's office.

The police station was large. It was mostly two floors of open space with unassigned desks. The people who had an official office were the sheriff and the undersheriff. There were plenty of rooms, but the layout furthered Collins's philosophy of chain of command. He was chief; everyone else was an Indian.

The door was open as Jack approached. Sheriff Collins was behind an ultramodern desk with little on it. Two large computer monitors reflected in his glasses. Picture frames, diplomas, and certificates covered the back wall. He swiveled in his chair and stood as Jack entered the room. His hand shot out. "My condolences, Jack."

Jack shook his hand.

The sheriff sat, and Jack remained standing. With Jack's Army background, it was routine for him, but some of the other officers still had a hard time with Collins's habit of having you stand while he asked you questions.

"You could have taken some more time, but I'm glad you're here." Collins didn't smile, but he wasn't scowling either, Jack noted.

"Thank you, sir, but I need to get some things settled now. First, let me offer my apologies for not notifying you directly."

"You didn't notify me indirectly either, Jack." Collins's eyebrow rose and his jaw slightly clenched. "Save the apologies and just tell me what happened."

By the book. I should have thought of something about the phone.

"This past Thursday night, my friend's sister came to my apartment."

Leave off the naked part and the fight with Gina.

"She informed me that my foster sister, Michelle Campbell, was missing. Her foster mother filed a missing person's report in Fairfield earlier."

Sheriff Collins nodded.

"Michelle's brother and I served in Iraq together, and it sounded out of character for her to just up and go. I thought I should look into it. We took a ride over to the college and spoke with Michelle's roommate and the campus police." Jack paused to see whether he should provide more details. Silence seemed to be permission to continue. "The campus police said Michelle had transferred but we…" He cleared his throat. "I decided to look up the car Michelle had been driving and located it at Sullivan's."

Sheriff Collins's eyes narrowed and deep lines formed on his tanned face.

He looks a little like Clint Eastwood when he's angry. Is he ticked at me for looking into the car or Murphy for not entering it into the database?

Jack cleared his throat again. "After speaking with Sully, I spoke with Ben Nichols, who had called in the abandoned car report." Jack pulled out his notebook and noted the approving look of the sheriff. "Mr. Nichols informed me he witnessed some teens around the car before he called it in. One of the teens had a distinctive helmet, and on the way out to Reservoir Road, where the car was found, I noticed the teen and followed him to the high school."

Sort of true. He doesn't need to know I went there to look specifically for the kid.

"The teen, Rick Matthews, indicated he'd been in the car and started the car. He also informed me he found this phone." Jack had placed the phone in a police bag, but he didn't look at Collins as he placed it on his desk.

"Immediately after that, I headed out to Reservoir Road, and it was then I followed the debris trail and located…the victim's body." His eyes burned as he spoke the last few words and he paused while he waited for the sheriff's reaction.

"Jack…" Collins fiddled with a pen on his desk. "Right now I want to apologize for Murphy. He's the one who should be apologizing anyway. You shouldn't have had to run this down."

Jack nodded. Collins released the grip he had on the pen. Jack's anger had started to rise too. Murphy's ineptitude had always made the sheriff's blood boil. With noticeable effort, Collins straightened his notepad and laid the pen next to it.

"You'll need to write it all up in a report. I'd appreciate it if you got to it directly. After that, take a few days. When is the funeral?"

"Saturday."

Collins gave a brief nod. "We'll talk again after that."

"Sheriff?" Jack hated to wait, especially for a reprimand. "I'm sorry, but can you let me know…?"

"Let you know?" Collins had started to rise but sat back down. His face turned red. "The same way you should have let me know but didn't." Sheriff Collins exhaled slowly but loudly. "As of now, you're going to help the traffic detail for the next month."

Not too bad. It's the night shift.

"On days when there's no traffic detail, Cindy needs assistance getting caught up on reports."

Suck. Jack hated paperwork.

"We will need to review your training schedule at a later date to see if that busy roster impacted your judgment."

Good and bad. Jack tried his best to keep an "I'm sorry" face and not show any surprise or anger. Collins said review, so he hadn't canceled anything, but I'm on notice. If I do anything else, he takes away my training. Collins might as well have said, "you're fired" because it would have the same effect.

"Jack, let me make this clear: this is Joe Davenport's case now. Additionally, Michelle is your foster sister; that's a conflict of interest. I've talked to Joe about reviewing the case, and I'll personally examine it. Now you have my utmost sympathies, but if you even think of going around me and looking into this, I'll have your hide. That is all." Collins turned back to his computer.

As Jack turned away, he let the mask fall off his face. He walked straight out of the office to the back room to complete the report.

Get it done and then get out.

Now it was Jack's blood that was boiling. He stormed by Cindy, and she held out a stack of papers to him. He grabbed them like a relay runner, never breaking stride, and headed to the back office.

He carefully shut the door because he wanted to slam it—badly.

Murphy's a stupid moron. If he'd done the bare minimum, they...damn.

Jack flopped into the chair and let his head fall into his hands. After a minute, he sat up and looked at the stack of papers. He couldn't help but smile a little. Cindy had filled out the sections she could. He flipped open a few of the pages.

I could be out of here in a couple of hours. He paused. Why rush, Jack? Where do you have to be?

CHAPTER TWENTY

So Much for Green

Jack rolled over and looked at the clock. One thirty. He was glad but also ticked off. He couldn't sleep, but he didn't want to get up before the bar around the corner closed. He didn't want a drink; he wanted nine or ten. His pain was still raw. That burn he couldn't put out seemed to be always on now. He tried to bury it, but it seared its way back into the open.

Drown it. Head off the rails one night and into oblivion.

He tried to convince himself it would be okay but fought that urge. He refused. He could be a blackout drinker. He knew that even before he enlisted in the Army. His drinking had never bothered him when he was younger, but it put a completely different spin on things when you woke up, clueless, surrounded by high caliber weapons.

He got up and headed into the kitchen for some water.

Don't drink. The service is tomorrow. Anyway, it's too late. Everything's closed.

"Nice butt."

Jack grabbed for the dishtowel and then dashed back into the bedroom as Replacement laughed.

"You should warn me," he called out as he pulled on a pair of sweatpants.

"Warn you?" She giggled. "How? Danger, Jack. You're about to come into the kitchen with your butt uncovered?"

"I didn't know you were up."

"Do you normally go around naked?" She kept giggling.

"You know…" he stammered. "I just forgot you were here."

He was beet red. Clearly, Replacement couldn't decide whether he was embarrassed or truly upset, so she changed her tune. "I'm sorry."

"Don't—it's my fault. This will take some getting used to." Jack tried not to shake his head. He returned and got a glass of water, and Replacement turned back to the computer. He poured two glasses and then walked back over to her, handing her one. "What're you working on?"

"Michelle had a fitness app on her phone. It's called Get in Shape Girl." Her eyes stayed on the screen. Replacement sat in her old Fairfield High jersey with her legs tucked underneath her.

"And?" Jack stood behind her.

"Part of the app monitors all of your exercise. There's a walking program that shows everywhere she had been."

"Great job, kid." Jack grabbed the back of her chair and leaned over her shoulder to stare at the screen too. "Does it give dates and times? Everywhere she had been?"

"It has everything. I just got in her phone—"

"Michelle's phone? But I gave it to Collins?"

"Umm…" She hunched up her shoulders and looked at him with emerald eyes that hinted at a secret.

"You couldn't have taken it. Did you switch it? How—?" Jack squeezed the glass.

She looked nervously at his tightening fingers. "I made a backup. That's all."

"You backed up her phone *before* I gave it to Collins?" His grip relaxed a bit.

"It's a smart phone, so it was easy. I did it after we came home from the hospital. I didn't think it was wrong."

"Don't think, ask. It's *my job*." Jack winced after he shouted the last two words. She looked hurt, and he felt sorry.

Don't feel bad, you idiot. He cursed at himself. *Keep your job. If Collins knew we went into the phone, he'd have your head on his wall.*

"How did you get in? Aren't they password protected?"

"They have a four-digit pin. Michelle always used the same one." Replacement shrugged.

He tried to glare at her, but she grinned like a little kid. Jack rolled his eyes and looked back at the screen. It looked like a spreadsheet of times and dates, and his thoughts shifted to the hunt for answers.

"Can you start backward? What were her last whereabouts?"

Replacement turned and began to type. "The phone was at Reservoir Road in the same place for twelve hours. December twenty-first."

"So Michelle got there on the twenty-first? What time?"

"Twelve thirty a.m."

She wouldn't just go for a drive out there after midnight.

"What happened to the phone after twelve hours?"

"The phone must have died then…" Her choice of words made her trail off.

"Where was she before? How long—"

"Hold on, I don't know the program that well." Replacement's fingers flew over the keyboard. "She was there for…almost four hours."

"Where?" Jack leaned in, but the data on the screen didn't make sense to him.

"I have to map the coordinates." She pressed more keys, and a mapping program appeared. "Here. General Alexander Davidson Circle."

They both stared at the map for a minute. There was a large building out there, but the location puzzled Jack. He hadn't been there. He'd driven around most of the county, but not out there.

"What was she doing out there?"

"The building is listed as a nature center." Replacement zoomed in.

"Why from eight thirty until after midnight?"

He looked at the clock. One fifty. Replacement raised an eyebrow, and he did too. "I can't sleep anyway."

They snuck out of the apartment like little kids, careful not to wake Mrs. Stevens. The ride to the nature center would take about twenty minutes because of the winding roads. It was below freezing, so Replacement ditched the seat belt along with any notion of personal space and shivered next to him as the car tried to warm up during the drive.

They rode with their teeth chattering. He was glad to be doing something, and she looked that way too.

"Life's hard." Jack rolled his eyes at his own comment. *Life's hard? What else was I going to say? How you doing? Her sister died. She's in pain. Stupid.*

"It is." Replacement smiled. "Thanks for everything." She curled up closer to him.

Thanks for everything? I gave her a couch instead of a closet. Everything wasn't much.

They drove past an old open gate as they made their way up the last curving road. As they neared the nature center at the top of the hill, they pulled into a small, empty parking lot.

The building was a large, two-story, circular structure. A curved driveway led up to a large entrance. It was a mixture of granite and stone, and looked as though it was constructed in the 1960s.

As they got out of the car, light snow fell. A large modern sign at the front of the building read: WHITE ROCKS EASTERN COLLEGE – NEUROPSYCHOLOGY CENTER.

"It looks like the college converted the nature center." Jack looked at Replacement.

Her face contorted. "So much for green," she mocked.

They both went to the door. Apart from a faint hallway light, the building looked closed. There was a large greeting desk in the front, behind which were two doors. Staircases led up on both the left and right.

"It's opened weekdays at nine o'clock." Replacement pointed to a blackboard with white snap-on letters.

Jack walked to the left to go around the building but stopped. The ground sloped off and revealed another level below. It had the same large windows as the rest of the building. Another look to the right showed there was not an easy way to walk around the building.

Replacement headed back to the car while Jack scanned the outside of the building once more.

"Wish I could get a look around back." He slid back into the Impala. "How accurate is that phone?" He chastised himself for shutting the car off as his hands shook with the cold.

"You mean distance?" Replacement slid up against him; her teeth chattered. He looked down and saw that her jacket was more suited to fall than winter.

"Can it tell if she was in the building?" Jack whipped his coat off, and before she could protest, he wrapped it over her legs.

"Thank you." She looked at Jack as if he'd just done something monumental. "The app gives a rough distance, like she was around here." She made large circles with her hands when she said around.

"So, she came out here at eight thirty at night. She had some reason. Did you find anything else on the phone yet?"

"I went through her emails and texts. It wasn't much. A bunch of school stuff. She didn't have many friends. She focused on school. I'll go back and check."

"She came here for something. We just need to figure out why."

"I'll go through her phone and look for any connection to here. When are we coming out on Monday?" Jack tilted his head, and he could feel Replacement stiffen next to him.

"Look…Collins is going to go after my head. I'm supposed to go through him." Jack shrugged.

"What if we came up with some reason you were out here? Some reason why you'd come back." She stopped when she saw Jack's face. "Jack?"

He gripped the wheel and stared straight ahead. His voice was soft when he spoke. "I'm sorry. I'm sorry I didn't come back."

"You should be." The words were softer than Jack expected, as was the hand that enclosed his, prying his fingers from the steering wheel. "But you're here now. And we're going to find who did this."

The certainty in her words calmed Jack, and he put the car in gear.

"We will."

CHAPTER TWENTY-ONE

Homecoming

Jack shifted in his seat. He sat next to Replacement, and she was next to Aunt Haddie in the front row. He hated funeral homes. Subdued lighting and the scent of flowers hung in the air. The thick carpet and chairs were in neat rows. Men in suits, who you'd never met, had looks of empathy and pity carved onto their faces. He hated it all.

People filled the funeral home. He couldn't believe how many were there.

How many really knew her? When someone young dies, every young kid turns out. It's their first taste of death for someone like them, someone who shouldn't have died. It makes them think, "It could have been me." How many here were really her friends?

Michelle had always been the quiet type. She was careful when she chose her friends. She wasn't arrogant at all, but she had high standards. Friends had to be loyal, honest, and truthful. Aunt Haddie used to say if you made it out of this life with one good friend, that you were blessed. Michelle was blessed.

Jack shifted. He forced a smile at Replacement, but she never stopped looking down at her hands. He closed his eyes and let his head fall forward.

The minister had already begun the service. He was a large man with a deep voice. They sang "Amazing Grace" and scriptures were read. Aunt Haddie and Replacement cried.

After they sang "When the Roll is Called up Yonder," a young girl around sixteen went up to the podium. Her curly dark brown hair came down to her shoulders. She was dressed in a simple gray dress, and her eyes flittered around the room. She unfolded a page from a notebook.

"Michelle was my mentor and my friend. I met her through the sisters…program where she…volunteered. She always tell…told me that I…" the girl said haltingly. It was obviously hard for her to read. She looked up and paused. She refolded the paper. "I'm going to start again." She looked forward and tried to stand tall. "Michelle believed in me. She taught me to believe in myself. I loved her very much. I was shy like her, but she showed me an example of what I could be. My life is much better because of her."

The girl took her seat. Four more girls from all different backgrounds came up and spoke about Michelle. They talked about the Michelle Jack didn't know. The Michelle who loved to learn and taught herself computers. The Michelle who helped her neighbors and underprivileged kids. A young woman filled with hope who passed that hope along to others.

A tall man, over six feet, with broad shoulders and finely groomed silver hair leaned slightly on a cane as he walked forward to speak. He was in his mid-sixties, dressed in a dark blue suit, and had a bit of a belly.

"Michelle was one of my brightest students. As evidenced by the words of the people here who knew her best, Michelle was an example for us all. She worked to create change. She was always willing to help her fellow students and workers. Her enthusiasm and spirit will be missed, but it won't be forgotten. Her legacy will live on in her work and accomplishments."

The funeral director came over and looked at Replacement. Her eyes filled with fear, and she went white. Aunt Haddie patted her leg, rose, and the director and Replacement helped her make it up to the podium. She looked so old. She stood there, bent over, gripping the podium for support, and looked down for a long time.

"Michelle," she began, and her voice broke. Replacement squeezed Jack's hand. "Michelle was one of my dear, dear babies. She was on loan from the Lord. She was such a precious girl. God abundantly blessed me by bringing her into my life. Michelle was truly special. The years she stayed in my home were so dear to me, but I don't feel this is a time for sadness. Michelle is home with Jesus now."

Aunt Haddie paused and wiped her eyes. "I remember when Michelle and Chandler first came home to me. Michelle always looked at the positives. She was like a little ray of sunshine all bottled up. We didn't have much, but Michelle was always looking at what we did have."

Everyone tried not to break down.

"They asked me to talk about some of my favorite memories of Michelle but how can I pick? I prayed about it. I tried to think, and then I remembered one—Michelle's bike.

"Michelle's birthday was coming up, and that year we had very little. I knew Michelle had wanted a bike; she'd been saving up for it all summer." Aunt Haddie was crying now. Replacement shifted.

"On the morning of her birthday, Chandler and Jackie came inside, smiling ear to ear. Their hands were covered in pink paint. They'd found an old boy's bike and they painted it bright pink. They put purple streamers on it. You'd think they both would pop the buttons off their shirts. They were so proud."

Jack rubbed his eyes.

"Michelle cried and danced and cried some more. Jackie and Chandler taught her for a day, but she took to it like a fish to water. She rode that bike everywhere. I can still see her smiling face riding out in the driveway. Her little wave…"

Aunt Haddie stopped, and Replacement's hand went a little limp. Aunt Haddie looked around. "I don't know what happened to the bike…she lost it…Michelle…" She stopped again.

The funeral director looked at Replacement and then they went up to the podium and helped Aunt Haddie back to her seat. The stress of the situation had clearly gotten to her.

Aunt Haddie turned to look at Jack, and he held her gaze, but he could see the effects of Alzheimer's. She looked at him, but he knew she didn't really see him. Replacement stroked the back of the old woman's hand.

Jack looked down. That bike. He and Chandler had found it at the dump. It was a boy's bike, and it had a flat tire. They'd stayed up all night painting it and trying to figure out the tassels. Michelle had teased them for two days because of the pink paint on their hands.

There was a little disruption to his right as a man tried to move around people to come forward. It was so quiet any noise would have caught people's attention. The man walked up to the podium.

"Hello." He coughed as he looked down and brushed back his hair with one hand. "My name is Robert, and I knew Michelle since we were kids." He was a young man in his twenties. He had dark hair and eyes and wore a nice suit. His red eyes made it obvious he'd been crying. "It was hard hearing about Michelle's bike." He cleared his throat. "I know what happened to it." He looked straight at Aunt Haddie. "I stole it."

The quiet room grew completely still. Jack could hear his heart beat.

"I was a kid, and the bike was outside the library, and I took it. I brought it home and painted it blue." He paused to blow his nose and looked up, but no one was moving. "It didn't matter that I painted it and pulled off the tassels. Michelle knew it was hers, and when she saw me riding it, she followed me home. She came right to my front door. I thought she was going to punch me in the nose.

"She asked me why I stole it. I said, 'What does that matter? It's mine now.' She wanted to know why. She said, 'You shouldn't let evil things just go.' That freaked me out. I was like, 'I'm not evil,' but she said, 'Well, you're a thief.'" The young man gripped the podium, and the tears rolled down his cheeks. "She asked me why again. I told her mine broke. The frame cracked. I couldn't fix it, and it was just me and my mom. I begged her not to tell my mom or Chandler. I knew she was Chandler's sister, and he'd have stomped me. I told her she could have it back.

"Then she looked at me, and I'll never forget her face when she said, 'You can keep it.' I couldn't believe it. I followed her halfway home, trying to get her to take the bike back, but she wouldn't. She told me I should have it since I didn't have one and since I wanted it that bad. She said God gave her a mom and two brothers and a bike. She said she should share. I was just a kid, but I never forgot that. She and I were always friends from then on." Someone handed him a box of tissues. He blew his nose, turned, and walked back into the crowd.

Jack's leg shook. He could almost see when they were kids in the driveway, laughing with Chandler and waving to him.

Two brothers. I love you, too, Michelle.

The black minister rose and came forward. He began to walk to the podium and then turned and came to Aunt Haddie. The large man took the old woman's hands in his, got down on one knee, and bowed his head. "Lord, I thank you for the time that you've given all of us to know Michelle. I thank you for her wonderful heart and the example she has been. Please, Father, be with us who are left here. Watch over us, guide us, and lead us to the rest that Your Son prepared for those who He has called. We pray this in the name of Jesus. Amen."

Jack kept his eyes closed. The ceremony was over and people got up. He ran his hands through his hair, wiped his eyes, and exhaled.

"Jack?" He turned. Michelle's teacher in the dark blue suit held his hand out. The man had a firm handshake and a bright smile. "Please accept my condolences for your loss."

Slight European accent.

"Thank you. You're one of Michelle's teachers at the college?"

"Dr. Alexander Hahn. Psychology. I cannot express my sympathies strongly enough. Michelle's contributions will be very much missed by the college and myself personally."

"Contributions?"

"Michelle worked for me at the psychology center. She was instrumental in bringing our computer technology into the twenty-first century. I meant what I said. Her legacy will live on."

"Thank you, Doctor." Jack shook the outstretched hand again.

"If you have the time, you should stop by the center. You would be very proud of her work."

"I will. You can count on it."

CHAPTER TWENTY-TWO

The Void Beckons

Jack opened one eye when he heard the knock on the door but then closed it again.

Knock. Knock.

He started to call to Replacement but then he heard her in the shower.

Ugh.

He rolled himself out of bed and grabbed a pair of sweatpants from the floor.

"Hold on," he called toward the apartment door as he hopped into the pants. "One sec."

Jack didn't look to see who was there before he yanked open the door. He was surprised to see Joe Davenport standing there. Joe was nearing retirement, and it showed. He liked to fish more than anything, and his wrinkled face and potbelly were the result. He seemed like a good guy, and Jack liked him even though he didn't have the best work ethic.

"Hey, Joe. Come in."

Joe always wore a tan hat with a brown and white band, a cross between an old fedora and a fishing cap. "My condolences, Jack." He shook his hand as he came in, but he only glanced at Jack's face before he turned away.

Spill it, Joe.

That was what he wanted to blurt out, but he decided to give the old detective some time. "What brings you around, Joe?"

The detective put his hands in his pockets and followed Jack into the living room. "I got some good news about the phone. The tech guys got into it with that code you thought might work."

Jack had given Joe a possible list of numbers they should try. Of course, Jack knew which code would work, but he put it second on the list to make it look good.

"They got in it? Great. Have they found anything?"

"They said they'll go over it with a fine-tooth comb." Joe had a habit of nodding his head a lot.

Nervous tic.

"That's good news, Joe. Do you have anything else?"

Joe nodded. "Yeah." He stared at his feet.

This isn't good.

He handed Jack the manila envelope. "Toxicology."

Jack opened the envelope. *Presence of benzaldehyde I, nitroethane, benzyl-methylnaphthalene.*

"I'm sorry, Jack," Joe mumbled. "There's been a huge increase in the county."

"An increase in what?" Jack's frustration turned into anger.

"Glass meth." Joe said the words with a shrug. "It's ninety percent pure. They've even had a couple of ODs."

"They couldn't have found meth. Michelle would never do it. That's impossible."

"Not a lot but… Even a little of that stuff can make you crazy. You can get real disoriented, and if she was driving… I've seen—"

"No way. Michelle would never do that crap." Jack kept shaking his head.

"Jack, I wouldn't say anything if it wasn't my place."

Jack's head snapped up. He wanted to shout, *it's not your place.* But it was.

Joe is the lead detective. I'm the victim's family. Joe is just doing his job. He has to point these things out. But, he's wrong.

"You've seen it firsthand, Jack. I was just reading about two kids in Nebraska who took crystal one time and ran out in the middle of a snowstorm, thinking mobs of people were trying to kill them." Joe looked back at the floor.

Jack was numb. He wanted to explode, but his anger was nowhere to be found.

"I'm sorry, Jack. Everything points to an accident."

Jack tried to think of some other argument.

Aunt Haddie? If I say Michelle wouldn't leave her, he'll say she might. Would she? What do I say?

Joe took one step forward. "I'm sorry, Jack. I'll keep it open, of course." Joe looked up.

Jack saw an old, tired cop who just wanted to make it to retirement with as little fuss as possible, but he looked sincere. Jack searched his face, but he knew Joe thought he was doing the right thing.

"Thanks for coming by, Joe." He leaned over and shook his hand.

Joe walked out but paused at the door. "I just…I just want you to know that I did go back over everything, and I think…I think it is what it is."

Jack nodded.

The door clicked shut, and Jack walked over and leaned on the counter. A wave of doubt crashed over him and swept his anger away.

Meth?

He went to get a glass of water but stopped himself. With his hand on the faucet, he listened.

The water had stopped. The shower wasn't running.

He straightened bolt upright.

He walked over to the bedroom and slowly opened the door. Replacement sat on the edge of the bed with her head in her hands, softly crying. He moved over and sat down next to her. She leaned against him, and he held her.

"I don't think…" he began, but she pressed her hand against his lips.

"No, Jack. Shh, I'm just gonna think for a minute. Go take your shower." She wiped her eyes and walked over to the door.

Jack sat on the bed, feeling stupid.

What should I say?

He brushed his hair back in frustration.

"We'll talk when I get out, okay?"

Replacement just nodded and walked into the living room.

For the first time in years, Jack wished he had a real guy friend. He missed Chandler all the time, but he wished Chandler were around right now. He had lots of acquaintances and colleagues but no real friends. The only people who got close to him were girls, but he never told them anything.

As he lifted his face into the water, he closed his eyes. He wanted to think, but his thoughts flew all over, scattering like scared sparrows. He felt old and tired like Joe.

Alone.

He stayed in the shower for a long time before he decided he should call his father. They hadn't talked a lot recently. His father knew nothing about police work. He was a math teacher, but he could read people.

After this was all over, he was going down to Florida. He'd take two weeks and go visit his parents. The water started to run cold. Jack realized he must have been in there awhile.

He shut the water off, stood in the warm mist, and tried to calm down.

Think of now. Screw tomorrow and yesterday; just think of now. What should you do next?

Jack's shoulders slumped.

I don't have a clue.

"Sorry, kid. I didn't mean to take such a—" Jack started to apologize as he came out of the bedroom, still drying his hair. He stopped. It was a familiar sight, just not with her. Replacement stood at the front door with her bags packed.

"Jack, I have to go." She shrugged but didn't look at him.

"Hold on. Can we talk about this? Why?" Jack's emotions shifted right to hurt.

Slow down, Jack. She heard Joe. She's just upset.

"It is what it is, Jack." She looked at him, and her eyes glistened.

"Don't listen to Joe." Jack remembered what the old detective had said on his way out. "I'm not. I was about to come out and start—"

"It's over, Jack. You heard him."

"That's stupid."

"No, it's not. Michelle was just going to leave. That's it. She did meth and drove off the road and killed herself."

"She didn't. You know her." Inside, Jack felt as if she were ripping him apart.

Why? Why are you doing this?

"I didn't know her. I was just chasing after her. She never…" Her voice changed. It was getting colder. "Did you know her? Did you know her really? What was her favorite book? How about her favorite movie? Color? When did she get her first kiss? Who were her friends?"

Jack burned now, not with anger but shame. Shame because he didn't know these things. Shame because he never saw Replacement thought of him like this. She was hurt because he never returned, but they'd gone through so much together he thought that had changed.

"I'm sorry." Jack took another step forward, and she held up a hand. "Look, I'm so sorry. I know—"

"What do you know? You don't know crap. You think she wouldn't leave Aunt Haddie? Why? You did. Michelle is like you in that. She got her chance to go, and she took it. That's what I'm doing."

"Don't. You can go but—" Jack grabbed onto the side of a chair.

"Don't what?" Her mouth was twisted. "Don't tell you the truth?" She glared; all drops of tears vanished, along with any trace of warmth.

Jack wanted to become as detached as she was. He wanted to let her leave and then he'd go back to the way things were. He'd get a bottle and leap headfirst into the void. He closed his eyes. His mouth was dry, and his throat was tight. They were on the edge of a cliff, and Replacement was about to jump off.

"You're not blaming Michelle; you're blaming yourself. You're letting all that crap get into your head. You said you were chasing her. Is that it? You want to try convincing yourself that Michelle wanted to escape her little tagalong?"

"Screw you."

"Say what you want to me. You're right. I didn't know her. You did. But you need to know this. You walk out that door, and you'll bury Michelle in your head. You'll bury her in your heart. You'll lose all the times you had with her because you can't look at them, because you won't be able to look at yourself. I know that. That's…that's what I did with Chandler."

Her shoulders trembled, and her hands shook. She began to wail, and she covered her face. Jack didn't hesitate. He moved and pulled her close; his arms wrapped protectively around her. She pushed her face against his chest and sobbed. Jack felt her legs wobble. He swooped her up and cradled her in his arms. She turned her head against his chest, hiding her face. He carried her into the bedroom and softly laid her down.

She curled into a ball. He sat on the edge of the bed and rubbed her shoulders until she cried herself to sleep, but he continued to sit there and look at her.

He was numb with pain. Pain immobilizes people. Pain locks them in place so they spend hours, days, and lifetimes held captive.

I need to talk to Mark Reynolds. He's undercover. He'll help me find the meth dealers. Then I'll go out to the psychology center. Jack began to make a new list.

Jack knew pain. He and pain were old friends. Jack knew only one way to deal with pain. Hunt it down and kill it.

CHAPTER TWENTY-THREE

Aluminum Foil and Other Kitchen Stuff

Jack was dressed and in the kitchen. He looked at the clock. Eight thirty. He wanted to get going, but he waited. Replacement had finished her shower, but she hadn't come out of the bedroom. He looked down at the two plates of food he'd laid out on the counter.

Damn. She went back to bed.

He opened and closed cabinets, but he couldn't find anything. He looked beside the refrigerator and over it. Nothing. He pulled open the drawer under the stove and found an oven tray. He frowned.

The tray was rusted in places, and covered with splotches of black charred remnants. He grabbed a roll of aluminum foil and covered the entire tray in it. He opened another drawer and took out two red cloth napkins that looked as if they belonged in a Chinese restaurant. He carefully laid them over the tray, put the plate on it, and arranged the fork and knife.

He opened the refrigerator, and his eyes went wide. Mrs. Stevens had left four bags of food. Jack didn't like that she'd used her key to come into his apartment and put the food in the refrigerator, but he was still very grateful. He poured a glass of orange juice and stood back to look at his handiwork.

I doubt she'll throw anything at me.

He picked up the tray and walked into the bedroom. Replacement lay on the bed, curled up in a ball. Only the top of her brown hair peeked out from the white and purple comforter.

"Good morning, kid." Jack stood at the side of the bed.

After a couple of seconds, she pulled the corner of the comforter back, and one of her green eyes peeked out. She took one look at Jack, sat bolt upright, and burst out crying.

"No. I just wanted…" Jack set the tray on the bureau and sat down on the bed.

Replacement grabbed him and pulled herself close. She tilted her head, pressed her face into his neck, and continued to wail. Jack tried not to cringe as she sniffled and blubbered all over him as she attempted to speak. He could make out every couple of words.

"Sorry…I don't…you mean…please don't…"

Jack just let her go on. After a few minutes, he realized her nose was so stuffed up, she couldn't breathe. He jumped up, grabbed a roll of toilet paper from the bathroom, and brought it back to her.

"Thank you. I'm so sorry. I…"

Jack grabbed the breakfast tray and held it out, eager to get her to stop crying. "It will get cold, and you'll hurt my feelings." Jack felt like a pansy saying those words, but they seemed to work.

Replacement took the tray and closed her eyes. After a few moments, she picked up the fork and started to eat. Jack started to breathe again.

He watched her as if she were an IED that could go off any second. After she'd taken several bites, Jack relaxed and leaned against the bureau.

"Wait." Replacement's voice broke. "What about you?"

Jack stood up straight. "What about me?"

"What're you going to eat?" Replacement's lip trembled, and she went to set the tray down.

"I made one for me too. I'll go get it." He hopped up from the bed, returning a few seconds later with his own plate. Only then did Replacement pick up her fork and eat.

After a few mouthfuls, she lifted her head and gave a sad smile, swallowing a sob. "Thank you."

"It's nothing." *Just don't cry again.* "I was thinking you could sleep in this morning. So after you've eaten, you can just watch TV or sleep. I'm going to run a couple errands."

"Where are you going?"

"We need some stuff. Aluminum foil and kitchen stuff."

"Okay."

They ate in silence, and Jack had to force himself to slow down. He timed it so he finished right when she did.

"All right." He put his plate on hers, took the tray, and set it down. "Back to bed with you."

Replacement scooted back under the covers. Jack pulled the comforter up and gave her an awkward tuck in.

"Good?" He leaned down, and she sat partway up and kissed his cheek.

"Good." She smiled and rolled over.

Jack hurried out of the room. He'd already put his holster in the hallway near the door. He didn't want Replacement to know where he was going today or why.

Jack drove straight for the psychology center. His hands were sweating. He couldn't have asked for a better excuse to go to the college, but he still had to be careful, invite or not. If he asked too many questions, someone could still call the sheriff. He could explain it, but if someone called from the college, it always went to critical mass on Collins's radar. WRE paid the most taxes and any issue there brought the most heat.

He turned off White Spruce Road and onto General Alexander Davidson Circle. His Impala raced up the road and hugged the turns. Speed felt good, real good. He loved a rush.

I like it too much.

He was always tempted to go all out. Go faster. Go harder. He took his foot off the gas and coasted into the small parking lot. There were a dozen cars in it. He parked, got out, and stretched.

Jack scanned all of the cars in the parking lot. None seemed out of the ordinary except a silver Audi. Parked at a slight angle, it took up two parking spaces. He was grateful for the brief walk to the front of the building because it gave him the chance to burn off his nervous energy.

He opened the large glass door. A gray carpet with black and red flecks covered the floor. The two staircases were a light oak, and the railing was metal and clear plastic. A very large counter stood before a light brown wooden wall. In the daylight, Jack could now see that four doors, not two, were evenly spaced along the wall, each with a name plaque. He liked the look. It was a mixture—modern with a natural feel. The place even smelled new.

A young, pretty girl with short black hair sat behind the big desk, but no one else was visible.

"Good morning." She seemed eager. "Can I help you, sir?"

"Good morning. I was wondering if I might see Dr. Hahn?"

"Do you have an appointment?"

"No, he asked me to stop by for a tour."

"May I have your name?" She was too perky for Jack.

"Jack Stratton."

"Certainly, one moment, please." She pressed some buttons on the phone. "Karen? Is Dr. Hahn in? Can you interrupt?" She covered the phone and whispered, "He's very busy." She looked up and grinned. "Okay." She hung up and looked back at Jack. "Just one minute."

"That's fine." Jack leaned onto the counter, and the girl leaned closer. "I didn't catch your name."

"Stacy."

"Do you have a long shift ahead of you, Stacy?"

"Yeah." She pouted. "I have to work until noon."

Three hours? Killer shift. Wait until you graduate, kid.

"That's rough." Jack tried to look sympathetic. "Do you ever have to work a late shift?"

"No. We close at five every day." She put her chin on the back of her hand as she looked up at him.

"Does the whole center close or just the reception area?"

"People with card access can stay after hours, I guess. Why?"

"I'm just curious. I hate those cards. Your picture always looks funny."

She sat up straight. "Mine doesn't look funny."

Jack rolled his eyes. "Sure."

"It doesn't. Look." She handed Jack her card.

Computer chip inside. Card reader. No key punch access. All doors monitored and recorded. The cards are color-coded. Hers is yellow.

"It's a beautiful picture, but it doesn't do you justice." Jack made sure that he brushed her hand as he handed the card back to her.

"Thank you." She sighed.

"You mentioned…"

Dr. Hahn walked through the door to the far left of the reception desk. A dark wooden cane was in his left hand, and he leaned slightly on it as he walked. He was dressed in a medium blue suit with a matching tie and flashed a confident white smile at the receptionist. A young man walked through the door after him. He was tall too, just over six feet, with blond hair and blue eyes. He wore khaki pants and a white shirt.

"Officer." Dr. Hahn's countenance became more somber as he approached Jack with an outstretched hand. "It's certainly a pleasure that you have accepted my offer so swiftly."

"I appreciate the invitation. I really wanted to see the work Michelle has done."

"If it is okay with you, I have asked Brendan here to begin the tour while I conclude a previously scheduled appointment."

"Certainly, Doctor. I apologize for the short notice."

"No trouble at all. I shall not be long. If you'll excuse me." The doctor hurried off, and Jack turned to look at Brendan.

The young man waved and then shook Jack's outstretched hand. "Brendan Phillips. I'm sorry about Michelle. She was very nice."

The strength of Brendan's grip surprised Jack. He looked Brendan up and down and instantly disliked him. The young man raised no suspicions but Jack didn't like the type of person he seemed to be: manicured hair, muscular, handsome, and preppy. It was a combination that reeked of privilege and always rubbed Jack the wrong way.

"Thank you. Did you know Michelle long?"

"Just a few months. She came to the center to work on the computer systems." Brendan walked over to the right-hand staircase, and Jack followed a step behind.

"And what do you do here, Brendan?"

"I'm working on my doctorate in neuropsychology."

"I'd have pegged you for a football player."

"I was in high school. Quarterback—but I tore my rotator cuff. I changed my major and never looked back."

"Do you take classes here?" Jack asked.

"Take? This semester I'm teaching," Brendan said. "I teach some of Dr. Hahn's introductory courses and I work here in the lab."

"Lab?"

"It's on the lower level. We do a lot of work on brain scans—brain imaging."

"Imaging? Like creating a picture of what people are thinking?"

Brendan looked away from Jack for a second, but Jack still saw him make a face and smirk. He turned back and explained, "No, that technology is still years away. We use the fMRI to perform scans and see patterns. Images of how different stimuli affect the brain."

Jack nodded.

If he keeps that smirk on his face, I'm going to smack him upside the head and see how that stimuli affects his brain.

Brendan pointed out various conference rooms and offices on the third floor. Jack noticed the many warning and danger signs posted throughout the building.

This looks like a fun place to work.

Jack pointed at the *Volatile Materials — Use Caution* sign and quipped, "I thought the most you had to worry about in the psychology center was falling off the shrink's couch and getting a headache."

Brendan frowned. "This is a fully functional laboratory environment. It's world renowned."

Jack tried to backpedal. "I'm sure it is. I just had different expectations."

Brendan turned and continued with the tour. The whole center appeared to have been recently remodeled; there was still that faint chemical odor of new that hung in the air. Everything seemed to have a plaque attached to it, indicating who donated the money for it. Jack was starting to get bored but nodded his head at the appropriate times and looked for any opportunity to question Brendan.

"What was Michelle's role here?"

"I'll show you on the second floor. That's where the new computer lab is. Michelle did a great job overseeing the backup generators, updating the servers, and increasing the storage capacities. More and more, we're moving to video, and that takes a lot of space."

"When did she find the time for all that?"

"It takes a lot of dedication. She was here all the time." Brendan paused outside a large glass wall. On the other side, computer lights flashed and flickered in three separate rows.

Jack noticed all of the security cameras around the computer room and the card reader attached to the door. "You have a lot of security here." Jack pointed at the card reader.

"It's almost all done. That was the last part Michelle was working on. I have one of the first new cards." He scanned it through the card reader at the door. Jack noticed it was a blue card with his picture on it.

He followed Brendan out, and the level they were now on was all glass to the rear of the building. The result was a panoramic view of the woods. A solid white wall with a large double door in the middle split the lower level in half.

Brendan gestured to the breathtaking view of the woods. "The college purchased it five years ago. The makeover has been going on as long as I've been here. This way."

He motioned Jack down a staircase that led to the lowest level. At the bottom of the staircase were two closed metal doors. Neither door had a sign on it, and Brendan wasn't offering any advice as to the correct way to go. Jack paused at the bottom of the stairs.

Like I'll ask for directions.

Jack opened the closed door on the left. A cement hallway stretched out into the darkness.

Brendan smirked and pointed to the other door. "That's a utility corridor. This way."

Jack let Brendan lead and tried to unclench his fists.

They walked down another corridor until they came to a large double door. Brendan swiped his card and the doors opened. A short hallway split left and right with doors at the ends. This section had the feel of a hospital, as everything was white and sterile.

"This way to the lab." Brendan walked to the left and into a small hallway filled with cubes along the wall. He pulled out a small plastic tray from one cube. "Do you have any ferromagnetic materials?"

"What?"

"Metal?" Brendan rolled his eyes as he pointed up to the caution sign. *No Metal Beyond This Point.*

Jack bit his tongue but made a show of it as he un-chambered his Glock .40 caliber gun and dropped the clip into his hand. "Do you have a secure location for this?" Jack pulled the slide back to remove the round in the chamber.

"We get all sorts of visitors." Brendan walked over and opened a safe. "It will be secure in here."

Jack took his time while he placed his gun inside. He closed the door himself and tried the handle to make sure it locked. "What would happen if I went in with it?"

"It would be bad. I've seen accident reports from other facilities where careless hospital workers brought wheelchairs, gurneys, and even floor polishers too close and they got jammed deep inside. Some police officer had his pistol fly out of his holster and shot a hole in the wall when it hit the magnet."

Jack raised an eyebrow. "Seriously?"

"Yeah. Google it. It was in a *New York Times* article recently. And that was only a regular MRI. The fMRI is twenty times more powerful."

"What about the metal in here?" Jack pointed to a fire extinguisher. "Why doesn't it get sucked up?"

Brendan patted the wall. "Shielding. It was part of the biggest expense but it surrounds the machine." He moved over to a door. Another swipe and it opened. "The fMRI is in here." Jack followed and found himself in some kind of control booth. A computer console in front of a large window looked out to a room that appeared as if it belonged in a hospital. A large circular machine was in the main room, centered over a stretcher, and looked to be in use. On a monitor in the control booth, Jack could see a smiling girl lying on the stretcher. Her body was inside of the long tube, surrounded by the machine. The ring was the size of two large tractor tires. It reflected in the pristine black tiled floor.

"Impressive, isn't it?" Brendan beamed. "It's a modified experimental design, 9.4 Tesla. One of the most powerful fMRIs in the world and twenty times more powerful than the average MRI. The University of Illinois at Chicago has been experimenting with a similar design for years with excellent results. The detailed brain scans can pinpoint reactions in nanoseconds."

"How does it work?"

"It operates by detecting the changes in blood oxygenation and flow that occur in response to neural activity. This control booth precisely controls and monitors the machine and the super magnet inside."

A young man, in his mid-twenties, sat at the console and clicked a mouse. Video monitors on either side of him flashed graphs and charts. "It takes almost a full day to power down," the young man chimed in.

"Pete, let him hear." Brendan tapped the young man's shoulder, and Pete flicked a switch.

Jack looked at the girl on the stretcher and realized she was watching a monitor inside of the machine. He could hear her laughing and with each laugh, the charts on the monitors in the control room jumped and changed.

"We're almost ready to kill the TV and let her pray," Pete said as he slowly turned a dial.

Jack looked at Brendan. "Pray?"

Brendan nodded. "This is a monitoring session for Dr. Hahn's class—The Evolution of Religion and the God Spot."

"The God Spot?"

"Dr. Hahn has a theory that there is one centralized spot in the brain responsible for religious thought. We can use the fMRI to see what areas of the brain are utilized for different functions. You can see from the pattern—"

"Excellent, you're here. Please accept my apologies for my tardiness." Dr. Hahn hurried into the room and shook Jack's hand. "I trust that Brendan is explaining everything?"

Jack nodded. "It's very impressive, Doctor."

"It represents countless hours and sacrifice by so many, including Michelle," Hahn said.

"How many students work here?"

"Several dozen. We're at full staff and have a number of students who volunteer too. Don't you wish that you could have been able to get credit for watching TV?" Hahn laughed.

"I didn't realize you had so much high-tech equipment in here. It's great that Michelle was getting it all locked down."

"This is a college psychology center. It's as quiet as a church. Still, the college wants you to follow procedures."

"How late are people here, typically?" Jack asked.

"Typically?" Dr. Hahn paused. "The hours are typically nine to five. It is, however, a college and in academia things are sometimes atypical."

"Dr. Hahn, what's your function here?"

"I am just a figurehead." He laughed. "They say I run the center, but you see that's better left to the young. They bring me out for fundraisers and to teach a class or two."

"He's being modest." Brendan stepped forward. "Dr. Hahn is director of the Neuropsychology Department. This whole center is his work. He's a real pioneer in fMRI research."

Dr. Hahn's hand rested on Brendan's shoulder. "My student's flattery is sure to positively affect his grades." He laughed again and patted Brendan's arm. "I do apologize, but I have a class this morning, and I need to prepare for it."

"Of course." Jack shook his hand. "Thank you for thinking of me."

"It was the least I could do for all of Michelle's work. Brendan will see you out." Dr. Hahn turned to go.

"Dr. Hahn, I was hoping that I could make a rather odd request of you. After seeing all of this, I just wish...I wish I could have been a fly on the wall and seen Michelle at work. Do you know what I mean?" Jack asked.

"I do. Maybe it's the researcher in me but wanting to be an observer is a frequent wish of mine too."

"Then do you think it would be possible if I could look at some of the video footage of Michelle working? I know it's not a typical request, but I think it would help me with closure."

"Sadly, that wouldn't be possible…" Hahn shook his head.

"I'd be happy to come back." Jack turned his hands out.

"Unfortunately, it isn't a matter of time. The security cameras were one of the last things Michelle was working on, and right now, they don't record anything. They only serve as a deterrent."

"That's too bad." Jack's shoulders slumped.

"Michelle would have been very happy you came out here today, Officer. I hope you can find some closure in the fact that her work here was meaningful and will continue."

After another minute and one wimpy handshake from Brendan, Jack walked back toward his Impala as it began to rain. He didn't change his pace or even react to the cold sting from the downpour.

Closure. I'll get closure when I find out what happened to Michelle.

CHAPTER TWENTY-FOUR

Ask a Better Question

Jack drove along the road through the state forest and looked at the clock. Twelve forty-nine. He was early. He pulled to the side at the third lookout spot. There were many staggered along the scenic drive so people could pull off, stretch their legs, and enjoy the view. He wasn't there for the scenery, and he didn't get out of the car. He was waiting for a silver Ford Taurus. It wasn't there yet.

It was cold out. He left the car running.

Jack shook his head. *Undercover detectives.*

You always had to meet them somewhere out of the norm. When he first joined the force, he had to make drops to an undercover at a golf course. They were a paranoid bunch, with good reason. If one wrong person saw them, months of work could go down the drain or worse, they could end up dead.

Jack was here to meet Detective Mark Reynolds. He was the man to go to for information about what was happening in Darrington County, if drugs were involved. Jack wanted to know as much about meth as possible. He needed to rule out a few possible scenarios.

To Jack, it didn't make sense that Michelle, who worked hard and never did drugs, would use meth.

Could someone have slipped it to her? Are college kids using it and, if so, who's their supplier?

As Jack worked on his mental list, Reynolds's car pulled in.

The silver Taurus backed up next to him and Mark slipped out of the driver seat and slid into Jack's passenger seat. Reynolds was in his early thirties but looked about ten years younger. Jack couldn't understand how, considering all the stress he must be under. Reynolds was about five foot five, and he was strong. His handshake was so firm Jack thought it should belong to a sheet metal worker.

His hair was black and wavy. He wore a tan work coat and blue jeans. His voice wasn't too deep, but it had a calmness to it, like a teacher.

"Jack."

"Mark. I appreciate you coming."

"I can't stay long. I'm supposed to be dropping off a package. You said you had some questions you needed help with."

"Yeah, they're about meth."

"This related to your foster sister Michelle Campbell?"

Jack nodded.

"She died in a car accident out on Reservoir Road?"

"Yes."

"She had meth in her system."

"Yes. How did you know all of that?"

"The ME's office always informs the drug task force. We keep track of any deaths involving drugs."

Jack nodded. "I have a few questions."

Mark eyed Jack. "What're you going to do with the information if I do give it to you?"

"Do with it?"

"Are you going to go kicking down the doors of all the meth dealers in the city?"

Jack thought for a minute before he responded. "I'll think about what you give me. If it leads me to the guy who gave her the meth, yeah…I'll kick his door down. You have a problem with that?"

Mark looked at him for a minute and then shook his head. He lit a cigarette and leaned back. "Okay. What do you want to know?"

"How can you take meth?"

"Shoot it. Smoke it. Eat it. Suppository."

"Is it big at the college?"

"Depends on what your definition of big is. It's available. It's always available. We shut one lab down and another pops up. Last year, there were two dealers at the college. I don't know of one operating right now. It's been quiet there lately."

"None?"

"Like I said, you can get it, but there isn't one dealer who's got it for turf. Too much heat now."

Mark leaned forward and angled his head down while he pretended to tune the radio. Jack looked up and saw a man riding his bike along the road. They both remained silent as he rode past. The detective leaned back and took a long drag from his cigarette.

"Could someone have forced her to take it?"

"Yeah, I suppose." He paused and looked at Jack. "Is that what you think happened?"

"Yes."

"Why do you think that?"

"She wouldn't do meth. She was a clean, hardworking kid with no previous drug use. If someone didn't do drugs, would their first choice be meth?"

"You need to ask a better question, Jack."

Jack's jaw clenched. "How so?"

"First off, you don't know for a fact the she hadn't done any other drugs, right?"

Jack nodded.

"Second, anyone might. It matters on the circumstances. I can't answer how likely. Who knew her best?"

"Her sister."

"Does she say that she could have done it?"

"She said no way."

"But she had it in her system. What did the ME say?"

"The body wasn't discovered for some time. They couldn't tell how much."

Mark took a drag on his cigarette and blew the smoke out the crack of the window.

Jack cleared his throat. "I appreciate you meeting me."

"I understand now why you asked. Family is important."

"Do you have any?" Jack asked.

Mark took another long drag and exhaled. The smoke wafted out the window.

"I have a wife who defies expectations. She's like a good doctor; she has a lot of patience." Jack smiled at the joke and Mark continued, "My daughter, on the other hand..." His voice trailed off and he looked out the window.

Jack debated for a second and then said, "She's like a pediatrician? She has little patience."

Mark looked at him, puzzled, and then burst out laughing. He laughed so hard he started to cough.

"That was funny." Mark tossed his cigarette out.

"I just made it up."

"Thanks. I needed a laugh."

"One more question?" Jack continued. "You said there are no dealers at the college now. Who were the dealers before?"

"Carl Finn and Mike Leverone. Leverone will talk with you."

"Why not Finn?"

"He's dead."

"Dead?"

"Suicide. Last year."

"Why will Leverone talk?"

"He had an accident. His lab blew up. Burned down his parents' house and got pretty fried himself. He flipped. He gave us everything and everyone he had. He does Scared Straight stuff now."

"How can I get in touch with him?"

Reynolds scribbled a phone number and address down and handed them to Jack.

"He's odd, but he's helping us, so don't go off, understand?"

"I just want to find out how she got it. I'm open to ideas."

"Talk to Mike. He knew how everything went at the college. If it were me, I'd consider starting with your sister's friends. Find out who she was with. Friends, start there. If not, you're chasing the wind."

"I appreciate it."

They shook hands and Mark started to slide out of the car, and then he stopped.

"Jack?" Mark held up one finger as he stared straight ahead.

"Yeah?"

"There was this one kid. We followed him a few times last year. We suspected he was a runner for one of the dealers at the college, but we never could catch him red-handed."

Jack opened his notebook again.

"Lennie Jacobsen. They call him Lennie J," Reynolds said.

"Thanks. I'll look him up."

"No problem." He gave a curt nod and then walked away.

Jack watched the Taurus pull out and started to dial. He wanted to see Leverone before he went home.

CHAPTER TWENTY-FIVE

But by the Grace of God Go I

It was a quiet tree-lined neighborhood and the small yellow and white ranch fit right in. An old red Honda sedan was in the driveway. Jack pulled in behind it and parked. He walked up a curved brick walkway to a red door with a big, pine wreath on it, rang the doorbell, and waited.

Someone yanked open the door. Mike Leverone stood, smiling, in the doorway. At least Jack thought he was smiling.

Look him in the eye and don't look away.

Mark Reynolds hadn't provided enough information regarding Mike's accident. The fire had scarred and burned his entire face. A baseball cap covered his head, but the rest of his face was extremely difficult to look at.

"Jack, I guess?"

Jack had been a soldier and had seen more than his share of horrifying accidents, but one look at Mike and he wondered how he'd survived.

"Jack Stratton." He reached forward, and his hand closed around Mike's prosthetic hook.

"Mike Leverone." The man smiled and nodded his head. "You're good. You didn't even flinch at the hook." He turned, and Jack followed him in.

The living room was clean and tidy. There wasn't a spot of dust anywhere. Everything was meticulously placed and arranged. There was an enormous TV hanging on the wall and facing it was a large couch. To the right was a black leather chair. The wooden floor in the entryway led to a gray carpet that headed off into the living room. The carpet stopped before the kitchen on the left.

"Thank you for seeing me on such short notice."

"Thank you for seeing me. I don't get many visitors." Mike held out his hand for Jack to sit in the leather recliner.

If a man's home is his castle, then his recliner is his throne.

Jack nodded his head at the gesture as he sat down.

Mike grinned. "Do you want a drink?"

"No, thank you."

"I don't have any alcohol. I'm on probation, so I stay squeaky clean. Coffee?"

"All set, really."

"Give me a minute then."

Mike wandered into the kitchen to a huge coffeemaker and reached into a cupboard for a new cup. His sweater sleeve slipped down; Jack caught a long glimpse at the scars underneath.

"Sure I can't get you one?" Mike turned. Jack quickly pretended to be checking out the magazines that were stacked in a neat square on top of the coffee table.

"No, I'm good."

Jack saw Mike shrug, pour himself a cup, and then come back in to sit on the couch.

"On the phone you said that you had some questions about meth and White Rocks."

"I do. I was told you had knowledge about the meth situation there. I need some help. The reason I'm here... Can I ask you to keep this confidential?"

"Is this the face of a talker?" Mike laughed as he pointed to his scarred features.

Defense mechanism. Self-deprecation. Laugh. Jack smiled.

"Unfortunately, I'm here because I'm looking into a murder. The autopsy showed the victim had meth in her system. There's reason to believe the victim didn't do drugs. We think someone forced her to take it and then killed her."

"Forced her?"

Jack paused. He was trying to read Mike's face. He thought that maybe he raised an eyebrow, but he didn't have any.

"Could someone have tricked her into taking it? Slipped it in a drink?"

Mike shook his head. "No. You can parachute it, but if you put it in a drink it's really bitter."

"What're the ways to do meth?"

"You could parachute, which is swallow. Snort, like coke. Smoke it. Slam it. You know, shoot it like heroin or booty bump."

Jack winced. He wasn't going to ask about the last way.

"If someone was going to force someone else to take it, how would they?"

"I'd think shoot it up."

"If someone does meth, do they get the effects right away?"

"Not necessarily. It depends on the person. The way you take it affects the speed and strength, too. Smoking is the fastest and gets you off quickest."

"Did you know Carl Finn?"

"Yeah. Good guy. We were in some classes together."

"What happened to him?"

"He sampled. One time. He thought spiders were in his brain. He used a nail gun to get them." Mike pantomimed the scene out as he spoke, holding his prosthetic hook up next to his temple and then jerking his head to the side.

Jack shuddered.

"He only sampled it once?"

"All it takes."

"How hard is it to make?"

"Hard?" Mike snorted. "It's not. Anyone can make it."

"Anyone?"

"If you have the Internet, you can figure it out. I learned at college."

"College? White Rocks?"

"Dr. Franklin's class. Will Franklin. He taught us how."

"He taught you?"

"Step by step. He gave me the idea. I thought he was a hero until I blew apart my life."

Jack glanced at the hook where a hand would otherwise be as Mike gestured wildly.

"Why did he teach kids how to make meth?"

"Showing off? Midlife crisis? Power to the people? Who knows? It was my fault for doing it."

"What went wrong?"

Mike shrugged. "The whole process is super combustible. You can see videos on the net. With me, it was solvents, I think. I was hurrying, and I left the cover off. Making meth is fire and explosive fumes. They mixed and boom. Fire all over."

Jack remembered the phosphorus bombs and swallowed.

Is that what happened to Mike? If Chandler hadn't broken down that door...

Jack could still see the blue and white flames swirl together before they turned crimson.

"You've seen it, haven't you?" Mike leaned forward, and Jack nodded.

Silence descended on the room as the men replayed the flames in their own minds. Jack closed his eyes and rubbed them with his hands.

"What does Franklin teach?"

"Psychology. I was taking Drugs, Youth, and the Mind. He's into imaging."

"Like pretending?"

Mike laughed hard. "Not imagining, *imaging*. Pictures. He takes pictures of your mind, with computers."

Jack grimaced. This was the second time this morning someone spoke to him as if he was stupid. "I just heard about that. Is that with the fMRI?"

I think that's what he called it.

"At the center? Yeah. They hook you up and take images of your brain. They give you different drugs and watch your head. They make you take off all your rings and stuff." He pointed at his earring that hung off what was left of his ear. "I was nervous when I first went in. I heard a story of this guy who was harpooned by a chair that flew up and crashed into the machine. It was something to do with the metal."

"Because of the magnets?"

"Something like that."

"Do they give you meth?" Jack sat up.

"Sort of. You can get a prescription for ADHD and stuff like that. They do studies at the school, and I think they used it. That was awhile ago. Anyway, the pill is super low dose. A regular street hit would be like a month's worth of prescription."

"So you can legally get meth? That's messed up."

"Not really. It's way harder to get the legal stuff than the street stuff."

Jack paused. "One last question. Anyone at the college I should talk to who could have given it to the victim?"

Mike shook his head and held his hand up. "Almost anyone. I haven't heard about anyone stepping up after Carl and me. There's still too much attention for one guy to set up shop, but you can still get it. You just have to ask."

"Did you know a Lennie Jacobsen?"

"A Lennie?"

"Lennie J? He may have been a runner."

Mike shook his head and looked down at his feet. "Meth attracts people like flies to garbage, hangers-on and wannabes." He stared down at the floor and swallowed. "For a while, I felt like a rock star with all my groupies. But they were just kids. Who knows what I turned them into? I burned myself on the outside, but they burned on the inside. I didn't even know most of their names." He looked up at Jack and his chin trembled.

Jack tried, but he couldn't hold his gaze. He stood up to leave. "Thank you for your time."

"Oh, okay." Mike looked disappointed.

"If you hear anything, please give me a call."

"Sure. If I can help at all, you can just stop by. I can't go anywhere, and I don't get many visitors." He lifted up his pant leg, and Jack saw the ankle monitor.

"Thanks for your time."

"Anytime." Mike followed him to the door, stood in the open doorway and waved with his prosthesis as Jack drove away.

Jack looked up at his reflection in the rearview mirror.

That could have been me.

He whispered to his dead friend, "Thanks, buddy."

Jack came home late afternoon, and Replacement almost bowled him over when he walked in the door. "Where have you been? What happened?"

"Give me a second, kid." He walked past her into the apartment.

"Does your phone work? Can't you hear it ring? I've been trying to get you all day," she whined and followed right behind him.

He pulled it out. It was off. He shrugged a sorry, and she glared.

"You didn't check your phone?" Her hands flew wide. "I was worried. I wanted to know—"

"Shut up."

She slammed both hands into his shoulders, though he could tell that she held back. "You shut up. I've been waiting."

"Okay. Get me a drink while I get ready for work and I'll tell you."

"I'm not your wife. Get your own—"

"You're nagging at me like a wife so get...fine." Jack paused and closed his eyes for a second. "I went out to the center this morning. I got the full tour from this pretty boy. I didn't get much of anything, but I'm going back for another look in a couple days." Jack left off about looking up Dr. Franklin.

"Can I go with you?"

"Last time didn't go too well. Remember Missy?"

"Funny you brought her up." Replacement walked over to the computer.

"Funny how?"

"Well, remember how you thought she was lying about Michelle?" She looked back at him. "I thought if we pushed a little more—"

"Pushed? I didn't say push. I said back off."

"It's not a big deal. I just sent an email..."

Jack marched over to his computer. Replacement backed away. She opened her mouth but closed it when he shot her a look.

"Log in." He pointed at the laptop.

"Me?"

"You sent it?"

"Well, it kind of came from...you." Her eyes grew large.

"You sent it from MY account?"

"I thought it would look more intimidating if it came from you."

"I don't want to be intimidating." He logged in to his computer and email and switched to his sent folder.

"DEAR MS. LORTON. PLEASE BE OFFICIALLY NOTIFIED THAT WE ARE CONTINUING TO LOOK INTO THE MURDER OF MICHELLE CAMPBELL. IT IS OUR HOPE THAT YOU WILL CONTACT ME REGARDING ALL INFORMATION THAT YOU HAVE CONCERNING THIS CASE. SINCERELY, OFFICER JACK STRATTON."

"Did you lose your mind? Do you know what she's going to do? You even included my cell phone."

"She didn't go to the cops before. This might shake her up. She might—"

"Yeah, she might go to the police now. But she'll go about me." Jack pulled the plug out of the back of the computer. "Stay off it." He stormed into the bathroom and slammed the door.

CHAPTER TWENTY-SIX

Dirty Dancing

Later that night, Jack was pulling traffic duty on the night shift.
Penance.

He shrugged as he zipped up his jacket and walked over to the work detail. They'd been working on this highway since Jack started on the force, leisurely making their way from exit to exit.

They've barely done two exits in the last six months. What a waste.

The smell of hot tar filled the air. There always seemed to be tar ready for pouring, but Jack didn't think it was worth the stench. The odor clung to everything it touched, and Jack was sure he'd smell it for days.

It was just warm enough for the rain not to freeze into snow. A light mist fell, and the drops glistened under the enormous arc lights. The pavement glittered with the mix of colors reflected off it.

Officer Tom Kempy waved and smiled at him. He was a little older than Jack and always seemed happy. Married with three kids and he loved life.

"Hey, Jack." Tom trotted up to him. "Billy said they're making good progress and should be done by four."

Four in the morning. Jack frowned. It's freezing, and pulling traffic duty on the night detail blows.

"It'll go by fast." Tom slapped him on the arm and then jogged for his car.

"Say hi to Amy and the kids," Jack called after him.

Tom turned back around. "If you ever want to come over for dinner..." Tom's words trailed off.

"I'd love to but don't worry, I won't bring a date."

Tom exhaled and smiled. "Okay. Great. Sure. I'll find out when and let you know." He waved and ran for his car.

Jack laughed. He'd brought a date to the Christmas party. Gina. He didn't know it was more of a conservative event for the police and all their families. Tom had been there with his wife, Amy, and all their kids.

The next thing Jack knew, Gina had bribed the DJ into playing some spicy music and then she'd started to dance. She cleared the dance floor as her drunken salsa began to look more and more like a striptease. She blew kisses to Jack. When her hand slipped to the shoulder strap of her dress, he rushed in, tossed her over his shoulder, and carried her out. He could still remember the look on Amy's face as he walked by. Gina was vividly describing all the erotic things she wanted to do to him. Jack didn't know whose face was redder, his or Amy's, but they were both very embarrassed.

Yeah. Definitely no date.

Five hours later, Jack felt like time had stopped. He stood on the side of a highway, freezing and bored. A car came by every twenty to thirty minutes.

I can't wait to get home.

Jack watched as stars began to peek out from between the clouds.

Replacement was trying to get her schedule to match his. She'd wake up when he did and try to stay up until he returned, even on days when he was pulling a double. It drove him crazy, but he had to admit he also liked it. She kept going over and over all the information from the phone. The emails were driving her crazy because they were so dull and there were so many of them. She was still going through them, studying each line, each word, in case there was a little piece of information that could hold some relevance.

He wanted to look up the information on that Lennie kid, but he was stuck outside directing traffic. Maybe he could email Replacement and get her to look it up.

Email.

Jack was still ticked she'd sent the email to Missy.

What the hell was she thinking? That Missy was going to confess to having a hand in Michelle's death? Most likely, she'll be going to a lawyer. The lawyer will call Collins. Collins will go mental, and I'm screwed. How screwed? I do have a police delegate. That won't matter. Collins will give me this job every shift. No training and I'll have the night shift on traffic detail, or he'll assign me to paper filing and answering the phone for the rest of my career. Thanks, Replacement.

He waved as a car made its way down the lane of cones.

And Replacement. What am I going to do about her? She won't take the bed, and she can't sleep on the couch forever. I can't kick her out. I'll have to get a two-bedroom place.

Jack laughed. It wasn't a little laugh but a big sidesplitting howl.

A couple of guys who were talking to the bobcat operator stopped and looked at him.

He held up his hands in a forget-about-it gesture. He was thinking about Missy Lorton rolling into her kitchen, squealing. She must have died when she got Replacement's email.

Jack had a second to react as he heard the car behind him speed up. He turned and saw the headlights come straight at him. The engine revved as the driver jammed down the gas pedal. Everything slowed as his adrenaline kicked in.

He tried to jump.

Too late. Pain. Protect your head.

The bumper had slammed into his thigh, and he crashed into the windshield. His back exploded; a million fires burned. Glass sliced into his shoulder.

Still spinning.

For a second, he looked at the stars. They were beautiful. They sparkled. He continued to spin around, and he could see the arc lights reflected in the water on the road. The lights twinkled and danced. His feet were going over his head. He could hear swearing from the guys at the bobcat.

Not back into the road.

He realized he'd be landing back on the highway. Jack thought about a guy who was hit by a car and then run over three more times. He was clear of the car, but he was still spinning.

Hold your head.

His left arm cradled his head, but his right just flopped, useless. He saw the car that hit him swerve back onto the road and keep going. He landed feet first on the pavement, then on his back, and then on his head. His left hand cushioned some of the impact, but everything flashed for a second and his eyes flew wide open. Pain. Pain everywhere. He burned like a match held upside down.

Roll, he commanded himself, but his body wouldn't respond.

Jack's eyes fluttered, and he tried to focus on the men who ran toward him. He could see them, but his ears didn't seem to be working. Everything dimmed. Then it went black.

CHAPTER TWENTY-SEVEN

Iron Man

The first sound Jack heard as he came around was a slow, steady beep. It matched the thudding of the pulse that echoed in his head.

Hospital. Not dead just yet, Jack.

Jack tried to open his eyes, but only one worked, and it wasn't working too well. He tried to blink, but everything was fuzzy. He let his head roll to the side. He could smell the odors of the hospital, and his stomach churned. He tried not to breathe through his nose but then he noticed the faint scent of flowers. Through the haze, he could see splotches of colors next to his bed.

Flowers? Maybe I'm dead. Body check.

Jack started with his legs. He flexed his left leg, but he couldn't move the right.

Immobile? Knee down. Hips? Check. Back? Pain but dull. Ribs? Lot of pain on the right side. Left arm and hand? Okay. Right? No.

He held up his right arm in front of the eye that was sort of working.

Splint.

"Jack?" A blurry shape called to him from past the flowers. "Jack." The shape lunged forward and came almost nose to nose with him.

"Replacement?" Jack's mouth was so dry that it sounded more like *placemat* but the form smiled.

"DOCTOR," she shouted, but kept her eyes on Jack. She screamed right in his face, causing him physical pain, and his eye fluttered.

"Sorry." She reached her hand out to touch his head but hesitated; her hand hovered. "Doctor." He was grateful she turned her head before she yelled this time, but his ears still rang. She turned back to him, and he could see the concern on her face.

"You okay, kid?" Jack shut his eye.

"Me?" Replacement drew back and frowned. "I'm fine. I have been so worried about you. Don't worry, though. You're going to be fine. You're good…Doctor…"

Darkness returned.

The next time Jack woke, he tried to open his eyes, but the left eyelid was like a broken garage door that went up a bit and stopped. He picked up his right hand, forgetting he had a splint, and because of its added weight, his hand crashed into his good eye.

"Damn." Jack swore at his own stupidity and jerked partly upright, coming to a sudden stop as new pain flooded his already battered body.

"Jack." Replacement was suddenly at his side, and she placed her hands behind his back to help him. The pain was intense, and the last thing he wanted to do now was to sit up.

"Stop, stop! You're killing me," Jack protested.

Replacement pulled her hands away as if she'd grabbed a hot stove, and Jack thumped back onto the bed with a loud groan.

"Sorry." Her face was once again inches from him, and she stared into his eyes.

She started to inhale in preparation of roaring for the doctor, but Jack interrupted. "No, I'm fine. Give me a minute." The little shake of his head hurt.

"Are you sure?" She leaned even closer as she searched his face.

He kissed her. It was a kiss like a little kid gives by puckering their lips way out. That was all he did but she was so close it landed right on her lips. She stood upright, and her eyes grew larger.

Jack giggled. The pain medicine he was on made him a little loopy.

"Jack?" She leaned closer, but he closed his eyes again and laughed.

"Miss me?" His speech was slurred. He opened his eyes, and the room spun.

"Jack, you're in the hospital." She spoke softly and slowly. "Do you remember what happened?"

Jack nodded. "I got hit by a green Toyota Corolla."

"What's my name?"

Jack laughed. *I'm screwed. I forgot again.* He laughed some more.

Her face grew concerned. "Jack, what's my name?"

He swallowed. "Replacement."

"What's my real name?" she pressed.

"I think I hit my head…"

Her frown morphed into hurt. "You can remember it was a green Toyota Corolla that hit you but you can't—"

"Alice." Jack felt as if he hit the game-winning shot at the buzzer. He giggled.

Replacement hugged him so tightly that she choked off his groans of pain. All he could do was grimace as he waited for her to relax her grip.

"Everyone was so worried." She stood up and wiped away tears.

Jack struggled not to groan. He was flat on his back, but now he wanted to try to sit up again. "Does this bed do that sit up thing without you having to lift me?"

Replacement grabbed the remote, and the bed began to raise him to a sitting position. He looked around the room. The first things he noticed were all the flower arrangements.

"How long have I been out?" The words were tough to say. His mouth felt dry and slimy at the same time.

Replacement held up a cup with a straw, and he took a small sip of water. It felt good against the back of his parched mouth. "You were out for a while. The doctors were worried about your head. Then they came back to say it looked okay."

"I've been out…" He tried to sit up more but realized that was a lousy idea as the room spun even more. "Traffic. It was a green…"

"They found the car. It had been stolen." Replacement stroked his arm. "We can talk about that later."

"Nothing off the car? Prints?" Jack closed one eye, and it helped bring her into focus.

"Nothing. Sheriff Collins came by. He said they had nothing on it yet." Replacement shrugged. Jack noticed how tired she looked. "Cindy came by too. She said they wiped it clean."

"How long have you been here, kid?"

She shrugged again, but the dark circles under her eyes provided the answer.

"You need to go get some rest. You look awful."

She shook her head at him but remained silent.

He took another swig of water and tried to wiggle his toes. They immobilized his right leg from the knee down.

"Did I break my leg?"

"Surprisingly not. They've been calling you Iron Man. The doctors thought you had at first because it was so black and blue, but all the x-rays came back negative. You did injure your right wrist, and your face got pretty busted up."

He didn't have to touch the left side of his face to feel the swelling. He knew his eye must still be bad since it wouldn't open all the way.

"Officer Stratton?" Jack looked up as a doctor and nurse walked into the room.

They're smiling. That's a good sign.

"I'd like to examine you if I may?"

Jack nodded.

Sure, give me the all-clear, and then I can go track down the bastard who did this to me.

Jack stared up at the ceiling. The long rectangular light fixture above his head created a strange yellowish glow. He was sick of spending time in the hospital. He was tempted to try to get his stuff and go.

"How long do they want me to stay here?" Jack was irritated. "I have been here almost two days." He hated sitting and hated the feeling of being trapped even more.

"Maybe this afternoon." Cindy patted his leg before she walked over and sat down in the lime-green chair.

"I'm fine. I have to—"

"Have to do what? What're you going to do, Jack? The doctor doesn't want you walking on that leg, and your right hand needs time to heal." She held up her hand. "Collins said you were to take some time off, too."

"You have to be fu—"

"Jack Alton Stratton." Cindy stamped her foot so loud that a nurse poked her head into the room.

"Sorry," he mumbled.

"You should not be speaking such language in front of a lady." She folded her arms and glared. "The sheriff is right. You can't stand on your leg yet, and you can't shoot. You need time to get well."

Jack looked up into her eyes but was unable to hold them.

He leaned over and picked at the flowers next to his bed. "These came without cards," he said with a sweep of his hand as he gestured to the half-dozen displays nurses had delivered to the room.

"Well, they all had cards…once…" Cindy chuckled.

"Once?" Jack didn't understand.

"Alice read a couple of them…"

"Replacement? Why would she get rid of the cards?"

Cindy looked at him as if he had three heads. "When it comes to women, you really don't know jack, Jack."

"Ha, ha. Why do I have to stay here so long?" Jack folded his arms.

"One reason is to give poor Alice a break. Do you have any idea how long she stayed at your side? She wouldn't go home until today, and I had to promise I'd stay."

"You're not staying."

"I told her I would."

"Go home, Cindy." Jack sulked like a little kid.

"I thought you'd want the company."

"I actually would prefer to sleep. You can go."

"Would that be okay? Really?" She leaned in. "My mother came for a visit, and if I leave her home alone with my husband… They get along like gasoline and a match."

Jack nodded.

Cindy picked up her pocketbook. "Don't you dare tell her I left. That one can be scary." Cindy gave his foot a little squeeze and headed out the door.

Jack leaned back and looked up at the ceiling.

Doc said nothing is broken in my leg, and I'll be on it in a week or two.

He arched his back and tried to flex his muscles. He still hurt, a lot.

The door to his room opened, and a young nurse came in carrying a bright red vase filled with yet more flowers. She set them down next to the bed.

"Someone must want you to get better," the girl gushed. "This is the second time they sent you flowers." She started to put it down with the others.

He reached toward her. "Can I see who it's from?"

She handed him a very large card.

Jack mumbled a thank-you. The card had his name printed on the front. Jack opened the card but then closed it quickly. The inside had no words, just a picture.

Marisa.

He could feel his face turn red as he slowly peeked in and opened the card again. The picture was a pencil sketch of museum quality. The problem wasn't with the piece but the subject. The drawing was of him lying on a tattoo table, a sheet partly covering him—just not covering the right parts.

Well, that explains why Replacement got rid of the other cards.

CHAPTER TWENTY-EIGHT

Drunken Grasshopper

Replacement propped another pillow behind Jack's back and stepped away, appraising her work with a triumphant grin. Jack surveyed her accomplishment. She had transformed his bedroom; it was now his hospital room, only nicer. There was a food tray and a TV. Pillows were everywhere, and his leg was now cushioned on two of them.

"Thanks, kid. I don't know how you pulled this off but here." He handed her a small pile of cash.

"I'm not taking that," she protested and pushed it away.

"If you don't, I have to figure out how you got this stuff or have you arrested." He gestured to the room.

"Donations." She turned her hands up. "Cindy hooked me up at the Salvation Army. They wouldn't take a dime."

"Take the money, kid." Jack handed her the cash. "We need groceries and stuff."

"We have tons of food. Cindy brought food over. I like her very much." Replacement sat down on the bed.

"I like Cindy too." Jack stared up at the ceiling. "I tried calling Sheriff Collins, but he won't return my phone calls."

"Jack, I don't think that you…right now." Tears formed in the corner of her eyes.

"You didn't say anything just then. Not a full sentence anyway." Jack tried to smile, but he ended up just staring at her.

"For right now you need to stop. Jack, please. For right now, just get better." She squeezed his hand. "Please."

"Okay." He pulled the blanket up a little farther. "I'll be good."

"Of course you will. Wait here." She was smiling and crying at the same time as she raced out of the room and came back moments later with her arms filled with DVDs.

"Pick a movie." She stacked them on the table and gestured like Vanna White.

"Here." He grinned. "*Rocky*."

She picked up the movie and hopped over to the DVD player. "A boxing movie?" She made a face.

"You've never seen it? You'll like it."

That night, Jack stared up at the ceiling and waited. Replacement had gone to bed an hour ago.

She must be asleep by now.

He slipped out of bed and winced when he tried to stand. He shuffled to the door and slowly opened it.

It shouldn't make a noise. I used a whole can of spray oil so I wouldn't wake Gina up when I came home.

Replacement lay curled up on the couch under the thick comforter. He couldn't see her breathing but was sure she was asleep.

Gritting his teeth, he shuffled over to the desk. He leaned against it and forced himself to breathe. A quick glance at Replacement ensured she was still asleep.

Click.

The cord made the slightest sound as he unplugged her laptop. Cradling it like a football, he limped for the door as quietly as he could. As he neared the end of the couch, he heard a soft scraping sound. He turned around, trying to pinpoint the source of the noise, and his eyes stopped on the desk.

The unplugged laptop cord was slowly sliding across the desk and fell. It landed with a crisp *thwack*.

He held his breath and looked down at Replacement.

She didn't move.

Jack turned and scurried back to the safety of the bedroom with his prize.

The laptop's screen flashed to life, and a password prompt appeared.

Jack grinned.

You're not the only one who can look over someone's shoulder.

He typed XmasR0$3 and the laptop booted up.

Christmas Rose for her password? I would have never guessed it.

Jack logged in to the police database and opened the file on Lennie Jacobsen. He was clean. No arrest, but there was a mug shot.

Why was there a mug shot, but no arrest records?

He searched further into the file. He found an arrest record from a few years back. Someone had voided that arrest. Lennie had been arrested when he was a teenager, but the juvenile record was now sealed.

Damn.

He knew what that meant. Juvie records were like vaults. He'd have to convince a judge to give him a subpoena and get them unsealed.

Mark Reynolds said Lennie was a runner for one of the dealers at the college. Maybe he was a student?

He started to write an email to Neil Waters.

The next couple of days, Replacement made him breakfast, lunch, and dinner and watched movie after movie lying next to him. If he tried to talk about the college or Michelle, she cut him off and reminded him he promised to wait until he got better. He couldn't remember making a promise, but he didn't say anything.

Every night, Jack would sneak Replacement's laptop and continue the hunt. He pored over all the files to search for anything he may have missed.

His leg healed slowly. The whole length of it was bruised and sore.

Replacement never left his side. When he woke up, she was there, and she tucked him in at night. She doted on him like a mother, and though he wouldn't admit it to her, he liked it. Even so, he was glad when the day finally came for his checkup.

Jack was excited to see the doctor and get clearance to go back to work. He'd been out of the hospital for a week and was hopeful. He was not as excited about *how* they were getting to the doctor's office. Because of his leg, he couldn't drive. That left Replacement.

He watched her carefully put the front seat all the way back to accommodate Jack's leg brace. As he settled into the passenger seat, he realized a big problem: the front seat in the Impala was one long seat. It was like driving sitting on a couch. The problem was, in order for Jack's leg to be straight out, Replacement now had to sit on the very edge in order to reach the steering wheel and pedals.

He looked at her and laughed. She looked like a little kid playing in the car. She made a face and sat up straighter.

"Okay. Just remember that the gas pedal is—"

The car shot forward like a rocket as she pressed down too hard on the gas. She countered by jamming both feet on the brake, and Jack had to catch himself on the dashboard to keep from going through the windshield.

"Very sensitive."

Before he could say anything else, she did the whole process again, and they were headed down the street with Jack feeling as if he were riding a bull in a rodeo.

They stopped at a light and, between the pain in his leg and the terrified yet determined look on Replacement's face, he burst out laughing. She muttered, which caused him to laugh even harder.

"I'm doing my best."

"You have to go easy."

"I am."

"Just press a little."

When they reached the clinic, they both were howling with laughter.

She followed him into the small exam room. Jack hopped up onto the examining table.

Just let this guy give me the green light.

He stared at the ceiling, and his mood shifted. As his thoughts moved back to work, he could hear Replacement move things on the desk.

"Don't touch anything, kid," he called out but kept his eyes closed.

"That's Doctor Kid to you." Replacement poked his leg.

Jack sat up, and his eyes went wide. Replacement had blue rubber gloves on her hands and a white mask over her mouth. She crossed her eyes and held up a tongue depressor.

"It's time for your full body checkup."

They both burst out laughing, and still were as the door opened and the doctor walked in. Jack swallowed, and Replacement spun around, pulled her mask down, and put her hands behind her back. The older doctor's expression lost the quizzical look and turned into a frown.

I'm an idiot. Now he's going to be bent out of shape.

"I'm Dr. Nieman." He shook Jack's hand. "I see you've met my assistant." He nodded toward Replacement.

Jack exhaled, and Replacement grinned.

Dr. Nieman walked over and removed Jack's leg brace. Jack winced. After a few minutes of prodding, Nieman leaned back.

"Officer, your leg is healing up quite nicely. If my assistant here keeps up with this quality care, you can head back to work next week." He winked at Replacement.

Jack and Replacement exchanged a quick smile.

"Thank you, Doctor."

Nieman shook Jack's hand, and as he turned to walk out of the office, he whispered into Replacement's ear. Jack watched from across the room as her eyes grew big and her face turned scarlet. She didn't say a word as Nieman chuckled and left the room.

"What was that all about?"

"Nothing."

He shot her a semi-mad look.

"He said that I can take the mask and gloves. If we want to play doctor and patient, you're healthy enough for that now." Replacement continued to stare at the floor as her face continued past scarlet to plum red.

The good news put Jack in a great mood for the ride home. They were soon howling with laughter again at Replacement's driving. She couldn't get the feel for the gas pedal, and they lurched down the street like a drunken grasshopper. Jack was amazed she parked the car.

They were both still in a laughing mood as they tried to get into the apartment. Replacement held a stack of mail as she propped the door open for Jack while he had to shimmy sideways on his crutches to get through.

Replacement dropped the pile of mail on the counter and headed off to take a shower. Jack couldn't wait to take one either. He hated the doctor's office.

Germ factory.

Jack made up two plates for lunch and hobbled over to the computer. Neil Waters wrote back. Jack read the email. Lennie Jacobsen had been a computer science student, but he'd dropped out in October. The only other information Neil had on him was a home address in Michigan.

Jack looked down at Replacement's notebook. She'd continued to read Michelle's emails and made notes. He flipped it open and checked some of the pages. She had circled a filename in red and wrote *Password?* next to it.

He logged into the file storage where Replacement had put the contents of the phone. A few clicks and he was at the folder. A video named "XPC 15 Interview — Part 1" was the only file in there. Jack double-clicked it, and a password prompt appeared. He read Replacement's note. She'd written "tried everything!!!" with an unhappy face.

He typed COOKIES and a message appeared: "Invalid Password. Type secure password and press enter."

Jack frowned, limped into the bedroom, and knocked at the bathroom door. He opened it a crack, and Replacement yelped. Jack jumped back and slammed the door shut.

"What's the matter?" he called.

"I'm in the shower."

"I have a quick question."

"Can it wait?" she asked.

"You walk in on me all the time."

"It's different. I'm a woman."

Jack laughed and shook his head. "What makes a password secure?"

"What do you mean?" She shut the water off and, in a few seconds, the door opened a fraction, her body hidden behind it. "What're you talking about?"

"That file that you can't open. Did you try any word like cookies?" Jack asked.

"A password doesn't have cookies." She looked at him as if he were stupid.

"No. For the password. Did you try the word cookies?"

"No. Why would I try cookies?"

"Michelle always used that for her password," he said.

"No, she didn't."

"Yes, she did, when she was little. It was her super-secret one you had to say." Jack could see Michelle with her hands on her hips and her little chin sticking out, demanding that he say the password before she'd let him go by.

Replacement yanked opened the door and raced to the computer. She was dripping wet but had a large towel wrapped around herself. She jumped behind the keyboard and pulled up another program.

"I'll run it through this." She pressed a few keys, and the screen flashed.

"What is it?" Jack leaned forward, but the screen was changing so fast he couldn't tell what was going on.

"It's a password cracker. It would take way too long if you didn't have any idea what the base password was. You'd need a super computer to crack it. But if you forgot your password and had some idea, this program tries the different permutations."

"You lost me with your geek-speak, girl."

Replacement frowned. "A secure password uses letters, numbers, capital letters, and symbols. I can put in a base word or words and let the program do all the combinations. There are thousands and it will try them, but it still may take a couple days."

"Days?"

"Yes, but that beats never."

Again, Jack thought she wanted to add the word *stupid* to her statement. "Okay." Jack got up and limped for the bathroom. "I guess we have time." He paused outside the bedroom door. "I'm real impressed. You really are brilliant."

Replacement jumped up and spun around so fast her towel started to fall. Jack couldn't help it. His mouth fell open, and his eyes widened. Replacement twisted and turned different shades of crimson as she tried to hold onto the towel and cover herself up.

As Jack quickly tried to look away, he slipped on the water on the floor. His full weight came down on his hurt leg, and he fell forward. He went to catch himself and realized it would be with his hurt wrist. He forced his hand up and landed flat on his stomach and face instead. The impact knocked the wind right out of him, and he groaned loudly.

"Jack." Replacement rushed over to him. "Jack, I'm so sorry." Her small hands pushed his hair back. "Are you okay?"

He tried to swallow and look just at her eyes, but he failed. He could hardly breathe, but he didn't know whether it was because of her, or landing on his stomach. Her skin was white and flawless. Her emerald eyes invited him to lose himself in them. Her mouth was only inches away, and her clean scent washed over him and drew him closer.

"Jack?" Both of her hands grabbed the side of his face; he lay there and stared at her.

His arms circled around her waist and lower back. They stared at each other. Her eyes widened and then softened. His hand glided up to her shoulder.

Jack leaned closer and placed his cheek next to hers. He could feel her heart beat against his chest. It matched the rhythm of his own. They both relaxed into each other, and Jack pressed his face into her neck.

Her breath was hot against his ear. He felt her leg slide up and he tightened his grip to pull her even closer into him. Her hand caressed the side of his cheek, and he trembled.

Don't.

The word of caution came from somewhere deep within his mind. It leapt out of hiding from some buried dark spot. His newfound desires for her vanished like mist at dawn.

"Fine, I'm fine." He closed his eyes. "Get dressed."

Jack waited, but her hands held his face. He could still feel her breath hot on his neck. He softly shook his head. She slid her hands down his cheeks, and he relaxed a little. Then he felt her hands move underneath his arms.

"Let me help you up."

Jack kept his eyes closed as she struggled to lift him. He felt her body press against his and he managed to stand and lean against the door. He felt her lean up to him as she held him upright; her arms encircled his waist.

He opened his eyes and looked at the ceiling. "I'm okay." His voice sounded odd, and he realized he held his breath. He looked down to find Replacement's eyes waiting to search his. Her mouth was open, and her lips glistened.

Jack could feel the heat radiate off her, and he panicked. "I'm fine." He guided her away from him and looked away. "Really."

"Let me help you," Replacement protested and began to slide her arm back around his waist.

Jack hurriedly turned. "Thank you. I'm okay." As softly as he could, he slipped away from her hold, opened the door, and retreated into the safety of the bedroom. Just before it closed behind him, he caught a glimpse of a pair of very confused emerald eyes.

CHAPTER TWENTY-NINE

The Tape

He'd tried to go to bed early but failed. Jack rolled over and looked at the clock. Nine forty-five. He couldn't sleep again. He rolled out of bed and hobbled into the living room. Replacement sat at the computer. She didn't turn around but waved him over. Jack limped up behind her and saw a video playing on the monitor.

"This is the file." Her voice was low and monotone, and for the first time he heard real fear in her voice. Next to her the notebook lay open, "Password = C00KI3$" scrawled on a page.

Jack turned to watch what had her so spooked. The tape showed a close-up of a man's face. A leather band strapped his head down to a bed. It was hard to judge his age, but he looked to be at least in his thirties. His hair was long, greasy, and unkempt. He had sores on his lips and face.

Drug addict. A bum too, from the looks of it.

His eyelids were taped open, and a plastic bit or gag was in his mouth.

"Is there audio?"

Replacement cringed, but she turned up the speakers.

Jack looked back at the man. They could hear him moaning. He'd seen the tape on the eyes before.

Iraq.

Jack had been doing a door-to-door in Iraq, chasing an insurgent. They'd come into a room with two dead bodies in chairs. Their eyes had been taped open. The torturers had wanted the men to see what they were doing to them.

Who tortures a homeless guy? And why did Michelle have a video of it?

Jack stood up and forced himself to put weight on his hurt leg.

The man on the tape made a gurgling noise as he tried to speak.

From somewhere off screen, they could hear a voice, but Jack couldn't make it out.

The room darkened even more, and they could hear some computerized clicks, beeps, and a strange humming sound. The man began to struggle against the straps. There was a loud crunching sound, and he screamed in agony. The gag in his mouth distorted his groans.

"Whaaa...why?" he managed to say.

From off camera, someone responded, but even though Jack turned the volume all the way up, they couldn't make it out.

The man started to thrash again. Tears poured over his face and sweat matted his hair. He frantically shook his head.

A massive sob erupted from behind the gag in his mouth, and he choked on his own saliva. Replacement looked away.

"Please." In spite of the gag, the word was clear. He thrashed against the restraints.

"I can't watch this." Replacement ran to the bedroom.

Jack took the chair. He was so angry he didn't feel human.

He couldn't tell what the person off camera was saying, but he knew the next sound they made. He heard someone laugh as the poor man on the table continued to sob. There was the sound of another bone being broken and the man's body flopped on the table.

The man's muffled voice called out, "Please, God! Please…" and the tape ended.

Jack found himself staring at the ceiling again. His whole body hurt, but his head was killing him. He checked the clock. Eleven ten. With a groan, he rolled onto his side and reached for the phone, and sat up as he dialed.

"Dad? Sorry to call so late."

"Hey, kid. How are you feeling?" His father was attempting to mask the fact that he'd been asleep.

"Good, good, much better." *Physically, that is.*

"What's up, son?" His father's voice always made him sit up straighter. He didn't know why. He was one of the kindest men he'd ever met.

"Dad, I need some advice."

Jack jumped back and forth as he relayed the events of the last few weeks, but he laid out everything. He spoke about Replacement, Collins, and Michelle as they talked for over two hours. His father listened and asked a few questions to clarify a point here or to have him repeat something there.

"What do you think?" Jack held his breath as he waited for a response.

"Jack, I know they found drugs in her system, but that doesn't match with the Michelle we knew. Michelle would never do drugs. She…" His voice trembled, and Jack felt as if someone had squeezed his own heart.

I'm a thoughtless jerk. Dad knew her. He loved her too.

"Sorry," his father continued. "You need to be careful. Jack, what do you think?"

"I have no real proof, but you're right, that isn't the Michelle I knew, unless I didn't really know her…" He almost whispered the last part.

"Now you're just beating yourself up, Jack. You knew Michelle."

"I pushed them out of my life. I didn't know anything about what she was like recently."

"Jack. The truth is I don't know everything about your mother." He paused. "I don't know her favorite movie. Do you know what that means? It means I should ask her. It doesn't mean I don't love her. You loved Michelle as a sister, and you knew her. Do you love me, Jack?"

"You know I do, Dad." Jack was now trying not to cry. He couldn't remember crying in front of his father—his mom, yes—but never Dad.

"What's my favorite movie?"

Jack lost it. He babbled, "Sorry," before he dissolved into tears.

He wiped his eyes and put his head in his hands.

"Dad, what's wrong with me? I've turned into a total pansy."

"No. You've always kept everything in, Jack. That's not good. I'm not telling you to go on Dr. Phil, but you have to let it out from time to time. You didn't do that when you were a little boy, and you didn't do that after you came back from Iraq, and now…now it's coming out. It's okay."

"It's not okay. I shouldn't…I got it good. I'm just…"

"Jack. I've always been one hundred percent straight with you, right?"

"Yeah."

"I'm no therapist, but the first seven years of your life sucked. Life after that wasn't a picnic for you either. You've had it tough. You've tried to bury all that crap like it didn't happen, and it doesn't bother you. That's like trying to bury toxic waste in your backyard. It doesn't work. It will kill you."

"What should I do? How do I let it out?"

"You have a choice, Jack. That stuff happened. You can't bury it. You have to face it."

"How?" he whispered, more to himself.

"It will come, Jack. Just let it."

"But Dad, I get…I get so angry…"

"Jack, I know you don't want to hear this but you have to face your demons. It happened. Life's hard. Yeah, you got knocked down, but wipe your nose and get up."

Dad, I can't. I can't face them. I can't win.

"Dad, don't tell Mom, all right?" Jack wiped his eyes.

"I won't tell her. If I did, she'd come up there and kick your butt for being such a baby."

Jack's mother was one of the kindest, sweetest people he'd ever met. He'd never heard her yell. His father's joke was so out of character for Jack's mother he laughed at the thought of it. They both laughed for a couple minutes. Jack's head hurt, and now his sides did too. He needed that.

"Dad, what's your favorite movie?" Jack sniffled.

"The Seven Samurai."

"The one where the Samurai help out the farmers?"

"Yes. Jack, if you're going to do what I think you're going to do…please be careful." His father sounded worried.

"I will. I'm not afraid of a fight, Dad."

"Well, I don't like you to fight, but remember, if you're going to fight, fight to win."

<u>CHAPTER THIRTY</u>

Following the Bread Crumbs

Early the next morning, Jack watched as Replacement checked her makeup in the hall mirror.

"Where are you going?" Jack asked her again.

"I'll be back in a few hours. I told you about a computer job I have. Well, I used to have it. I do their website, and they need me again. The extra money would help out around here." She shrugged.

"You?" Jack couldn't help making a face.

"Thanks." She spun back around, and he hardly recognized her. She'd come back that morning with a new hair trimmed and colored. Her medium brown hair was now almost black. Her ponytail was gone, and her shoulder-length hair hung down. It was a business look that went with her blue skirt and blouse. "Can I use the car?"

"*The* car? *My* car." Jack groaned, but then tossed her the keys. "Now I'm trapped."

"I won't be late. Mrs. Stevens is right downstairs. Bye." She waved and headed out the door.

Jack flexed his wrist; his arm felt fine. Next, he tested his leg.

Yeah, still hurts like hell.

The bruise on his thigh was fading, but the muscles still throbbed.

He forced himself to walk normally into the kitchen. After filling a large cup with coffee, he headed back to the computer.

No reason I can't work.

Jack sat down and propped his leg up on a little footstool under the desk. The computer beeped as he logged in to the police database. He wanted to look for the guy from the tape again.

Jack pulled up the mug shots and tried to limit them by gender, race, age, and arrests. He shook his head. The list was huge. He took a swig of coffee and forced himself to stop and think.

There are too many results. Narrow the field. I need to break it down somehow.

He flipped back to the video file and just stared at it. "XPC 15 Interview — Part 1." The date was December 19.

That's when she put the file on her phone. The nineteenth. Michelle died on the twenty-first. Two days. Two days.

He looked at the file. "XPC 15 Interview – Part 1." Date Created: December 19. Jack tapped his fingers on the desk. He switched over to the Internet and searched for DATE CREATED.

"The Date Created is the date the file was copied. When you copy a file, you CREATE a copy of the file in the new location."

So the nineteenth is when Michelle copied the file to her phone, not when the video was recorded.

"DATE MODIFIED is the last time the file was actually changed. Moving or copying doesn't affect the Date Modified."

The date modified would be the date inside the computer when the file was last modified or recorded. That's the date the video was recorded.

He opened the video and selected the properties. Date Modified. October 20—one year ago.

Bingo.

He switched back to the mug shots, this time calling up old photos. Male, white, twenties, meth.

Yes.

The man from the video was on the first page. Charlie Harding. He was twenty-three.

Twenty-three? He looked forty.

Charlie had been arrested a number of times. All of them were for either drinking, drugs, or because it was cold. Jack shook his head. Being homeless in winter meant that you got creative. If the shelters were full, you could freeze to death, so a few homeless people would try to get themselves arrested so they could get a warm bed and some food. Trespassing or shoplifting was the usual ticket.

Someone reported Charlie missing in December that same year. Jack frowned. It took two months for someone to figure out he was gone? The person who reported him missing was Hank Foster. Under "Relationship," the file said, "Sponsor."

Must be an AA sponsor.

There was an address and number listed for Foster. Jack knew he should call first, but it would be just as easy to swing over, and he preferred that.

He got up, grabbed his jacket, and headed for the door but then stopped.

I don't have a car.

Throwing the jacket down, he went back and reread the missing person report. Hank Foster listed Charlie as having "substance abuse issues." Charlie's rap sheet was long. They'd arrested him for drugs, alcohol, and meth numerous times.

Jack leaned over, grabbed the phone, and dialed.

"Hello?"

"Hi. I'm looking for Hank Foster." Jack smiled. On an interview course, he'd learned that people could hear a smile in your voice, so he forced himself to smile when he spoke on the phone.

"You got him. How can I help?"

"My name is Jack Stratton. I'm a police officer with the Darrington County Sheriff's Office and I'm calling about the missing person's report that you filed."

"Oh, okay. What do you want to know about her?"

Jack paused.

"Hank, I'd like to swing by and speak with you. Are you still located on Pine Hill?"

"I am."

"Will you be around…later this evening?"

"It matters how late. I have an AA meeting at eight o'clock, and it can run late."

"Where would that be?"

"It's at the VFW out near Houton's Pond. Do you have any more information about Tiffany?"

Tiffany? Another missing person? One guy files two different missing person reports?

"I'll meet you after your meeting. Hank, I'm reconciling the reports and need Tiffany's middle name. Can you confirm it for me?"

"Tiffany Marie McAllister."

"Thank you. I'll see you tonight."

Jack hung up the phone and started to type. The case came up on the screen. Tiffany McAllister had gone missing five months prior to Michelle.

Looks like Foster was a little late in reporting her missing.

They had found her body a few days before he filed the report. The medical examiner had listed her as a Jane Doe.

At least the report he filed attached a name to the body.

Jack read the police report. The cleaning crew found her behind the Imperial Motor Lodge. The ME listed the cause of death as a meth overdose. Shot it.

The Imperial is a popular hangout for prostitutes.

Jack switched programs and ran Tiffany's information. Prostitution and drug arrests scrolled up the screen. He looked at her age: nineteen.

He printed out the report and then pulled up her picture. She looked younger than nineteen. She also looked ashamed. With her short brown hair and green eyes, she could have passed for Replacement's sister.

Jack ran Hank Foster. He'd done time for assault and armed robbery fifteen years ago. He had arrests for drugs and prostitution at that time too. The arrest wasn't for being a john. He'd been a pimp. Jack continued to type. Assault on girlfriend. Assault on a police officer. Hank served five years and got five years probation.

Habitual offender. Now he files two missing person reports? One was tortured. Replacement had best be back in time.

Jack printed out a still from Charlie Harding's video and pushed the mouse away. His head pounded, and he wanted a drink, but that was also the last thing he wanted. With a groan, he grabbed Tiffany's report from the printer, walked over to the couch, and stretched out.

A few minutes later, the papers fell to the floor as Jack fell asleep.

CHAPTER THIRTY-ONE

Girl Jacked

IRAQ

Jack's shirt clung to him like a damp towel. He shifted his assault rifle in his arms and continued to scan the crowd.

A lot of people moved by their checkpoint. The families going home chattered back and forth. Besides the heat, the feeling was upbeat.

He turned to Chandler. "Are you hot?"

"Yeah." A cocky grin spread across his big friend's face as he nodded his head. "That's what all the ladies say."

"Shut up."

"You shut up," Chandler shot back. "It's two hundred degrees out. What a stupid question. I'm about to spontaneously combust." He laughed and finished off another bottle of Gatorade.

Jack turned to look at the approaching crowd. Something was wrong. People talked all around, but a strange pocket of silence approached them. He scanned the faces and noticed the source of the silence. A woman dressed in a black burqa walked with a little girl dressed in the same head-to-toe black dress. He could only see their eyes because of the slit on the front. Other than that, they were covered.

Many women wore burqas, but there was something wrong with this pair. The mother kept the girl at arm's length as they walked.

"Chandler. One o'clock." Jack nodded toward the approaching pair.

Chandler stood next to Jack on the left. His smile vanished when he saw them approach.

"The mother is freaked." Jack's chin tipped up. "She's probably being forced to wear a vest and is trying to keep the little girl out of the way. Can we separate them?"

"I can get the girl." Chandler walked toward the edge of the crowd.

Jack moved to the right.

Chandler looked back, and Jack nodded. Chandler kept moving.

The crowd kept shying away from the pair. The mother and daughter picked up the pace as a pocket formed around them. Jack looked at the girl. Judging by her height, she was six or seven years old. He could see her rich brown eyes. They gleamed. She was happy. She had no idea of the danger she was in.

Jack watched the mother. Her eyes darted all over, but she never looked directly at Jack. He glanced over and saw Chandler make his move. His friend took two huge strides, scooped the little girl up in his arms, and headed back to the checkpoint.

"STOP," Jack commanded in both Arabic and English. "Hands up."

The mother watched as Chandler carried her daughter away. She then turned back to look at Jack. He saw her eyes as they changed from fear to relief and then as the relief changed to a look of hate.

"Hands up," he shouted again at her as the crowd scrambled for safety. With his finger on the trigger, Jack hesitated. He'd never shot a woman before. She raised her arms up slowly.

It was then Jack realized his mistake.

He saw the large hands of a man.

It wasn't a mother worried for her daughter. It was a man worried for his own safety. He was scared because it was the little girl who'd been forced to wear the suicide vest.

"CHANDLER," Jack yelled.

Chandler looked back at Jack as he cradled the little girl in his big arms. Their eyes met for a second before the white flash.

The explosion knocked Jack to his knees. His hands hit the dirt. He couldn't breathe. He couldn't see clearly, and his ears rang. His fingers clawed the ground in front of him. The hard dry ground had now turned soft...

He opened his eyes and stared down at gray carpet with black flecks. He gazed at the pattern he was sure he'd seen before but couldn't place where.

The funeral home.

Jack stood up. He was at the funeral home where they held Michelle's service. Chandler stood at the rear, near an open coffin. He wore his dress uniform and tears rolled down his face. His arm was around Michelle's shoulder. She wore her long hair pulled back, and she had on a simple charcoal dress. She glanced at Jack, and she was crying too.

Jack staggered forward. They both gazed into a coffin. It was purple and white with pink flowers.

Aunt Haddie? No...

It felt as though he were walking through knee-deep mud as he forced himself to keep moving forward. Chandler glared back at him, and Michelle wept.

"My babies!" The cry behind him caused him to turn around.

Aunt Haddie stood in the doorway of the funeral home. She looked even frailer as she took small steps forward.

"My babies," she cried as she held her hands out. "All of my babies are gone."

Jack turned back around and raced to the coffin. Replacement's body lay inside. Her emerald green eyes were now gray and lifeless. Her mouth was frozen in a twisted scream. Her eyes had been taped open.

"Alice, no...ALICE!"

Replacement was shaking him. She said something, but he couldn't hear clearly. His trembling hands gripped the back of his head. He gasped for air.

"Jack? Jack?" Replacement held his shoulders at arm's length. "It's just a dream. You were dreaming. You must have taken a nap."

Jack grabbed her and pulled her close. He was panting, but he still crushed her to his chest. He straightened his arms and looked at her.

Concern filled her eyes.

"You're okay. It was just a dream," Jack muttered and stood up.

He swayed like a drunken sailor as he turned around.

"I just walked in and you were…yelling my name." Alice looked up at him.

"I'm sorry." Jack shuffled into the kitchen and looked at the clock. Eight fifteen.

Damn.

"I need my car." Jack rubbed his eyes.

"What? Why?" The color drained from Replacement's face. "I was going to borrow it tomorrow too."

"You can. I'm meeting a guy tonight. Hey, how is the website job going?" He tried to smile.

"Good. It's nothing special." Replacement followed him into the kitchen. "They need some updates. Nothing big. Who are you meeting?"

"Guy's name is Hank Foster. I also got the name of the guy on the tape. Charlie Harding. Hank Foster reported him missing."

"Good work. Are you sure you're okay?"

"I'm fine. The problem is that Hank Foster also reported a girl named Tiffany McAllister missing five months ago."

"He reported both of them missing? Are you sure that you have the guy from the tape?"

"Yeah. I found out the video was filmed a year ago. That narrowed down the field."

"Nice work." Replacement smiled.

"I need to ask Hank about Tiffany. She showed up dead. Then I'm going to ask about Charlie. Keys?"

She handed him the keys, and he grabbed his jacket.

"What about your crutches?"

"I need to strengthen the leg," he called back.

Replacement shut the door and hurried to catch up to him.

"You're not coming. Go get something to eat."

"What? No. I'll drive."

"No." Jack stopped and turned to her. "You can't come. Don't even try."

"I can help." She raised herself up on her toes.

"No. Listen. It's not happening." Jack shut his eyes, and the images from his dream flashed into view. "Seriously, no." Jack tried to soften his voice, but he knew it still came out cold and angry.

Replacement didn't say anything. She turned and went back to the apartment.

Jack pulled up in front of the small VFW hall. Twenty to thirty cars were in the parking lot. He headed for the main door and scanned the faces of the few people outside smoking cigarettes. Hank Foster's last mug shot was ten years old, but he didn't appear to be one of the smokers huddled next to the building.

Jack opened the door to a medium-sized room with folding chairs set up in neat rows. Less than a quarter of them had someone sitting on them. It was your typical AA meeting. He picked a half-empty row and sat down.

A man at the front was speaking about how he stayed sober. Jack didn't pay too much attention to him at first. He looked at a man seated three rows from the front next to a column. The man was ten years older, but he was sure he was watching Hank Foster.

"How many people right now want to drink?" Hands shot up all over the room, and then the man speaking raised his own hand. "I do. The problem is, I won't stop. I'll just keep going. I drink because I'm a drunk."

The man behind the podium had everyone's attention now, including Jack's. "There's only one way I have stayed sober. How? My higher power? Get real. That self-righteous crap doesn't keep you sober. I know what power is, and it ain't me; it's God, pure and simple. He keeps me on track one day at a time, moment by moment. But, *He* expects you to step up, twelve steps exactly. Don't drink, work the program, and ask for help. That's how I have stayed sober for fifteen years."

Jack shifted in his seat.

After he finished, there was a small round of applause as an older man rose and moved next to the podium.

"Ten minute break. Smoke 'em if you got 'em."

People stood up and filed for the doors. Jack's eyes stayed on Foster. He rose and shook a woman's hand. He watched them talk. After a few minutes, Foster headed for the back door too. Jack moved right behind him.

Jack walked out the door and onto the big porch filled with smokers.

"Hank?"

Hank Foster turned to stare at Jack. He was in his forties, but he looked older. Rough. His long hair, pulled back into a ponytail, was predominantly gray, but black streaks still ran through it. A full beard and mustache partly covered his pockmarked face. The well-worn leather jacket seemed too large for his slim frame.

"You the cop who called?"

Jack got the feeling Hank wanted to talk alone and his saying cop as loudly as he did had the desired effect. Everyone else left the porch, leaving the two of them alone.

"I am."

"What did you find out about Tiffany?"

"You're aware that she's dead?"

"Yeah. Who do you think paid for the funeral? You got anything new on her?" The man took a step forward.

Jack's rear foot shifted, and he let his center of gravity drop lower. The veins in Hank's neck stood out, and he clenched his jaw. Jack could see he was trying to control his anger but was losing the struggle.

This could break bad.

"No. I was calling about Charlie Harding, but you brought up Tiffany. Do you file a lot of missing person reports?"

Hank took a drag off his cigarette, and Jack noticed he switched hands when he took it out of his mouth.

He's a righty. His cigarette is now in his left hand. He's getting ready to punch.

"I filed two."

"One of them is dead. I'm concerned for the safety of the other."

"Me too; that's why I filed the missing person's report."

They stared at each other for a moment and then Foster relaxed.

"So you still have nothing. Jeez."

"How did you know Tiffany?" Jack asked.

"Man. I try to do the right thing and I get looked at?" Hank flicked his cigarette off the porch.

"If you want to do the right thing, just answer a couple of questions."

"Fine."

"How did you know Tiffany?"

"I was her sponsor."

"I thought AA didn't allow different sex sponsors?"

Hank straightened up, and he peered at Jack. "You in the program?"

"Was. You sponsored a girl?"

"Not officially. She was the same age as my daughter. I thought I could help."

"What happened?" Jack relaxed his guard a little but resisted the urge to lean against the railing.

"She missed a meeting. I called her—nothing. She missed more. I freaked. I kept going to the police, but they don't care about whores, even if they're kids. I filed the report, but they came back a couple days later and said she was already dead."

"She OD'd injecting meth."

"That's a lie." Foster jumped up so fast that Jack's hand instinctively went out in front of him.

"Easy." Jack shifted.

"You don't give a—" Hank snarled.

"Hey, I'm the cop who's here right now looking into this, so how about you just answer my questions? First, why do you think it's a lie?"

Hank paused. "She didn't do meth."

"She did drugs."

"Not meth."

"Could have been the first time?"

"Not meth."

Jack was getting frustrated. "She did drugs and was a prostitute. Why would she not do meth?"

"She was a person, too. She said she'd never do meth because she thought it would make her go instantly crazy. She said she saw someone go nuts and start ripping at their skin. It freaked her out. I know it sounds weird, but she was different. And, she never shot up. She never would. She hated needles."

"She hated needles enough to never do meth?" Jack shook his head. "Even if she was desperate?"

"Even if she was in total withdrawal. I went through that with her. It was bad. Real bad. She didn't do needles. Do you know people who are so freaked they don't fly? They wouldn't get on a plane for any reason? She was like that with needles."

"So what do you think happened?"

"I don't know. I've gone over it in my head. She was trying real hard. She was clean. No drugs and no booze."

He's not telling me everything. He's holding out.

"Hank, look, I'm the guy who's trying to find out what happened." Jack took a step forward.

Hank looked up at the night sky. "She was having money issues. I offered her what I could, but it wasn't much. She couldn't ask her parents. It might have been she ran down for a quick trick."

That would explain why she was at the motel.

"Okay. What can you tell me about Charlie Harding?"

"Not much."

"Were you his sponsor?"

"Yeah. Not long. He was a good kid. He had it hard. Him, there wasn't a drug that he wouldn't take."

"What happened?"

"He disappeared. I haven't heard of him since. He was living at the shelter so the stinking pigs...sorry...police just assumed he moved on."

"Why do you think differently?"

"Because he was happy. He just got a job. Crappy gig doing dishes, but it was work."

"What do you think happened?"

"I don't know. He just vanished. I filed the report and checked a couple of times but nothing."

Jack held out the still picture from the video. "This him?"

Foster held the picture and stared at it for a while. He didn't say anything but he nodded.

"Thanks."

"Is he dead?"

"I don't know. This picture is from a video taken late last October."

"It must have been around when he went missing. It was before Halloween. What happened to him?"

"I don't know...yet. Do you know if he'd ever been to White Rocks Eastern College?"

"He went there."

"How do you know?"

"Because I took him there. I do a Scared Straight thing every semester. We go and scare the crap out of rich kids. Tell them how screwed up drugs make your life."

"Charlie went with you? When did you go?"

"When school first started. What's that, September? The professor uses us to kick off the class. Tell the kids about drugs. I know it's a dog and pony show, but it's a chance to warn them." Hank shrugged.

"You know the teacher's name?"

"Franklin. Dr. Franklin. He teaches out at the college."

"Did Tiffany talk in front of the class?"

"No."

"So she never went with you?"

"No."

"Did either Charlie or Tiffany ever say anything about going there again?"

Foster shook his head as he lit another cigarette.

"Okay then, Hank. Thank you for your time."

Jack nodded. Hank did the same, but he didn't extend a hand, so neither did Jack. As Jack walked away, Hank called to him.

"Hey. I'm telling you straight. I know Tiffany didn't do meth, no way. I'm telling you, she got girl jacked."

CHAPTER THIRTY-TWO

Speed Kills

Jack spent the next few days going back and forth over all his notes and the police reports. He started a new notebook and copied everything over to organize it. He created a timeline, starting with Charlie Harding right up to the present day.

He groaned and rubbed the back of his neck.

Six o'clock. Replacement's still not back.

Jack pulled his sweatshirt on and headed out for his walk. He needed to think and build up his strength. His leg was still killing him, though he wouldn't admit that to the doctor. He was good at masking pain.

He looked down the stairs with dread. The deep muscles in his thigh still throbbed. The hardest part of going down the steps was trying to bear all his weight on one leg. After he finally made it out the front door, he was glad it wasn't that cold. He'd walk down to Finnegan's and then up toward the library and back. His usual two-mile lap.

I have to get to Aunt Haddie's tomorrow. I'm not going down that road again.

He'd been calling her every few days, but she was adamant he visit in person.

Jack picked up the pace as his thoughts turned to Replacement. She borrowed the car every day to get to her job. She wouldn't talk about it, so he gave up asking. He was considering picking up a used car for her. Not having his was getting to be a logistical pain.

Great, we need another car and a new place.

A car horn sounded and Jack turned to see Mrs. Sawyer pull up alongside him and crank down her window. The boat of a car she drove made her appear even smaller in the front seat.

"I'm so glad to see you up and about, Jack. Did you like my flowers?" Her old eyes twinkled.

Replacement throwing out the stupid flower cards is still causing me grief.

"I loved them. Thank you so much."

As he got close to the car, she pulled him halfway in the window and gave him a big hug.

"You'll have to stop by. I made cherries jubilee that will put you into sugar shock." She patted his cheek and winked.

"I will. Has everything been nice and quiet?"

"Not a peep around the house," she proclaimed and squeezed his hand. "All thanks to you."

"Well, I'd better get back to my walk."

"Don't dawdle. It looks like rain. Be sure to stop by." She waved and jammed on the gas.

Jack cringed as she drove in the wrong lane for fifty feet before she slowly crossed over to the right lane.

He hurried to the library and turned around without going in. As he headed back into town, he realized it was Tuesday because of the increase in foot traffic. Forgetting what day it was made him yearn for a work schedule. His frustration caused his body to tense. He uncurled his clenched fists and shook his hands.

I need some way to ask questions at the college. Dr. Franklin. Two people have brought him up, so I should call Hahn and see if I can go back out. I can say that I'm organizing something from Michelle's friends for Haddie. A remembrance book. Yeah, that should work. While I'm out there, I'll look up Franklin.

When Jack looked left to cross the street, he noticed a guy in an oversized blue parka. It was the second time he'd noticed him. The first was two miles back when he'd come out of his apartment.

The guy was following him.

Walk calmly. Don't rush. Left. Right. Left. Right. Swing your arms normally. Look around a little.

He kept walking straight and strained to hear anything behind him. He took a left down a little side street. A couple of people walked down the sidewalk; a few cars were parked. He jumped into the shadow of a large doorway and pressed his back against the wall.

Wait. Listen.

He tried to drown out the sounds of the cars.

Footsteps. Running.

The guy in the parka ran past him down the sidewalk. His face was gaunt and marked with sores.

Another addict.

He was about an inch taller than Jack and from his thin face, he figured he weighed under one eighty.

Great time to have left your gun at home.

"Looking for me?"

As the man spun around, Jack could see a pair of glazed eyes that gave away a world of information.

He's wired. Scared. Mad. Crazy.

His pupils were gone, and there was a creepy grin on his face. He lunged.

Jack sprang forward as the man moved. Jack's hand came down to block, and he saw a knife headed for his gut. He scooped it to the side, but as he went to grab the guy's wrist, he realized something was wrong. The thumb is the weakest part of the grip, but as Jack twisted the addict's hand, it wouldn't open.

Because Jack pushed forward and stepped to the left, it took him out of the knife's path. It also moved him into the middle of the sidewalk. Jack pivoted, but the motion placed too much weight on his injured leg. Pain shot up his thigh, and his scream of agony turned into a guttural growl. His leg shook and then went limp.

Jack fell backward. He pulled the man with him as he fell. He held onto the guy's hand with the knife, and they crashed into a parked car and then landed on the sidewalk.

The damned knife is duct taped to his wrist.

He knew from personal experience that homeless people do that to hold the knife while they sleep.

He twisted the guy's wrist.

Fast and hard.

He heard something snap.

The guy screamed, but so did Jack as the man's knee landed right on his injured thigh. Jack's hand reflexively opened, and the man pulled his injured arm away.

With his other hand, he punched Jack in the face. It was a quick punch, but it had a lot of power. The blow caught Jack across the chin. He saw stars and his vision blurred. He could taste blood in his mouth.

Day after day, his instructor had drilled the science of martial arts into his head.

Force equals mass times acceleration. You can't make your hand any bigger, but you can make it faster. Speed...Speed kills.

Jack brought his right hand up to the left side of his face, and his fist flashed out. His arm moved so fast it was a blur. The bottom, meaty part of his hand connected with the guy's jaw and continued through. Jack felt the jaw break.

The guy was smashed backward. A muffled wail burst from his broken mouth. He spit blood and teeth onto the sidewalk.

Jack rolled on his side and pushed himself up. His thigh muscles contracted, and he fell back down.

His attacker scrambled backward and got to his feet. Jack pulled himself up to his knees.

The man saw Jack getting up, turned, and ran. Jack howled in frustration. He knew he could barely walk, let alone catch the guy. As he fumbled for his phone, he noticed a small crowd rush toward him.

People asked, "Are you okay?" and "Are you hurt?" Jack punched in a number he could dial in his sleep.

"Darrington Police."

"Bev, this is Jack. A guy tried to knife me, need pursuit."

"Where?"

"He's running south down Oak. Male suspect about six feet, one eighty, dark blue parka with blue jeans and boots. He has a knife taped to his broken wrist."

"Broken wrist? So he has a cast on his arm?" she asked as she repeated his information over the radio.

"No, but his wrist is broken..."

"How do you know?"

"I broke it."

Jack glanced around.

"I'm on Laurel Road."

Jack stretched his leg to try to get blood back in it. He winced and his eyes narrowed.

Finally, a live suspect.

CHAPTER THIRTY-THREE

Loose Ends

"I'll see you later. I won't be home until late," Replacement called on her way out of the apartment. Jack heard her pick up the car keys from the hall table, and then open and close the front door.

"Bye." Jack stared at the door.

Damn. Something is up. She's not talking about work, and she's coming home later and later. She's wearing makeup and perfume now.

He shook himself out of his thoughts and moved back to the computer. After a swig of coffee, he got back to work. His attacker had vanished. They had an APB out with all the surrounding towns, but he was a ghost.

He'll turn up.

Jack had picked the man's mug shot out in under thirty minutes. He was from Rockland. Bennie Mayer. He had a long list of priors: B&E, assault, marijuana, cocaine, and meth. Bennie also did time off and on.

Jack stared out the window, aggravated. He'd rather be out looking for Bennie the Goon right now.

The guy was watching my apartment. He was waiting for me. It wasn't random.

Jack saw his face, saw his eyes.

I don't think he started out to kill me. He must have wanted to follow me. When I surprised him, he panicked. He was scared, but he turned into a scared killer.

He'd seen it before. He'd never met anyone who didn't care about killing. Taking another person's life freaked out most people; very few were just plain evil. Most were scared, but their own anger or hate overcame their fears, and that's when they killed.

That's what the guy looked like. He was going to kill Jack. It may have been the drugs, but Jack saw him make the decision. He could have run, but he chose to kill instead.

Could it be that someone wanted me dead because I was asking questions? I need to find that goon.

He pulled up the list of hospitals in the surrounding area and groaned. It was going to be a long day.

Jack spent hours calling every hospital. When that turned up nothing, he called every regional clinic. Finally, he ran through the alphabet to call doctor's offices. No one had a walk-in with a broken wrist and jaw. Nothing. He was sure he'd snapped the wrist and broken the jaw, but no one who matched the description showed up.

Switch gears. I'm spinning my tires.

Jack changed back to looking at Tiffany McAllister. He flipped to her autopsy report. No sexual assault. Meth OD. As he expected, there was a ton of medical jargon. Jack kept hitting the page-down key.

Then he thought of something.

Pictures.

The autopsy photos were all high resolution and took forever to load. They photographed the entire body, but Jack wanted to see a close-up of Tiffany's face. The pages continued to load until that face filled the monitor. Jack shut his eyes for a second. He'd seen death many times, but it was still hard, almost surreal to him.

Maybe all I can do for her is find the monster that did this.

He scanned around her eyes. He was looking for something. There was slight bruising around the right eye. He clicked and zoomed in on it. There it was. It was very, very faint but clear. There was a small square patch on her cheek. He zoomed in as far as he could: a rectangle.

Her eyes had been taped open.

The medical examiner can find out a lot more, but it's there. The tape on the eyes links the two cases—Tiffany McAllister to Charlie Harding.

Jack leaned back in his chair.

The computer lab has Michelle's phone with the videotape of a guy getting tortured. I have proof it's related at least to Tiffany's death. That's enough for them to go on. They'll be able to get a warrant with that. Tomorrow...I'm back at work tomorrow, and I can get down to Joe and lay it all out to him face to face. Once they get the video, I can fill in the details of who and what and then lead them to Tiffany. They'll also have to reexamine Michelle's autopsy photos to look for tape around her eyes.

Jack got up and stretched. His leg hurt from sitting for so long. He paced the floor.

Damn it. He picked up the phone and dialed Joe Davenport's cell phone.

I should tell him right now.

Joe's voicemail picked up. "Detective Joe Davenport. I'm currently unavailable. Detective Flynn can be reached by contacting..."

He hung up the phone. He looked up at the clock. It was six twenty.

Maybe he's eating dinner...I'll try again later.

He looked over his notes.

Loose ends. Lots of loose ends.

He decided to call Western Technical University.

"Registrar's Office, how can we help?"

Jack had to explain who he was to three separate people. He looked at the clock. One hour and he hadn't asked a question yet.

"Mr. Wellington's office, how can we help?" The woman on the other end of the line had an irritating singsong voice.

"How can you help? Miss, I have been on hold for over an hour. My name is Jack Stratton, and I'm calling concerning my sister Michelle Campbell. She supposedly transferred to your college but...she was killed." Jack heard the woman gasp. "Can you please answer a few questions about her transfer?"

"I'll certainly do whatever I can to help, sir."

"Her name is Michelle Campbell..."

"I'm looking at her transfer now, sir."

"Did she register for classes?"

"Yes. She signed up for a full course requirement."

"Did she sign up for housing?"

"No."

"Meal tickets?"

"No."

"Library access?"

"No."

"Anything besides the classes?"

"Not that I can see."

"How long does it take to get approved for classes?"

"Instantly."

Jack held the phone away from his head. "What? How can you get accepted to a college instantly?"

"Well, she's just transferring classes. We're a sister college. She can take any classes here that she wants."

"So she just signed up for classes there? She didn't transfer?"

"We're a sister college, so technically, yes."

Technically I'm going to strangle you.

"When did she apply for the classes?"

"December 20."

"How do you know that?"

There was a pause. "I know it because it's the date that's written on the form."

"Lady…" Jack's frustration was getting the better of him. "Is there a way you can tell when they electronically submitted the form?"

"Hold please."

"No."

Jack waited for over fifteen more minutes.

He looked back up at the clock. *What's it…four forty-two on the West Coast? I need this information today.* By the time the hold music stopped, he didn't know whether he'd be able to speak without swearing.

"Hey. You still there?" A young man spoke on the other end of the line.

"I'm on hold for…" *Damn. I don't have her name.*

"Are you the guy looking for the date on the form?"

"Yes."

"I'm from the computer help desk. How can I help?"

"Can you get a date…can you please tell me the date that Michelle Campbell signed up for those classes? Electronically. Not the date that's written on the form."

"Sure, dude. Hold on."

Jack could hear someone type in the background.

"The time stamp on the doc is December 20 at ten oh three p.m."

"Are you sure?"

"Yeah. The computer stamps it. I'm looking at the electronic time stamp. December 20 at ten oh three p.m."

She could have signed up herself while she was still at the school. Dead end…. Wait.

"You're talking Pacific Standard Time. Eastern would make it December 21, one o'clock a.m., one oh three a.m. here?"

"Yeah."

"I need a copy of that report."

CHAPTER THIRTY-FOUR

The Pit

Early in the morning the following day, Jack walked through the doors of the police station with a large folder in his hands. Even though his first shift back wasn't until later that afternoon, he had Replacement drop him off this morning. He stayed up half the night getting everything prepared to give to Collins. As he marched down the corridor, other police officers came over and patted him on the back or shook his hand. He hated the attention.

"Jack?"

He turned around just as Kendra crashed into him to give him a big hug. She wrapped her arms around his waist and pressed her cheek against his. Jack stood there with his hands at his sides.

"This is getting awkward," he joked after a couple seconds.

She stood back and tried to appear more stoic, but she was still beaming.

"When did you get back on?"

"Tonight. I have to see Collins first."

"He's out."

"How long is he out?" Jack groaned.

She shrugged. "Are you cleared to come back?"

"Healthy as a horse. I have a hard head."

"Everyone was worried about you. Did you get my flowers?"

Jack chuckled. "I did. Thanks. I have to go check in." He nodded down the hallway.

"Welcome back." Kendra started to open her arms as she moved in but caught herself. She gave him a quick shot in the arm and turned around.

"Not here? I didn't know he'd be gone," Jack complained.

The police secretary looked up at him and smiled. "I was not aware you were on the list of people to be informed of scheduling."

Jack exhaled and his lips pressed together.

"He's at the National Sheriff's Association Conference in Charlotte," she added and then swiveled around to her keyboard.

"When is he coming back?"

"He left Wednesday. I think it's a five-day conference. So, he should be back on Monday. He can be reached if it's an emergency." She looked up and stopped typing.

"Not exactly an emergency. Um, do you know when Joe Davenport is in?"

"Nine a.m." She went back to typing. "When he gets back."

"What?" Jack snapped.

"Detective Davenport is on vacation, a fishing trip to Canada." She continued to type, but she was striking the keys with more force now. "If you want a copy of the schedule, it's posted near the water cooler."

"Do you know when he'll be back?"

She stopped typing and swiveled back to glare at him. "It's posted on the schedule." She leaned forward and read his badge. "Officer Stratton. Detective Davenport will return on Saturday. If you—" She stopped and her eyes went wide. "Jack Stratton?"

Jack nodded.

"I'm so sorry. You should have said something. How are you?"

Said something? Yeah, I'm the guy who got hit by the car. Can you be nice and answer a simple question?

"Much better, thank you. I just need to speak to Collins or Joe."

The woman's hands went up and out. "Sheriff Collins checks his messages between meetings or you can text 911 if it's an emergency. Undersheriff Morrison is available, and Detective Flynn is covering for Detective Davenport. Can they help?"

Jack tapped the folder against the edge of the desk.

I'm screwed. I don't think Collins likes Morrison so much. I can't give it to Flynn after what happened. Joe's not back for two days.

"Thanks."

Jack shook his head and walked away.

Jack held the phone up to his ear, and he didn't have to wait. Davenport's voicemail picked up.

"Detective Joe Davenport. I'm currently unavailable. Detective Flynn can be reached by contacting…"

Jack hung up and tried Sheriff Collins. His message clicked on right away too.

"Sheriff Ethan Collins. I'll be in and out of conferences all day. If this is an emergency, text me and I'll call you back immediately. If not, then Undersheriff Morrison is covering and can be reached by contacting…"

He debated for a second and then hung up.

He called Detective Davenport again. "This is Officer Stratton. Can you give me a call when you get a chance? It's in regard to my sister's case. My number is…"

Jack had to force himself to put the phone down on the counter and not out the window.

Later that afternoon, Jack stood in the police parking lot again. He was still on the night shift, four to midnight. He shrugged.

At least getting hit by the car got me off traffic duty.

Jack's anger and frustration vanished for a moment when he saw the Charger was all his. He slid behind the wheel. When he turned it over, the engine purred as if it were glad to see him again.

He had the freedom to patrol where he wanted, within boundaries, and he let those boundaries bring him out of town and close to the college. He needed to clear his head. He needed speed.

He drummed the steering wheel as he waited to reach the back roads and open the Charger up.

"Ten-ten in progress at WRE," the dispatcher's voice said over the radio.

Jack heard the location and jumped for the radio.

"This is car sixty-eight. I'm north on Piedmont crossing Bridge Street."

"Ten-four, car sixty-eight. The location is Two Jefferson Avenue."

Jack hit the lights and sirens and punched it.

Two Jefferson Avenue was the address for the Pit, the campus bar at White Rocks. He settled back in the seat as adrenaline flowed along with the gas. He kept his foot down, and the Charger roared its approval.

Two campus police cars were parked outside the Pit, and a large crowd was already forming.

The Pit was in the basement of an old administration building the college had converted into a bar. As he walked up, it looked as though they'd set up some type of temporary triage at the picnic table outside. A couple of guys held bloody towels to their heads, and people chattered at them as Jack passed.

Chad Tucker, one of the campus cops, stood in the doorway and shook his head. He was busy trying to hold back Milton Anderson, another campus cop. Milton's nose was bloody, and he held a towel to his face.

"Chad, Milton, what's going on?" Jack inquired.

"Inside." Chad motioned with his head. "We got two guys with cuts and another one who may never have kids, if you know what I mean." He adjusted himself.

"What happened to you, Milton?" Jack looked at the tall, thin man who was trying to hold his head back to stop his bleeding nose.

"The psycho hit me in the face when I went to break up the fight." The towel muffled his voice.

"Show me who." Jack motioned to Chad.

Chad led the way but stopped at the door. Jack pushed by him as he descended the stairs and opened the front door. The Pit was never much on looks, but you could tell a good fight had taken place. Tables were overturned and in one corner, glass littered the floor.

Chad followed him in. "Careful, Jack. She doesn't look tough, but she's dangerous," he whispered.

"She?" Jack turned to look at him. "A girl did this?"

"Shh." Chad's eyes went wide, and he pointed as he moved behind Jack.

I'm so glad they don't give them guns.

Jack turned, and observed the girl who sat at the end of the bar facing away from them.

She's like five foot tall and a hundred pounds.

Jack shook his head as he walked closer. Chad followed just behind him.

"Excuse me, miss?" Jack held his hands out with the palms up.

The girl swung around on the stool. Jack gasped and stepped back on Chad's foot.

"Yes, sir?" Replacement said as her face contorted.

Jack just stood there with his mouth open.

Replacement was trying to convey something, but the sight of her had thrown him so he struggled to respond.

"Chad, I've got this. Go check on Milton," Jack ordered without turning around.

"You sure?"

Jack turned to glare at Chad, who quickly headed toward the door.

Replacement watched the campus cop walk away. "Don't say anything," she whispered.

"Don't say anything? What the hell are you doing? Did you kick the crap out of—"

"Shh, I'm undercover."

"You're…undercover? What the…?" Jack stammered.

Milton and Chad walked in.

"How come she's not in cuffs?" Milton demanded as he glared at Replacement.

Damn.

"Once I ascertain…what happened to this poor girl—"

"Poor girl?" Milton said. "I think she broke my nose."

Replacement let out an enormous wail and covered her face, sobbing. "I'm sorry. I thought you were one of them…one of the men who attacked me," she bawled.

"Attacked you?" Jack moved forward, anger now on his face. Replacement was hamming it up, but something had happened to her.

"Ken put something in my drink. Him and his friends." There was real anger and disgust on her face.

She'd never make that up about someone to get out of a bad situation.

"Bring them in but keep them separate," Jack demanded to Milton and Chad. "I'm speaking with the girl first." He took Replacement by the arm and led her across the large dance floor into a backroom.

"What the hell are you doing?" he whispered.

"I told you, I'm undercover." She glared back.

"Well, your cover is blown. What happened?"

"It's not blown. They don't know who I am." She crossed her arms and huffed. "I went to go talk to this guy, and Ken put something in my drink. It freaked me out."

"How do you know? Did you drink it?"

"I saw him do it, and he told me." She stamped her foot.

"What do you mean he told you?"

"We were over in that corner. I came back from the bathroom, and I saw Ken put something in my drink, and when I confronted him, he had the nerve to say, 'I *just* put in a little something to help you relax.'" Her hands turned into fists. "So I punched him in the face. Then his friends came up and tried to grab me, and I had the glass in my hand, so I whacked one with it."

Replacement acted it out. "The guy behind me had both my arms, but I pulled one free and he pushed me into the table. There was a beer bottle on it, so I grabbed it and hit him like this." She was relishing the moment as she mimed smashing a guy in the head with the bottle. "It didn't break, but he sure did scream."

Jack cringed. "What happened to Milton?"

"Who?"

"The campus police officer whose nose you broke."

"It's his fault. He snuck up behind me, grabbed me, and said, 'Settle down, girlie.' He didn't say he was a cop, and I didn't know until after I elbowed him in the face." She shrugged.

"Replacement—"

"Alexis." She corrected him.

"Who?"

"That's me." She smiled and pointed at herself. "My undercover name, Alexis Holmes."

"Will you forget about that for now? You're not undercover."

Jack walked her back into the bar and sat her at a table. Then he motioned for one of the guys. A tall man, around twenty, with a bloody towel pressed to his head walked forward.

He led the man into the backroom. Jack's face was hard as he shoved him into a chair.

"ID?" Jack waited for him to hand it to him.

Dillon Cole, twenty-one.

"Were you the guy who grabbed her from behind or came at her from the front?" Jack took out his notepad.

"What?" Dillon leaned forward. "No, you don't understand. I saw Ken get punched in the face, and I came over, and she hit me in the head with a drink."

"Listen, Dillon." Jack leaned in too. "What we have here is an underage girl who says you were part of a group of guys who tried to drug her."

His eyes went wide and his mouth flopped open. "I didn't know she was underage, and I had no idea Ken was going to do something like that. Honest. I wasn't even near him."

"Do you have any drugs?"

"No, nothing." He stood up and turned out his pockets.

"Did you see any of the other guys with drugs?"

Dillon nodded. "Ken said he got some Ecstasy or something to impress Alexis. She asked me if I had some drugs, but I don't do drugs. I don't even know where to get any. Honest."

Jack turned and called, "Chad?"

The young officer's head appeared.

"Stick this guy in the corner and send the next one in."

Another student walked in and slumped forward in the chair. Paul Denning, age twenty-two. Jack could see the bump on his head through the towel. The cut was small, but the bump was a whopping goose egg.

It might have been better for him if the bottle had broken, and he didn't get clubbed.

Paul's story matched Dillon's. Jack shook his head, pointed to the door, and waited for the final kid.

After a couple of minutes, Chad and Milton appeared. They were helping a guy in obvious pain through the door.

"Is this Ken?" Jack asked.

"Yes."

"Sit him down," Jack ordered. "Everyone else, clear out."

Jack looked down at his license.

Ken Fenton, twenty-one.

"What's your version of the events, Ken?"

"I met that crazy bit—" The look on Jack's face made him stop. "I was having a drink with Alexis, and she freaked out and smashed me in the face."

"Was this before or after you put drugs in her drink?" Jack's voice was as cold as his darkening eyes.

"What? I, I don't know—"

Jack put his face inches away from Ken's and glared. Jack didn't move. He didn't say a word. His eyes smoldered.

"It was Ecstasy. I asked. I asked her." Ken leaned away from Jack.

"You asked her?"

"I swear. I did. I told her it was in there."

"Why?"

"She wanted it."

"What did you say? You're saying she wanted you to drug her?" Jack grabbed the arms of the chair and shook it hard again. Ken's face contorted in pain.

"Crystal," he whined. "She kept asking for meth. I didn't know where to get any, but she was real insistent. I asked around, and this guy had some Ecstasy. I wanted to impress her. Before she went to the bathroom, she asked me if I could find some drugs. She said she wanted some. I just wanted to surprise her, so I put it in her drink. She must have seen me do it and misunderstand. I just wanted her to have fun and relax." Ken was on the verge of breaking down now.

Jack just glowered.

"Who was it that sold you the Ecstasy?"

"I don't really know him. I have seen him around campus. I think his name is Lennie."

"Lennie Jacobsen?"

He shrugged.

"When did you see him before?"

"Just around the school. He was in one of my computer classes. He's a little weird."

"What do you mean weird?"

"I mean that he doesn't look like a typical student. He's Goth and has long black hair."

"Can you point him out to me?" Jack gestured toward the door.

"Yeah, but I'm pretty sure he's gone. When I was outside and heard everyone start moaning that the cops were here, I saw him hop in a car and take off."

"What did the car look like?"

"It was silver."

"Do you know what kind of car it was?"

"No, no clue."

"What was Lennie wearing?"

"A black hooded sweatshirt and black jeans." Ken shifted in the chair.

"When did you get hit in the groin?" Jack tried to think of how to control this.

"After she hit Paul with the bottle, she walked over and kept kicking me."

"All right, go sit back there in the corner."

Jack walked back out and waved Replacement over.

"Listen to me, okay?" Jack hoped his tone conveyed the gravity of the situation. "Ken in there said you asked him to score meth for you. True or not true?"

She gave him a *duh* look. "I'm trying to find out how Michelle got meth in her system. I figure someone must have slipped it to her. If I can find out who—"

"So that's true."

"Yes, but—"

Jack held up a hand. "Listen. If I take him in, it will come out that you asked him and the other boys for drugs and it's going to turn into a he said/she said. Then your whole impersonating someone else is going to come out."

And I have to waste time on this when I have a solid lead to hunt down.

"But—"

"I think this whole thing was one misunderstanding after another, so do you really want me to arrest him?"

She scrunched up her face. "I guess not if it blows my cover. And I doubt he'll ever do it again." She grinned.

"Your cover? Get that smile off your face. You beat the snot out of three guys and broke Milton's nose. I have to figure out how not to arrest *you.*"

Jack walked her back out and looked at the three students and two campus policemen.

"Don't say anything," Jack whispered as he brought her back. "But cry…" She started to wail, so Jack quickly added, "A little. Cry a little."

Jack sat Replacement at a table in the middle of the room. He motioned for Milton and Chad to bring the boys over to the table.

"Milton, Chad, I'm going to try to contain this for your sake."

"Ours?" They both looked at each other.

"Right now I have an underage girl in *your* college bar accusing one of your students of providing her with illegal drugs, and she's alleging that you manhandled her and didn't disclose you were law enforcement." He raised an eyebrow toward Milton.

Milton looked away and muttered.

"But if it was all just a misunderstanding and no illegal drugs were visible," he glanced around the room, "then I'd be fine considering this just a mix-up. Unless, of course, you want me to file a report that she"—he pointed over to Replacement, who still pretended to cry—"gave you a bloody nose." He looked again at Milton. "And beat up the three of you." He glanced at the boys now. "We would then have to close the bar down indefinitely and then we will have to go through every drink here to determine if there were"—he looked at Ken—"any drugs on the premises. And that would lead to other charges."

The boys' and Milton's face turned different shades of crimson.

"So I believe this situation was due to 'misinterpretation' and may best be handled as a White Rocks matter." Jack exhaled as everyone relaxed at his words. "That's if no one requires medical attention?"

All of the students shook their heads and Chad chuckled under his breath. "We'll take it from here, Officer. Everyone is fine. It was a misunderstanding that will be addressed." Chad saluted Jack until Milton yanked the young man's hand down.

"Don't salute him, you twit," Milton snarled. "Yeah, we got it."

Everyone moved toward the door.

Jack walked out to the car, shaking his head. He needed to speak with Replacement, but it would have to wait. "Undercover?" he muttered to himself as his anger rose with each step.

What was she thinking?

As he started the car, the image of her in the coffin flashed in his head.

Wait until she gets home.

Jack spent the next couple of hours vainly driving around the campus to look for the silver car and Lennie Jacobsen.

CHAPTER THIRTY-FIVE

Stupid but Brilliant

Jack paced the floor and glanced at the clock. Twelve forty.

"Why isn't she home?" he muttered.

He stormed over to the window, yanked the curtain back and glared into the darkness. He grabbed his jacket and headed for the door.

When he reached in his jacket pocket, he stopped. He jammed his hand in the other pocket. With a snarl, he ripped his jacket off and beat it on the floor.

She has my car. I had to get a ride home from Donald.

Keys jingled in the lock, and he froze. The door slowly opened, and Replacement peered in.

"Get in...NOW," Jack's voice rumbled.

"I'm sorry." She stopped halfway in and held onto the doorknob.

"Get in here."

"You're mad." She came in with her head down and shut the door.

"No. I'm way beyond mad. They need to come up with a new word for just how angry I am." He stalked forward.

"I had to." Her head snapped up, and she glared at him.

It was exactly the wrong way to handle Jack at that moment.

He exploded forward, and his hand slammed into the doorframe to stop himself. Wood cracked.

"Three people are dead. Three. You're hunting a monster, yet you don't have a clue. Are you that stupid? Do you have any idea what Chandler would say to you?"

She burst into tears and shook her head. "No," she whispered and huddled against the door.

"He'd tell you that you were out of your mind for what you just did. If it was any other cop, they would have arrested you. You assaulted a police officer. You solicited drugs. Do you know what Chandler would say? He'd say just what I'm saying."

Jack towered over her, and she slid down the wall and pulled her legs up. She was sobbing.

"No." She shook her head. "Chandler never yelled at me."

Jack turned and took four steps away. "Don't. Don't turn this around on me. I'm not Chandler. He would...he'd handle it. I don't know what he would have done." He stormed over to the bedroom. "Don't leave the apartment EVER AGAIN," he yelled and slammed the door.

After tossing and turning for two hours, Jack opened the bedroom door. Replacement was asleep on the couch, curled up in a ball. The comforter had fallen off onto the floor. He picked it up and glared down at her. He fanned the comforter out and gently laid it over her.

Replacement's eyes fluttered open, and she sat up.

"Jack, I'm so sorry." She gathered the comforter tightly around her.

"I, I shouldn't have yelled. You're right. Chandler wouldn't have yelled. I was…upset. I don't want anything to happen to you."

She nodded.

"We need to get one thing straight."

"I can't leave the apartment." She bowed her head.

"No. That was stupid to say. But this whole undercover thing is done."

Replacement took a large breath.

Jack held up his hand. "I'm not arguing." He gave her a look.

She started to speak again.

"Wait." He walked over and picked up his notebook and pen. "Start at the very beginning. How did you get into the college?"

She tossed the comforter off and jumped up. "Getting into WRE was sort of easy. I already had an alias. Alexis Holmes. I've had it for like two years."

"How did you get it?" Jack paused and sat down in the chair at the computer.

"The lady from youth services wrote all her log-in information on a folder she left at the house. I figured I'd just make someone up to see if I could. I was just messing around. I figured I'd just keep it if I ever needed it. Well, I needed it."

"How did you get into the college?"

"When we went to the campus security office, and you were talking to Neil Waters, I saw May's log-in. She had full access to the college computer system."

"You didn't tell me?" Jack was too surprised to be angry.

"I didn't know if I could get into either of the systems until after…after you were in the hospital." She started to move forward and stopped. "I made a push after that. I got into the college's system, so I just made myself a student. I don't think I could take it to graduation or anything, but I got into classes and passes and all that stuff."

He looked up. "Why did you leave me out?"

"Jack, you'd lose everything. You told me about what your boss said."

"I won't lose my job. I don't care if I do." Jack grabbed her by the shoulders. "Did you think about you? What could happen to you? I have training. I have a gun. What do you have?"

"Nothing to lose."

They both stared at each other for a minute before Jack continued. "If you ever pull something like that on me again…" His anger rose as he struggled for the words.

"I won't," she whispered. "I promise."

He hugged her.

It was stupid. She could have gotten herself killed. No. Not stupid…fearless. Like her brother.

He held her for a moment and let himself relax. Replacement's hand moving at the small of his back felt good. He closed his eyes and embraced her.

She feels good.

She made the slightest sound. It was a faint, soft moan. Jack sat bolt upright and held her at arm's length.

"Did you find out anything?" He picked up his notebook as a barrier between them and scooted back in his seat.

"Not too much." She scrunched up her face.

"You getting into the college was brilliant. Stupid but brilliant."

Her smile vanished. "That's dumb. How can I be stupid and brilliant?"

"Not you…what you did. It wasn't stupid, but it was dangerous. Three people are dead. This isn't a game."

She nodded.

"Have you seen any drug use around campus?"

Her hands balled into fists. "Besides that spineless—"

"Besides him." Jack nodded.

"Not really. I haven't been out much. Besides the bar, I had a couple of study dates…" Her eyes widened, and she looked up at him as though she were caught doing something wrong.

Jack cocked an eyebrow. "Do you know a Lennie Jacobsen?"

"No, never heard of him."

"He was at the bar tonight. He was dressed in Goth. He has long hair and was wearing a black sweatshirt with black jeans."

"No, I never noticed him. Wait a minute. A Goth? I think I've seen a guy with dyed long black hair hanging around the school."

Jack pulled out the mug shot photo.

"Yeah, that's him. I've seen him in the computer lab."

"The lab on the second floor of the psych center where Michelle worked?"

"No, the one at the student union."

"Did you see him with anybody?"

"No, he was just sitting there by himself."

Jack stared down at the picture with a look of hatred.

"Is there anything else you can remember?" He gritted his teeth.

Replacement paused for a moment, and then shook her head. "Do you think he was involved?"

Jack flung up his hands. "I don't know. After what just happened at the Pit, Lennie is probably going to go into hiding."

"Sorry."

Jack continued with his semi-interrogation. "Have you had any classes with Dr. Hahn?"

"I think he's boring. He was great in the class, but you get him in the lab? He's cold. Like Spock or a robot. And he's super focused. Everyone has to be quiet. No sound. Nothing." She rolled her eyes, and Jack suppressed a smile.

She must have had quite a time trying to be silent.

"Have you talked to him one-on-one?" Jack was taking notes and trying to reference his old ones, so pages of his notebook flew back and forth.

"Nope."

"What about Dr. Franklin?"

"I don't have him for class, but I have seen him. Rumor is he hits on the girls. I heard he's married, but he takes his wedding ring off before class. Nice."

"Have you talked with him?"

"No. I've only seen him. People say he's a nutcase."

"How so?"

"I heard a guy say he can be charming one minute and then flip out the next. A girl in my psych class said he's a few fries short of a Happy Meal."

"Are you out at the center a lot?"

"All the time. If we're not in a class there, we're in the lab. It's a super pain."

"Are you ever there late?"

"No. We have to go by seven, but we start early. We have to do a mountain of homework. One of the grad students has been helping me."

"Who?"

"Just a guy. His name's Brendan."

"Phillips?" Jack's eyes narrowed.

"Yeah. How did you know his last name?" She stopped pacing and looked at him.

Jack didn't look back.

"He only helped me study."

"I met him when I went to go on the tour. He's the pretty boy who showed me around. How did he seem? What read did you get?"

She shrugged. "He seems nice."

"Hold up. He's Dr. Hahn's assistant, right?"

"Yes. He's going for his doctorate or something. He teaches one of my classes."

"He had a blue security card. Does that get him into the computer room?"

"I don't know. I knew he was Hahn's assistant; that's why I picked him. He has access to the other parts of the building. He likes to show off, as if he's a bigwig. I'm working on getting closer to him."

Jack's eyes narrowed. "Was…I mean you *were*. You're not anymore."

Replacement's grip tightened on the comforter.

"What about Missy Lorton, Michelle's roommate? I thought she wasn't telling us the whole story. Did you find anything out about her?"

"Fat thief?" Replacement spat. "She took some of Michelle's stuff. A box of it. I think that's what she was hiding."

"How do you know?" Jack stopped writing.

Replacement rolled her eyes. "Come on. I'm undercover. I can do that, right?"

Jack sat back. "Do what?"

Replacement's shoulders popped up and down. "I peeked."

"Peeked? Did you…did you break into her apartment?"

"It isn't breaking in since I'm undercover."

"You're not undercover. You have no right…even undercover." He could feel the blood rush to his face.

"I didn't take anything so I wouldn't contaminate the crime scene." Replacement gave Jack her "that explains it all and everything is okay" look.

"You made it a crime scene. It's called breaking and entering."

"She made it first. It's called fat-jerk-stealing."

"Stop. Okay?" Jack rubbed the sides of his head before he continued. "You didn't take Michelle's box, then?"

"No."

"Did you see what was in it?"

"No, it's just a big box of Michelle's stuff. Tubby must have wanted it. Can I get it back now?" Her lip trembled, and she looked down at her hands. "It's all…it's all I have left of Michelle."

Jack melted. "I'll get it. I promise." He put his hand on her shoulder.

She leaned her head onto his hand and closed her eyes.

"Thank you," she whispered and then her eyes snapped open. "Nothing I'm doing is going to get you in trouble, right?" Her eyes rounded in concern.

"Trouble?" Jack stuck his lower lip out and shook his head. "Nah, you've pretty much blown up my life. What more trouble could you cause?"

"Are you serious?" She grabbed his arms. "Don't say that. You're good, right?"

"I'm good. It's not your fault. Look. I've gone at this the wrong way. From the beginning, I should have gone to Collins, but I didn't." Replacement started to speak, and Jack held up both his hands. "Joe Davenport is…damn it. I forgot to try him again. I wonder why he didn't—" He looked down at his phone: two missed calls. "My phone rang, and I didn't hear it? Stupid thing. Smart phone my ass."

"Let me see." She took the phone from him. The sound of a dog barked out. "It's working."

"What the hell was that?"

"Your new ringtone. I thought it fit you better than that old grandpa one you had."

"You messed with my phone?"

"No." She shook her head. "I just updated it into the *twenty-first century*." She waved the phone over her head. "If you can't even change your ringtone, how am I going to start getting you to use a computer instead of a notebook?"

"You won't. Don't change my phone and *don't* try to change me."

"Fine."

Jack paused and rubbed his eyes with his thumb and index finger. "I'm going to Joe and give him everything."

"But you'll lose your job." Replacement's shoulders slumped.

"I might and I might not."

I might wish I had.

"Either way, we know someone who has access to the center has killed at least three people: Charlie, Tiffany and…" He hesitated. "We know that Michelle didn't apply for a transfer because the transfer went through on December 21 at one a.m."

"What?"

"I didn't tell you? I called Western Tech. They're a sister college, so you just have to apply for the classes and you can do that online. Someone just filled in December 20 on Michelle's form. I called and found out the time stamp on the application was December 21 at one oh three a.m."

"Michelle was already…at the reservoir. That was at twelve thirty. Someone else submitted it. But—" Replacement looked away.

"But what?"

Her mouth opened, and she looked at the ceiling as she thought of what he just said. "If it was electronic, then they'll be able to tell the IP too. It will say what computer it came from. Move."

Replacement shoved Jack out of the chair as she handed him back his phone.

As she logged in, Jack moved over to the window and pressed buttons on the phone.

"I kept thinking I was hearing dogs barking all night," he muttered to himself.

"What're you saying?"

He shook his head. "Nothing."

"If you can just sign up for classes at Western Tech, then WRE and their system are linked. I didn't even think about it. I'm a dork. I should be able to get into their system too."

Jack watched in amazement as Replacement's slender fingers sped across the keyboard. They were a blur. Every couple of seconds she'd huff or shake the mouse as she waited for a screen to catch up with her commands.

"Got the IP." She hopped up and down in the chair.

"Will that tell you the computer they used?"

Her fist smacked the desk. "No. It's the forward facing IP of the psych center."

"Can you translate that geek-speak back into English?"

"Every computer has an IP address, but if you connect in a building, all of those addresses can get funneled together for security and then go out as one IP. That's what they do at the psychology center. This IP is the address that covers the whole building."

"But you're sure it came from there?"

"A hundred percent."

"Now we're a hundred percent sure it's someone who has access to the building and the computers there."

"But we don't know who. Do you have any ideas?"

"Yeah. I'm going to go back out there tomorrow and talk to Dr. Franklin. He's like Dr. Meth. He also knew two of the victims. There's also Hahn."

"Hahn?"

"Well, he's in charge of the center. The person in charge either knows everything or nothing." Jack sighed and ran his hand through his hair. "It could also be a student or a janitor. I need to find this Lennie kid, but right now Franklin is the best fit. He also knows how to cook meth."

"I couldn't get meth anywhere. It must be tough to find."

Jack tried to hide his smirk. He faked a cough.

"Can you give me more time?" She pouted and made a begging face. "Before you go tell Davenport?"

"No. We have a lot. We have enough for them to get a warrant."

"Jack, do you remember that guy at the funeral who talked about Michelle tracking him down when he stole her bike? Michelle was like that. She didn't give up. Michelle found the video of that poor guy. I bet she found it in the psychology center."

Jack paced back and forth. "She was overhauling the computer systems, so she'd have had access to everything."

"If Michelle found that video, she'd have kept digging," Replacement said. "There's no way to log in to the center from the outside. She'd have had to go there."

"That's why Michelle was there so late?" Jack stared at the floor.

"She was looking for more information. I'm trying to get into the computers there right now."

"How are you going to get in? Don't you have access already?"

"No. The lab computers are completely separate from the college system. I used a student's account that has limited access, so I wrote a Trojan."

"A what?"

"A Trojan. I named a file 'SuperHotPornBabes.' The antivirus program will flag it and move it to a holding folder. Most computer administrators are horny computer geeks, and when they see that title, they'll want to see what it is. Once they run it, it will run under their permission. Get it? It will run with administrator rights, and it will create another admin account for me."

"I got about half of that. You wrote a program that will give us access?"

"Yeah."

"Did it work?"

"Not yet. I only put it on today so I'm hoping I get a hit by tomorrow, but I have to go there to log in."

"No way. Could you talk me through getting into the system?"

Replacement shook her head. "I can't get you to use your phone. No. If you let me, I can be in and—"

"No. Then that's off the table. I have the next two days off. I'm going to the campus in the morning by myself. Do you need the car?"

Replacement turned back to the computer. She whispered, "No."

CHAPTER THIRTY-SIX

Pendulum

Jack's phone woke him: Bark, Bark, Bark.

Stupid ringtone.

"Hello?"

"Jack? Undersheriff Morrison. Can you meet me down at the morgue?"

Jack straightened up. "Yes, sir. How soon?"

"How soon can you get here? It's eight now—let's say eight thirty?"

"Yes, sir."

Damn.

Jack wouldn't have time for a shower. He shaved and brushed his teeth. He was going to head to the college later so he dressed in black slacks, a gray sweater, and black shoes. He tossed his toothbrush into the sink and rushed into the living room. He scanned the area for his coat and grabbed it from the door.

Replacement was looking out the window and jumped when he walked into the room. "Are you going out?"

"Yes. I just got a call to go and meet the undersheriff at the morgue."

"Undertaker?"

"No. The guy who's next in line to Collins is called the undersheriff."

"Yeah, um…I was going to run a couple of errands."

"Sorry, kid, but I need the car. I can drive you when I get back."

"It's not far. I'll just walk, okay?" Replacement bit her lip but didn't say anything else.

Jack eyed her as he ran out the door. He hurried to the Impala. As he pulled out, he looked up to see Replacement was still standing at the window. He sped down the street and pulled onto the main road as a silver car took a right down his street.

The black tiled room felt like a crypt. He hated it even more than the hospital.

Jack stood next to Robert Morrison, a tall, African-American man in his late fifties. Morrison wore the tan uniform of the sheriff's department without the hat. His curly black hair was short and graying at the temples.

A petite woman dressed in a white hospital coat stood behind a stretcher with a corpse laid out on it.

"That's him."

"You sure?" Morrison asked.

Jack nodded. He looked down at Bennie the Goon's corpse. His face was heavily bruised, especially around the jaw where Jack broke it, but he was sure it was Bennie.

Morrison nodded, and the woman pulled the sheet back over the corpse.

"Did he have anything on him, Mei?" Morrison addressed her.

"Just these." She adjusted her rectangular blue and pink glasses and moved over to a metallic cart.

Jack looked down at the items: a crushed package of cigarettes, a fast-food receipt, three quarters, and a scrap of paper smeared with black ink.

"Looks like he had to bum a light," Morrison pointed out. "No lighter."

Jack leaned down so he could read what was on the scrap of paper.

"It looks like an address," Mei offered as she smiled sweetly at Jack.

"It is." He smiled back. "It's mine."

Morrison's eyes narrowed. "You never saw him before that night?"

"No. I noticed him when I came out of my apartment and he started following me."

"Thanks, Mei." Morrison turned to go.

The two men walked out of the cold room into a slightly warmer hallway. Morrison took out a pack of gum and handed Jack a piece.

"You'd just been clipped by the drunk driver, right?" Morrison pondered out loud.

Jack nodded.

"And you hurt your leg. You still have a little limp; how's it feeling?"

The observation took Jack aback. "It's much better, sir."

"You can save the sir stuff for Collins. Call me Bob." Jack gave him a short nod of respect before Bob continued, "Anyway, is it *possible* that maybe the guy thought you were an easy mark?"

Jack bristled at the comment and straightened up.

Bob looked at him and chuckled. "Then again, maybe not."

"They have no cause of death yet?" Jack looked back into the room.

"Preliminarily, it's an OD."

"Mei said they found him out behind a motel, but she didn't say what motel," Jack said.

Bob stuck two more pieces of gum in his mouth. "Imperial Motor Lodge."

"Are you sure?"

"There's only one Imperial."

But now we have two bodies found there.

"Okay. Thank you for letting me know, sir," Jack said.

Morrison's phone rang. "Morrison." He listened for a second. "Listen, I'll be over as soon as I can." He hung up. "Fatal car accident on the highway, two semi tractors."

Jack nodded his head.

"Jack?"

"Yes"

Morrison's voice got even deeper. "We have to have a conversation."

"Yes, sir?"

"I've been doing this too long to think that two close calls in short order don't warrant closer attention. Do you think they're related?"

Jack scratched his neck and looked down the hallway before he admitted, "Yes sir, I do."

"If you have any ideas, now's the time to speak up." Morrison eyed Jack for a moment before he continued. "I don't know you that well, Stratton, but all I can say is…trust your gut. If you think I'm the type of guy who's going to jam you up or throw you under the bus, shut your mouth. If you think you can trust me, tell me what you've got, and we'll take it from there." Morrison turned his hands out.

"Sheriff Collins is by the book. I don't want to get jammed up, but someone has to know, now."

"I'm not Collins."

Jack brought Morrison up to speed. He laid everything out. Morrison cracked his gum occasionally but remained silent.

"Okay, you have this video?"

"Yes, sir. The guys in the IT lab have it. They also have the password. I don't know if they've looked at it yet." Jack clenched and relaxed his hands.

"If the guys at the lab haven't seen the video yet *then neither have you*," Morrison pointed out. "Chain of custody is already gone with the phone, but it's explainable given the circumstances. Davenport is back tomorrow. I'll call the lab and the forensic people, and we'll all sit down first thing in the morning."

"Yes sir," Jack replied.

"Do you have any idea who at the college it could be?" Morrison asked.

"Nothing definite."

"Okay, we'll go over it all then."

Jack shook his hand, and Morrison's phone rang again. "Yes, I'm on my way." He nodded back to Jack and then he headed out the door.

Jack turned to go.

"Officer Stratton?" Mei ran around the corner after him.

"Yes?"

"Oh, I'm glad I caught you." She smiled up at him and adjusted her glasses. "We found a baggie with some money hidden in his left shoe and a small piece of torn stock paper."

Jack looked down at the evidence bag. The piece of paper was about two inches by one inch. It was off-white paper and one edge was jagged where it had been ripped. The only thing on it was the printed letters "lin."

Not much to go on.

"Thanks." Jack nodded. "Can you make sure that gets over to Undersheriff Morrison's office first thing in the morning?"

"Of course." She grinned.

"Well, goodbye."

She nodded her head and watched him leave.

Jack eased back on the gas as the Impala swung into the turn. The veins stood out on his neck, and he had a stranglehold on the steering wheel. Bennie the Goon had been his best lead. *Best living lead.* He could have led Jack to whoever hired him to watch his apartment. Now he was dead.

No money to follow. They'd have paid him in cash. And what would he have gotten? For fifty bucks, he'd have watched my place all day and night.

Jack was still bothered. It felt as if something was about to break. He'd felt that way before.

Weird.

He was apprehensive, as though time was slipping away.

Think, Jack, think: a crushed package of cigarettes, typical. Fast-food receipt, could be nothing but maybe he met someone there. The money, nothing unusual about that. The scrap of paper, stock paper...card stock...why would a junkie have—

"Business card," he shouted.

Jack watched the Impala's speedometer rise as he headed toward the college. The three letters clicked into place.

His hand pushed a Johnny Cash CD into the player. "God's Gonna Cut You Down" blared over the speakers as he flew out to the psychology center. The ride took fifteen minutes. He went through "Walk the Line," "It Ain't Me Babe," and "Busted." "Ring of Fire" was just finishing as he pulled into the parking lot.

Jack combed his fingers through his hair as he walked into the center and smiled at the blonde behind the counter.

She leaned forward and looked Jack up and down. "How can I help you?"

Jack grinned. "I'm here to see Dr. Franklin."

"Is he expecting you? He's in class right now."

"I just have a quick question. Is he in the new classroom upstairs?" He was guessing. "Can you show me?" He leaned in close and smiled.

"I can't leave the desk." She shrugged and leaned closer.

"That was room..."

"Two ten," she said.

"I'll only be a second. Be right back."

"You have to sign in...and you can't go unescorted," she called out.

"It's our secret." He winked and hurried up the stairs but the girl still reached for a phone.

Jack took the stairs two at a time without looking back. When he reached the top, he turned right and looked for the classroom. He scanned the room roster next to the doors. "Psychology Classroom 210." There was a rear door farther down the hallway that he headed to. He tried the handle on that door and then slipped into the room.

It was smaller than Jack expected. It would hold about fifty students, but thirty or so were there now. Dr. Franklin stood behind a large wooden desk. In his early fifties, he was tall with sandy brown hair that was on the long side but pulled back. Tweed jacket, jeans, and round glasses finished off the professor look.

Franklin was reading out a list of different topics: "Astrocytes, cluster, dopamine..." He was going down a list of possible topics for assignments.

"The parts of the Pleasure Pathway." Franklin leaned up and smiled at a young girl in the front row. "Once we're done, come up and pick up the list of possible topics. Your assignment will be a pro and con, not a right or wrong, nor a this or that. Short. Four pages."

Jack looked down as the student in front of him raised his hand.

"We can pick anything on the list?"

Franklin looked at the ceiling and sighed mockingly. "That's why I'm providing the list." The girl in the front giggled. "I want you to pick a subject and give a view on that subject and then select an opposing or differing view. For example, if you selected dopamine, you could write about its function in the Pleasure Pathway versus the view of its role with motivational or motor function. Or if I said nucleus accumbens, you could say…" He pointed to a young man in the front row who shifted in his seat.

"Um…right lobe?" he stuttered.

"Right lobe? And…?" Franklin inquired.

The student cleared his throat and settled back in his seat. He cast a glance at the girl seated next to him, and she smiled. Jack leaned onto the desk.

This should be good.

The young man started to speak. "I have been thinking about the connection between the nucleus accumbens and the right lobe and the theory that there's a connection between the two as far as spirituality…" He hesitated as Franklin walked around the podium and approached him. "Some theorize, and I concur, that, according to—"

The young man stopped speaking as Franklin came to a stop directly in front of his desk.

"You concur? Mr. …?"

"Ross."

"Mr. Ross concurs." Franklin held his hands out to the class, and nervous laughter flitted around the room. "And must I assume that you're taking The Effects of Trauma on the Brain this semester?"

Ross gulped and nodded.

Franklin exhaled and walked the length of the room. "For those not so privileged to be taking Dr. Hahn's class, please enlighten us with a brief preview of your synopsis."

The girl who sat next to Ross reached out and squeezed his arm.

He straightened up, puffed out his chest, and addressed the class. "We have been discussing how the nucleus accumbens produce pleasure and how it works in the reward pathway. In this process, the neurotransmitter dopamine is released, and I think there may be a link between that and the front right lobe—"

"EUREKA," Franklin shouted so loudly that everybody jumped in their seats and turned to look at him. "Mr. Ross has done it. He has accomplished what countless before him have strived for. He has discovered…" He mockingly and dramatically raised his hands above his head. "The God Spot."

Franklin clapped and walked back toward the shrinking student.

"Mr. Ross, the problem with your conclusion is—it's wrong." He leaned forward and flipped Ross's closed notebook back open. "Perhaps you should write this down."

He turned and smiled at the girl next to Ross, and she turned and stared at her desk.

"For years, scientists have been looking for a certain part of the brain. The God Spot, as it's sometimes called, is the area of the brain that's responsible for spirituality. I say this with the highest regard for Dr. Hahn, but for the twenty years he has spent looking for that one spot, he has been digging in the wrong place."

Franklin looked around the room, but most students peered down instead of meeting his eyes.

"Others, like myself or Dr. Melding, believe that it isn't one, but many spots. There have been many studies regarding this. Several have been performed in this university. Various methods have been employed to locate it."

He walked to stand before the girl who sat with her head in her hands and ogled him.

"They have tried love, meditation, happiness, fear. None have worked." He sauntered back over in front of Ross. "I have myself researched this exact topic you have selected for your paper. My study took the opposite path of the one that you concur with. In my humble opinion, it would be relatively easy to prove through the mapping of dopamine release that it isn't one spot but many spots." He leaned in and emphasized the words.

As Franklin turned to go back to the podium, he leered at the girl seated next to Ross. Jack shook his head as the student inhaled.

"Easy? Then why haven't you proved—"

Kid, you should have stayed down. It's a no-win fight.

"Why?" Franklin's hand crashed down on the podium, and he spun around. "Knowing and proving are totally separate. If they—" The professor grabbed the sides of the podium and inhaled. Jack could see his knuckles turn white as his hands clutched the wood. "I digress." When Franklin continued, his voice was calm but cold. "I await reading and *grading* your paper with bated breath."

Franklin sneered and Ross deflated.

"The assignment is due next class. As always, thank you." Franklin's attention turned to the girl in the front row who hopped up and rushed to his desk.

The rest of the students stood, and Jack wove his way to the front of the classroom. The young girl now turned back and forth and giggled. She kept leaning into the doctor, who was more interested in looking down at the view her low-cut blouse gave him.

Jack waited. Dr. Franklin looked up and frowned. So did the girl. She picked up her books, gave Jack a dirty look, and stomped past him.

"Dr. Franklin? Jack Stratton." Jack smiled. The doctor didn't.

"Yes?" He looked past Jack, leering at the girl as she walked out of the classroom.

"I have a couple quick questions for you."

Scumbag.

"I have another class. Can you get the notes from another student?" Franklin turned back to his desk.

"I spoke with Mike Leverone—"

Franklin's hand slammed down on his desk with such force that everyone left in the room turned and stared.

Damn. I should have said Hank Foster.

The doctor's voice was clipped and rapid fire. "Mike Leverone making his own meth lab and blowing his face off had nothing to do with me. Who are you? Get out."

That was a mistake. Take it down.

"I didn't say you had anything to do with it. I just need to ask you—"

"You need to get out of my classroom. Are you a lawyer? I'll call security." He turned and walked toward Jack.

Jack shook his head and held up his hands. "You have it wrong. I'm here for your professional opinion. I'm a police officer and I'm looking at a missing person case. I've spoken with a few different people who recommended I speak with you, including Hank Foster."

Franklin stood there and glared at Jack and then it was as if someone flipped a switch. He smiled. "My apologies, Jack. The situation with Mr. Leverone was…traumatic for me as an educator. You said you're a police officer? You're working a missing person's case? I don't see how I could be of any assistance with that."

"I'm looking for a girl who did meth. One time."

Franklin frowned and looked at Jack with a mixture of scorn and pity. "People don't do meth one time."

"They do if they die."

"That's a trick question then." The doctor's lips pressed together.

"The question I had is, how does meth influence someone the first time they take it psychologically?" Jack added the word *psychologically* at the last second to try to hook the doctor back into the conversation.

"Another trick question. There are too many variables and too many inconsistencies. What's the person like physically? Tall? Short? Fat? Thin? What's their emotional state? The drug? What's the mixture? How much? How taken? I could go on and on. A trick question again." Once more his hand came down on his desk.

This guy is way off the reservation.

"Doctor, thank you for explaining the complexity of how meth affects people. Since there are so many variables, how do you figure them out? You mentioned in class just now there are research studies."

"There have been a number of studies on the effects of meth and the mind, including my own. My personal study has been placed in a status of indefinite hold thanks to the aforementioned Mr. Leverone."

"That's unfortunate—"

"You've no idea of the hours wasted, not just mine, but my students'. The whole study was frozen, just like that. Now the data is useless. You can't just pause a study. Gone. All of that research is gone."

"Doctor, for the test subjects, did you accept volunteers?"

"Of course. We don't pay more than a small stipend, if anything, but…" His eyes widened and his nostrils flared. "This supposed missing person case…who? Who's missing?" Dr. Franklin pointed a finger at Jack.

This guy may be on meth. He's wacko.

"I can't divulge—"

"Get out. Now. I have a class." He took two steps toward Jack.

Talk him down.

"Doctor, I'm sorry I imposed. I just have one more question. Do you know a Lennie Jacobsen?"

"Yes…no…maybe. I have so many students," he spouted as his head shook. "Get out." He waved a hand at Jack.

"Thank you for your time. You've been very insightful." Jack forced a smile.

Franklin looked confused for a second and then smiled. "I'm so glad I could be of assistance. I have another class. You can make an appointment, and we can discuss this further. Good day." He turned his back on Jack and arranged his desk.

Jack headed for the door and slipped past some more students coming in.

That guy isn't right in the head.

Jack ran his hands through his hair and exhaled.

I shouldn't have opened with Mike Leverone. Of course it would get him upset.

Jack wove through the groups of students who headed to their classes. He stomped down the stairs and stormed out the door. One look at his smoldering eyes and the snarl on his lips caused the students coming toward him to move aside. He jumped into his Impala and gunned it out of the lot.

The Impala didn't hug the curves like the Charger and Jack kept having to slow down.

Tomorrow. I'll talk to Morrison and have him look at Franklin. The doctor is a lunatic. I think he's taking meth himself. He's his own research subject...

Jack pulled over.

Research subject. Charlie Harding. Was that torture...or research?

CHAPTER THIRTY-SEVEN

Box Full of Memories

Jack paced back and forth in his apartment as he waited for Replacement. He looked at the clock. Six o'clock.

He walked over and checked his phone. *Nothing. No word from her.* He tossed it down on the counter next to Replacement's note.

She said she's running errands. She has no car so she must have gone downtown. Get a grip, Jack.

As he headed for the window, the phone rang. He reached the counter and hit answer before the first ring stopped.

"Hey. Where are you?"

There was a pause.

Jack checked the number. He didn't recognize it. "Hello?"

"I'm looking for Jack Stratton." It was a girl's voice.

"That's me."

"This is Missy Lorton. Can we talk?"

"Certainly. Where are you?"

"My apartment. I'm not in trouble, am I?"

"You're off to a good start at getting out of any trouble by calling."

"I…I kept some of Michelle's things. I want to give them back."

"Okay. You're at your apartment now? I can be there right away," Jack said.

"I'll wait here." Click.

He gathered up his jacket, keys, and gun as fast as his leg would allow, and two minutes later raced to the college.

Stop by Missy's. Get Michelle's things for Replacement. Michelle may have said something to her, too. Something that Missy didn't want to share before. I can lean on her now. Not too hard; she's a crier.

Jack tried Replacement again, but she didn't pick up her phone.

Damn.

Jack parked right outside Missy's apartment. This time she immediately buzzed him in. He hurried up to the third floor and knocked. Missy opened the door. Her face was splotchy, and her eyes were red.

"Thank you for calling, Ms. Lorton."

"I don't want to be in trouble." She was hard to understand, garbling the words while she tried to hold back tears.

Crier. Not too hard.

"I do have some additional questions."

Missy nodded and moved into the apartment. "I'll get the box. I need a tissue." She hurried down a little hallway and through a door at the end.

Jack walked into the apartment. It looked as if she still didn't have a roommate; half of the apartment was still empty.

"I'm sorry I kept some of her stuff." Missy called from what Jack assumed was her bedroom. "I just…I thought that she was throwing it out. What's going to happen to me?" She came back into the room and placed a large cardboard box on an end table in the living room.

"Ms. Lorton. Can you tell me anything about Michelle on December 20? Did she say where she was going that night?" Jack opened the box.

"No. She just left."

"She didn't mention anything about going to the psychology center?"

"How do you know she was out there?"

"I spoke with Dr. Hahn about it. Are you familiar with the psychology center, Miss Lorton?"

Jack looked into the box. There were some clothes and a pair of shoes on top.

To Replacement, these things will mean the world.

"Yeah. I take some classes there."

"Did Michelle talk to you about transferring?"

"Yes. She was terribly excited about it." Missy leaned against the wall.

Lie. She also said he told her about Michelle transferring before.

As Jack lifted out a blanket, he heard a faint click behind him. He shot bolt upright and started to push to the right, but it was too late. A Taser's barbs embedded in his side and the electricity froze his muscles, but he didn't drop.

He'd been shot with a Taser in training before, so he knew he could ride this wave of pain. Whoever shot it had made the mistake of being too close to Jack when they fired. The prongs need to have distance between them to affect the most muscle groups, but they were too close together.

It's a knockoff civilian model. A ten-second burst, and then it's my turn.

Jack bellowed when the second Taser hit him. His muscles seized, and he pitched forward. As he lay writhing on the floor, someone ran up and placed a wet cloth over his face.

Jack's vision blurred, and a chemical smell filled his nose. He fought, but he knew it was a losing battle. The blackness rushed up to envelop him, and he toppled into the abyss.

CHAPTER THIRTY-EIGHT
Under the Rocks

Jack woke and opened his eyes a fraction to check out his situation. What he saw didn't look good. Thick leather straps bound his arms and legs to a hospital stretcher.

Just like Charlie Harding.

He pulled against the restraints, but they held him fast. His head pounded. He was in some kind of medical room. As he looked up, he saw the large circular machine above his head, which told him exactly where he was, even before he saw the control booth.

The center.

Through the large viewing window in the middle of the wall, he could see Missy in the control booth. She talked with someone just out of his view. The conversation seemed quite animated.

Slowly he moved his head, and he could see the edge of the heavy door on the right wall. Jack tried to remember the layout of the lab on the bottom floor of the psychology center. He remembered a corridor ran along that wall.

Jack closed his eyes so they were slits and he tested the restraints. He'd seen people restrained many times. These straps were leather; there would be no breaking them. His wrists were fastened, and a strap went over his legs. Anger rose up in him, and he tried to drive it away.

Stay calm. Remember your training. You're a cop. Try to get them talking.

The door swung open, and he heard someone walk into the room from the right. A chair scraped on the floor, and the person sat down next to the stretcher.

"Hello, Jack."

"Brendan." Jack buried his anger and his voice was steady.

"You surprise me, Jack. You're so calm. Did they teach you that in the Army? You're a soldier, right? You served with Michelle and Alice's brother in Iraq." Brendan smiled.

Jack's rage seethed back to the surface.

He knows about Alice. Bluff.

"So you figured out that you're under investigation? The police have been looking—"

"Very good." Brendan chuckled. "You're clever. You should have gone into acting, Jack. But you've got it all wrong. You see, you were the one under investigation. I've known all about you and Alice for a while."

Jack's muscles exploded against the restraints to no avail.

"Good. Good." Brendan smiled but he still leaned back. "I need you to help me today, Jack. Your anger issues will play a part in that." He lifted a syringe and held it to Jack's arm. Jack gritted his teeth as Brendan inserted the needle into his arm and pushed the plunger. "You ever do meth? This is the good stuff. I added a little extra kicker for you."

Jack felt his arm burn as the drug raced through his system. The door opened, and Missy pulled another stretcher in.

"Missy," Jack called out.

She turned her head, and the scowl on her face twisted into a sneer as she rolled the stretcher around. They had strapped Replacement to the gurney. The side of her face was red; blood trickled from her nose and the corner of her mouth.

"I'm going to kill you," Jack yelled.

"Not today, Jack." Brendan shook his head.

"You're a limp-wristed loser," Replacement spat. "If I wasn't Tasered, I would have kicked your teeth down your throat, and I'm going to rip Missy's fat face off."

"Screw you, you scrawny wench," Missy hissed before she turned to Brendan. "What happened to your arm?" She pointed at the bloodstain on his shirt.

"She bit me in the chem lab."

"What was she doing up there?" Missy demanded.

"She ran in there when I went to grab her. We have to clean it up after we're done tonight. She trashed it." Brendan glared at Replacement.

"Are you out of your mind?" Missy looked furious. "Everything in there is combustible. You'll blow this whole place up."

"Calm down. I got two batches of the stuff." Brendan held up two syringes. "I gave him one already."

Missy huffed. "Hold off on hers. It may be a long night."

"Now that everyone is here," Brendan leaned down, so his face was inches from Jack's, "let's get started."

"Wait. Right now everyone knows I'm watching you. Do you seriously think you can get away with this?"

"Yeah, I do. Tonight, both you and Alice will die."

"I'm a cop." Jack spoke calmly although his heart raced and his mind was clouded. "They'll come straight here." Jack tried to derail the scene that was unfolding. "They know I was investigating the psychology center. They know about Charlie Harding, Tiffany McAllister, and Michelle. It will lead them right to you. Get out now while you still can."

Brendan shrugged. "I know they'll come, but it won't matter." He placed his hand on the side of the large machine. "As for you and Alice…Missy wants to keep it simple and just have you disappear. To keep her happy, I could just cut you up and toss your bodies deep in the woods. I think a fire at your apartment building would be better. They'll find you and Alice in bed with some empty rum bottles and some drugs. The police will want to cover that up, and that's that."

Jack's head spun. "We have proof. It will lead them here."

"Proof? You met Dr. Franklin. He's my backup plan. With all the rumors about him using meth, a suicide note and his corpse would end any investigation. How do you think Bennie Mayer had Franklin's business card tucked into his shoe? That's why you came by today, right?"

Dammit.

"You think I fell for that?" Jack asked. "I know all about your research. That's what this is about, research? You're looking for the God Spot."

Brendan's eyes widened. He looked down at Jack and studied his face. "Impressive. You're correct. I'm almost there. I'll be the one who finds it. You think I want to wind up like Hahn and be the butt of everyone's joke? They'll all realize that Hahn was right, but I'll get the credit. Once I locate it, I'll shut everyone up. Do you have any idea the significance of finding it?"

"The God Spot doesn't exist." Replacement picked her head up as she spat and started to struggle. "You should take Dr. Melding's neuropsychology class, you moron."

The veins on Brendan's forehead bulged. "It is there. She's a fool. She always attacks Hahn but she's the imbecile. Did she say that? Did she say that in class?"

"Yeah. She said Dr. Hahn is a loser who wasted twenty years of his pathetic life. Any undergrad could poke a million holes in his theories."

Brendan cut off her shouted tirade by slapping her. "Silence," he commanded.

"I'm going to rip your heart out," Jack yelled.

"She's the fool, Alice." Brendan turned back to Jack. "Dr. Hahn is too merciful a man to do what needed to be done to get there. He's been looking for the God Spot but he used different emotions like hope and love to try to locate it; they didn't work. I found the key. Pain."

Replacement laughed. "If you think pain is the way to find God, then all you had to do is take your class. It was so *painfully* boring I prayed a piano would fall on my head. Or better yet, yours."

Brendan slapped her again.

"Stop." Missy's order was low and commanding.

"Better behave, Shrimpie." Replacement laughed, but Jack could see she was hurt. "That's what the girls in class call you. Did you know that? Did you *date one*?"

Brendan punched her in the face.

"Stop." Jack's body lifted off the stretcher as he screamed and strained against the restraints.

"Hit her again." Missy's voice crackled over the speaker as she glared out the control room window.

"Your boss hits like a girl." Replacement lifted her head and looked into the control room. Her eye started to swell shut.

"He's not my boss," Missy snapped and then smiled suggestively at Brendan.

"Ewww." Replacement's reaction wasn't taunting but honest disgust. "Brendan, you're banging Miss Piggy? That's gross."

Missy poured a stream of profanities over the speakers.

"Shut up," Brendan shouted. "As for you…" He grabbed a plastic bit and forced it between Replacement's teeth and silenced her.

CHAPTER THIRTY-NINE

You Are Sick

Brendan sat back down. "Now, where was I? Ah, the methods used to locate the God Spot. Dr. Hahn tried love, meditation, happiness, and then fear. None worked. I thought of pain. I know that Dr. Hahn thought my idea was credible but there are so many rules in science now about the methods you can employ. Human subjects were a necessity, but I had to pick ones who wouldn't be missed: drug addicts, prostitutes, and such."

"They're not subjects. They're human beings." Jack tried pulling the rail attached to his wrist up, but it held. "You're like that sick Nazi doctor. Mengele."

"Mengele understood it too. They're a means to an end. People like that are invisible. No one cared enough about them to even look. At least their lives were useful at the end, but their lifestyles deteriorated their minds. That made them inferior test subjects. Even though I gathered so much data, it was still flawed."

Replacement continued to struggle against her restraints.

"Then I looked into Dr. Franklin's research and found that meth enhanced the brain scans. I learned to make it in Dr. Franklin's class. That's another thing that's wrong with academia—doctors are too worried about their egos to work together. Some of Franklin's work is brilliant. I had to tweek the meth a little so it will cause pain. That's what I injected you with, Jack. It's a derivative of methamphetamine. It opens all the pain sensors in your system to make them even more receptive to pain impulses. That's the warm glow you're feeling right now. Soon you'll feel as if you're being roasted alive."

Jack's whole body felt as though it was smoldering.

That's what was in Michelle's system.

"Their research is why I came to this college. It was so easy. It only took me a year to go from Hahn's gopher to his protégé. He gave me the keys to the kingdom." He patted his security badge. "All I needed was subjects."

"How many?" Jack recoiled at the thought.

"Nearly a dozen. Because of the people we select, no one had actually looked for them before you. It's sad, really. If one disoriented dolphin swims into New York harbor, it's national news. Everyone rushes to save it and worries about its well-being. Yet, all of these people have disappeared, and all you hear is silence."

"Why Michelle? She didn't fit your pattern."

"No, Michelle was…unfortunate. I had no intention of using her for my study but she was too gifted with computers. She found a hidden file on our research."

Missy's voice crackled over the speaker. "She came back to find more information. Her mistake was being so trusting. She told me, so I told Brendan."

"We didn't think she had any living relatives, so I decided to include her in the experiment." Brendan shrugged. "There was a bonus, though. Her brain images were spectacular. C'est la vie." He smiled.

Jack screamed and thrashed against his bonds. Brendan looked backward, and Missy smiled as she looked at the readouts on the monitors.

"I didn't believe it when you showed up claiming to be her foster brother. I still thought our little ruse about Michelle transferring across the country would hold up."

"It would have if you just put the car in the lake," Missy chided.

Brendan shot her a look.

"I was a little nervous when you came snooping around, but after you sent the email to Missy, I felt we needed to act."

Replacement gasped.

"How's the leg?" Brendan's fist slammed into Jack's thigh and he screamed. "I'm sorry I didn't steal a bus to run you down with," he confessed.

Jack groaned.

"It's taking effect, I see." Brendan leaned in to examine Jack's eyes. "In some ways I'm glad you weren't killed instantly. Now I get to use you." He laughed.

Replacement thrashed against her bonds.

"Now, when we found out that Alice had come to our school, we welcomed her with open arms." Brendan leered at her. "We still needed a way to keep watch over you and wait for another time to remedy the situation."

"That's when Brendan hired a meth addict to keep an eye on you." Missy's voice was shrill, even over the speakers.

"Leave her out of this," Jack growled as the pain intensified.

"That was your mistake, Jack," Missy taunted. "You screwed up, bringing her along."

Replacement stopped struggling and stared at him. There was something in her look besides fear.

Hope. For some reason, she thinks I can do something still. She thinks I'm going to get her out of this. Stupid kid. I don't save the day. I got Chandler killed. I got you into this. Brendan knew we were coming. I'm no hero. I'm not even a good guy...

Jack's shame added to the burning in his body, and he groaned.

Now I've gotten her killed too.

CHAPTER FORTY

The Beast

"Let's get started." Jack was helpless to resist as Brendan taped Jack's eyes open, strapped his head in place, and then slipped a bit into his mouth.

"Did you check him for metal?" Missy joked.

Brendan positioned the gurney inside the fMRI scanner and slid it into the tube. Behind the glass was a video camera and monitor. Brendan used a remote control to angle the screen directly over Jack's face.

"You should be feeling quite a bit of discomfort now." Brendan reached in and squeezed Jack's upper arm again. This time it wasn't daggers; it felt like a chainsaw ripped into him.

"Good. You see, physical pain is quite effective. But for you, I think emotional pain will be far more efficient. Pain that hurts you at the core of your being—agony that crushes your heart and defeats your will." He turned toward Missy in the control room. "Put the imager up to full power."

Brendan walked around to the back of the machine. As he leaned down above Jack's head, he spoke. "I really hope you have some shrapnel embedded in you."

Jack struggled against his restraints.

Brendan headed to the safety of the control booth. The sound of a low buzz vibrated around Jack. Then the hum increased. He tried to calm his breathing, but his heart pounded louder than the roar of the machine as it whirled.

Brendan's voice echoed out over the speakers. "I had planned a tape of the battlefield to show you. I thought maybe reliving some of the horrors you saw in Iraq might help elicit that mental punishment, but then you gave me the perfect idea."

The monitor crackled, and a video played. It was of Michelle. Her eyes were taped open, and she was strapped to the stretcher. Her nose was bloody, and her cheek was swollen. She was terrified.

"Do you remember when you asked Dr. Hahn to see video footage of Michelle? You wanted to be a fly on the wall. Well, here's your chance."

"No." Jack attempted to break free from his head restraint, but all he could do was watch.

"Missy, please turn up the volume," Brendan ordered.

Jack heard Michelle pleading as she cried and begged, "Help me. Please!"

He lay there, powerless. Jack knew her cries for help would never be answered.

"Please stop." She wept. "Please."

Her mouth twitched and trembled. The memory of her when she was a little girl crying after she broke her leg ripped through him. She continued to plead for her life. She screamed as he heard something snap. Bile rose up in Jack's throat. He broke. He stopped struggling. He stopped fighting. Jack hadn't surrendered. He was defeated. All of his demons rose up inside him and tossed him into the void. He felt himself tumble down into the nothingness. No feeling. No pain. Nothing. He lay there with his eyes forced open but saw only the abyss. His mind had lowered an invisible curtain.

How long he stayed shrouded in the empty shifting mist, he didn't know. It enveloped him. A grayness swirled around him and, senseless, he hovered. The only thing he could tell was the vapor became darker. The murky gray haze transformed into ashen clouds.

Far away, he heard a sound. He wanted to continue his free fall into the vacuum and embrace death but from somewhere outside the ether, a voice called to him.

"Jack."

The mist began to vanish, and he could see the monitor.

It was Michelle's voice. She looked directly at the camera, straight at him, and called out his name.

"Jack," she called to him again.

"Jack," Replacement's voice echoed in the tube.

"Please," Michelle and Replacement called out at the same time. One voice in the here and now and the other from the tape, but their pleas blended together.

"The scrawny bitch is loose," Missy shrieked. "Brendan, you idiot. I told you to make sure she couldn't get out of the restraints."

Jack felt the stretcher being pulled out of the tube. Replacement tugged at the strap on his wrist.

As Replacement yanked on the restraint, Brendan rushed up behind her. He grabbed her around the waist and hoisted her into the air as her legs flailed wildly.

She twisted around in his arms, and her fingernails raked his face.

Brendan shrieked.

He dropped her, and she fell down against the stretcher.

"Punch her in the head," Missy screeched.

Replacement turned and tore at Jack's leg straps. She managed to pull the first part of the restraint out of the buckle. She flashed a brief smile before Brendan's fist slammed into the side of her face. The strike was so hard her head snapped around. Her body went limp, and she crumbled over Jack's legs. He looked down into her face. Her eyes were open, but they were black and dilated. Jack knew the vicious blow had knocked her out cold...or she was dead.

Brendan grabbed her limp body and pushed, dumping it on the floor.

"What're you doing?" Missy hissed. "Make sure she's dead."

Brendan looked toward the control booth. "Fine. We can't use her now anyway." He walked over to a cabinet, reached in, and took out a syringe.

Deep down inside, Jack knew he was a violent man. There had always been a beast inside him, wanting to break out of its cage. He feared it. He knew what it was: hate, pure and simple. He'd locked it away, but the monster didn't die; it grew. Finding Michelle that day had begun to release it. The hate remained just below the surface, semi-restrained inside its broken cage. Part of him wanted to close his eyes and run from the blackness that burned through his veins, but now Jack embraced the hate. He released the beast.

Jack yanked up, his chest muscles tightened, and he felt as though his ribs splintered apart. He was frothing at the mouth and biting the gag as he screamed. Spit flew upward into a red mist. Jack felt something on the gurney crack as he contorted his body. The burning from the drugs flowed even hotter through his veins, but he didn't feel the pain. He only felt the hate. He pulled his arms down tightly against the restraints, and his eyes rolled back in his head. His legs shot up as fast as they could, and he felt the gurney bend. Screaming, he pushed with everything he had.

Brendan walked over and stood next to the stretcher. "Go ahead and fight. You'll never break those straps." Brendan pushed the plunger of the syringe and a reddish liquid sprayed out. He walked around the gurney and began to lean down over Replacement.

Alice. Not her. Don't let her die.

Jack planted his heels and thrust with all his might. The restraints on his legs ripped free from the stretcher and pieces of molded resin flew through the air.

Brendan turned, and Jack kicked him squarely in the face. The force of the blow sent him back into the glass wall, and he fell to the floor.

Jack struggled to release his arms, but the restraints held them fast.

Brendan shook his head as he stood back up. He looked around for the syringe.

Jack roared in frustration and pulled against the wrist straps.

Brendan picked up the syringe from the floor. He sneered as he slowly approached Jack and raised the syringe in the air.

Jack twisted and angled his legs toward the oncoming attack.

Brendan chuckled.

"Get him, Jack!"

The familiar but unsteady voice came from below him. As he turned, he realized his restraints had been set free. Replacement slid out from underneath the stretcher. She held up two cotter pins in her trembling hand. Tears mixed with the blood on her face, but she still smiled up at him. "You want at him, boy? Go get him."

"He's loose. Kill him." Missy's shout echoed over the speakers.

Jack leapt to his feet, and Brendan stepped back, surprised by the sudden turn of events.

Jack staggered, and his vision blurred as he ripped the bit from his mouth and the tape off his eyes.

Brendan charged with the syringe held in front of him. Jack's left leg flashed out and smashed into the side of Brendan's hand. The syringe flew out, but Brendan's momentum kept him coming forward. Jack stepped to the right, and his elbow crashed into the side of Brendan's head. He grabbed Brendan by his collar and belt. Pulling him against his leg, he twisted his body and pivoted his hip. Brendan's feet went straight up, and Jack cried out in agony.

As Brendan reached the pinnacle of the flip, Jack slammed him down. Brendan hit with a sickening thump and his body went limp on impact.

"Jack," Replacement cried and pointed to the control room.

As Jack spun around, he saw Missy through the glass. She held his gun and pointed it straight at him. Her lips curled back in a triumphant snarl. Then she turned and aimed the gun at Replacement's chest.

Everything slowed. Jack stumbled sideways. He pushed off his rear foot; pain tore along his thigh as he ran forward.

He was too late. He saw the muzzle flash. Small flames flicked out of the barrel of the gun, and the recoil kicked it up and to the left. The glass in front of Missy spiderwebbed.

"Alice." Jack heard a high-pitched scream as he lunged forward and tackled Replacement. They crashed onto the floor and slid across the black tiles.

He jumped up and knelt over her. His hands frantically searched her body to look for the entry wound. Replacement gazed up at him in bewilderment and shook her head. She turned her palms upward. They stared in disbelief at the window. The round lodged in the thick glass; the bullet hadn't passed through.

Missy was screaming and holding her bloody hand.

Jack smirked. He knew what had happened. She had wrapped her fingers around his gun too high and the slide action had probably broken if not removed her thumb. Jack and Replacement got up and stumbled for the door. Jack attempted to turn the handle, but it was locked.

As he turned to look at Replacement, he saw her eyes go wide. "Jack!" He tried to move, but he wasn't fast enough. Brendan smashed into his back and slammed him up against the wall.

Brendan's fist caught him in the jaw, and Jack's head snapped to the side. He saw stars and his feet slipped. His left arm grabbed for the wall as Brendan's weight drove him to the ground. The back of Jack's head smashed into the floor, and his whole body shook.

Brendan knelt down on top of him and raised his fist.

Block.

Brendan punched right and then left. Jack's head whipped to the side with each blow. Jack knew what to do, but his body was not responding. Pain burned through every fiber of his body as the punches continued to rain down on him. A blow from the right split his lip open.

A loud twang rang out, and Brendon's eyes rolled back. Replacement stood triumphantly behind him with the stool clutched in her hands.

Jack screamed in pain as he pulled his hands up and then thrust them down.

Spear hands to the groin.

Brendan groaned and fell forward, his hands landing on either side of Jack's head. Jack reached up and grabbed the back of Brendan's hair in his left hand. He pulled down as he struck Brendan's jaw with his right hand. Jack's hands moving in opposite directions twisted Brendan's head with such brutal force that his neck snapped. Brendan's body fell forward like a marionette cut from its strings.

Jack shoved the body off him and despite the agony, he forced himself to sit up. He struggled to stand as each movement sent a wave of pain crashing over him. His hands violently trembled as he tore through Brendan's pockets. "Where's his pass?"

Suddenly, the whole room shook, and a muffled roar thundered from above. The lights flickered, and dust fell from the ceiling.

Jack looked to Replacement. "That was an explosion."

He turned toward the control booth and saw that Missy was also perplexed.

The second explosion was so loud and powerful it knocked Jack off his feet. Ceiling tiles fell to the ground, and the lights went on and off as a power surge raced through the building. Sprinklers hissed, but no water came out.

"Replacement?" He crawled to where she'd been.

"Jack?" He heard the panic in her voice.

Emergency lights flicked on. The small lights cast a strange glow around the room.

"What the hell happened?" Jack pulled himself to his feet and helped Replacement up.

"I may have done that..." She smiled sheepishly.

The large machine sped up and whirled faster and faster. The electrical wires and lights hanging down bent toward it, as even without power, the uncontrolled magnet continued its insatiable pull.

"We have to go," Replacement cried out.

Jack slipped his arm around her waist and moved for the door. He tried the handle. Even with the power cut, it still wouldn't turn.

"It's still locked."

"It's a keypad." Replacement ran to the wall and frantically punched in codes. "Four digits. I saw the first three." Replacement muttered as she kept typing and pulling the handle after each attempt. "Bingo."

The door swung open. Jack stepped back. Smoke was visible in the hallway.

"Wait!" Missy's muffled scream came from behind the glass. "Wait."

Jack looked back into the control booth. Missy pounded on the window.

"I can't get out. Something fell in front of the door. I'm trapped," Missy yelled.

Jack took one step toward her, and Replacement grabbed his arm. He could see that the explosion had bent the control room door out of its frame.

"You're going to get what you wanted, Missy. You wanted to find the God Spot? It looks like God has come looking for *you*."

"Please," Missy begged. "You have to help me. You're a policeman," she pleaded.

Thick black smoke drifted into the room.

Hate flooded Jack's heart as he glared at his torturer. Jack gritted his teeth, but then he grabbed the stool and rushed toward the control room. He slammed it against the window, but the glass didn't break. He groaned and swung the stool again.

The fMRI whirled louder and louder. A metal pipe blasted a hole behind Missy as it ripped through the wall.

Missy shrieked. "The shielding's broken. Please!" She screeched and ran into the corner of the control room.

Metal objects from the hallway flew through the air and slammed into the glass. The sound of twisting metal made them look toward the ceiling. The sprinkler system in the lab was plastic tubing, but in the building, it was metal pipes. All of that metal started pulling toward the colossal super magnet now that the explosion had cracked the shielding.

The whole wall cracked as the metal bent toward the machine. Missy's screams stopped as the ceiling in the control room collapsed in a deafening roar.

Jack grabbed Replacement and hurried through the door as they raced out into the hallway.

Holding each other up, they limped down the corridor. The smoke was already thick along the ceiling, and they walked hunched over. Jack was in agony with each step. Beneath his feet, the floor was moving.

Through the smoke, they could just make out an emergency exit sign and they stumbled toward it. There was a loud crash, and they were flung forward. Ceiling tiles and lighting strips rained down on them as the hallway behind disappeared into rubble.

"Jack, come on. Jack!"

Replacement's voice, and the need within it, gave Jack just enough strength to shrug off the debris that littered his shoulders and pull himself up. He staggered back onto his feet. Keeping low, he grabbed Replacement's hand and made a final dash for the exit sign.

They reached a stairwell that led up into the building.

"Here." He took off his shirt and ripped it in half. He handed half to her and put the other half over his face.

"We can't go up," Replacement cried as she looked up the staircase filled with thick black smoke.

"Over here." He led her around the staircase to the utility doorway at the bottom of the stairs.

The door opened to a narrow service corridor that had no emergency lighting. Blackness loomed in front of them.

"Follow me and don't let go."

He gripped Replacement's hand and started down into the darkness. The smoke burned his eyes, and his chest heaved with the effort of breathing. With his right hand, he felt his way along the corridor. The whole building continued to shake, and Jack could feel the dust raining down on them.

He reached his hand out and felt the cold touch of metal. He waved his hand around until he felt a handle.

A door.

They burst through the door, out into the night. Coughing, they staggered forward as glowing embers fell all around them. Broken glass and debris, flung outward from the explosion, crunched under their feet.

A light snow was falling and the flames engulfing the upper floors cast strange shadows on the trees. Stumbling, they climbed the small hill and found themselves at the corner of the parking lot.

Replacement reached out and took Jack's hand. He looked at her. The thoughts in his head swirled like the snowflakes that drifted around them. The rising flames drew his eyes back toward the building. Half of the psychology center had blown up, and the entire structure was now engulfed in flames.

They could feel the heat where they stood. He wasn't cold; his body still burned from the drugs. He looked back at the fire and once again realized his fate could have been quite different.

Replacement must have realized it too. She closed her eyes and whispered, "Thank you, God."

Jack pulled her close. The snow sparkled in her hair, and the fire reflected in her eyes. They held onto each other as they watched the large snowflakes fall to the ground.

Jack could hear the sirens approach in the distance. As they waited, he watched the snow create a veil of white on her hair and shoulders. He smiled. One of her eyes was swollen shut; her face was stained with soot, blood, and tears, but she smiled back.

"How did you do that?" He nodded toward the fire.

"Brendan chased me into the chem lab. I started trashing the place and mixing everything together, hoping it would set off the fire alarm. I didn't think…" With wide eyes, she gestured to the destroyed building.

Jack laughed so hard that tears ran down his face in spite of the pain. He looked down at Replacement, and his smile changed to a crooked grin as he shook his head.

"Only you, kid."

Replacement pushed him back and then pulled him even closer than before.

CHAPTER FORTY-ONE

I Got This One

The Impala cruised down the highway toward Fairfield. Replacement stretched her legs out onto the dashboard, and Jack winced. Her ankles were bruised from the restraints. Her jaw was swollen, and her eyes were black and blue. He frowned and looked forward.

He looked in the rearview mirror and caught a glimpse of himself.

I won't be winning any beauty contests, either.

"Replacement?"

"Yeah?" She turned her head to look at him.

"What's your favorite color?"

"What?" She wiggled around in her seat.

"What's your favorite color?" he repeated.

"Green."

"Green?"

"Green like my eyes." She perked right up. "What's yours?"

"Black, like my heart." He laughed.

"Seriously, what's your favorite color, Jack?"

"Pink."

"Hey. You're the one that started this." She crossed her arms.

"Fine. Red."

"Okay. I start next." She sat up and turned to look at him, clearly enjoying the game.

"What's your favorite movie?"

Jack smiled. "*Rocky.*"

"That boxing movie that you made me watch?" She rolled her eyes.

"It's a great movie. It won an Oscar." He saw her making a face. "Whatever. What's yours?"

She wrinkled her nose as she thought. "*The Wizard of Oz.*"

"The flying monkeys didn't freak you out?"

"I just like it." She sighed. "It's like my life."

"Your life?" Jack raised an eyebrow. "And who are you, Dorothy?"

"Yes." She impishly grinned. "You're in it too."

Jack sat up. "Me? Who am I? The Tin Man?"

"Nope." She shook her head.

"If you say the Cowardly Lion…" Jack scowled.

"Nope." She giggled.

"The Scarecrow?"

"No brain? A possibility but…nope." She hugged her legs to her chest.

"Who then?"

"Toto."

"The dog? I'm like the dog?" Jack looked at her in disbelief.

"Yeah. You're always running around, barking at me. You follow me everywhere but…you're loyal too."

"Seriously?"

"See. There you go getting yappy, but if I give you a pat on the head you're all loveable again."

Jack frowned.

"Why do you think I gave you that ringtone?" Her hands shot up.

"The stupid barking dog one? Because I remind you of Toto?"

She burst out laughing. Jack shook his head, but he still smiled.

Jack winced as he shifted his legs.

"Do you want me to drive?" she offered.

"No."

"Fine. Sport?"

"Baseball," Jack replied.

"Football," Replacement shot back. "Superhero?"

"Iron Man."

Replacement closed her eyes for a second. When she opened them, they glistened. "Batman."

Jack swallowed and looked at Replacement. He remembered how she thought Chandler was Superman, and he was Batman.

"Thank you for coming back." She smiled. "TV show?"

"*The Rifleman*."

"The what?" Replacement laughed.

They kept playing the game until they reached Fairfield. As they drove into the town, they both drifted off into their own private thoughts. The silence that followed ended the game, but not in a bad way.

Jack parked the car and looked at Replacement. Her eyebrows rose, and he understood the unspoken question. Jack started to get out of the car.

Replacement reached out and grabbed Jack's hand. "Do you want me to do it?"

"No, I got this one."

He looked down as he walked slowly. He stuffed his hands into his pockets and hunched his shoulders to avoid looking around. He was not looking forward to this, but he knew he had to do it himself. A few moments later, he stopped and stared at his feet, unable to look up.

"I'm sorry I'm late," he muttered. "I put off…coming to speak with you. I didn't want to…you know," he inhaled deeply, "but I need to tell you what happened. They caught the people responsible for Michelle's murder. It was this guy who worked at the psychology center with Michelle. It was him and Michelle's roommate. They're both dead. The sheriff's department is opening cases to look into the other people they murdered too. They'd been killing people for years and the victims' families should know what happened." Jack cleared his throat. "Replacement should get the credit. If it wasn't for her…"

He stopped talking. He wrung his hands together and waited. He was nervous when he heard nothing but silence.

Jack tried to keep going. "She's going to stay with me now. I'm going to get a two-bedroom apartment. My landlady already offered me the apartment below mine. She said the people moved out because the guy above them was too loud." Jack shrugged and faintly smiled. "That's me. Anyway…" He closed his eyes and exhaled. "I miss you. Both of you. I'll take care of Alice and Aunt Haddie. I promised her I'd stop by a lot."

He walked forward and placed a flag in front of the left side of the tombstone and flowers on the right.

Jack looked up and sighed. "I've been thinking about it. If it weren't for Replacement, no one would have known what happened to Michelle. More time would have gone by, and we might never have known. You can tell she's your sister. She has your courage, Chandler. You should have seen her at the Pit." Jack laughed. "Michelle, she said you taught her computers. She's quite good at them. Anyway, I see both of you in her."

Jack started to turn to go but stopped. "Thank you, for everything," he whispered. He closed his eyes. He could almost see them. Michelle was riding her bike, and Chandler ran alongside her. They both waved and smiled. Jack laughed and waved too.

He opened the door and sat back in the seat.

Replacement turned and looked up at him, hopeful. "How did it go?"

Jack gripped the steering wheel. "Good." His fingers tightened until the leather creaked, and then he relaxed his hand. "Are you ready, kid?"

Replacement grinned and rolled down her window.

"Ready." She smiled, and they headed down the road…together.

Epilogue

Replacement's hand covered the phone as she tried to muffle the beep. She held her breath as she peered back at the couch. Jack was still sleeping.

She bit her lip as her eyebrows knit together.

He hasn't slept the whole night through since the lab.

Jack moaned and rolled over again. She waited a minute until she was sure he hadn't woken up. She picked up the phone and checked the email that set it off. It wasn't her phone; it was Jack's. She tapped the display and the message opened.

Hi Jack,

Just checking in. Hope you're feeling better. I just read about your exploits in the paper. Like to get together sometime?

Marisa,

P.S. If you need any nursing, I give great sponge baths. ☺

"He doesn't need your nursing," Replacement muttered before she hit Delete.

She turned back to the computer and continued her hunt. Every night for the last few days, Jack had woken up screaming and covered in sweat. He wouldn't tell her what the nightmares were about, but she knew. She'd gone through his search history on the computer and saw what he was looking for—his mom.

As the case grew and the police found additional victims, he seemed to grow more and more restless. She wondered whether all the victims who were prostitutes had something to do with his angst.

Replacement had wanted to help, but she knew he'd say no, so she didn't tell him she'd started to search too. Every chance she had, she scoured through online records and hunted databases to look for clues.

She first found out that Jack's adoptive father had to hire a private detective to track down Jack's birth mother for the adoption. Reading through the court documents was frustrating because her name had been blacked out on every page. Replacement hit pay dirt when she discovered one page where the photocopy of the old records had bled through. His mother's name was Patricia Cole.

After that, Replacement followed her trail through the police database. The mug shots told her tale. Prostitution and drugs had worn down the beautiful woman into a shell of what she once was. Replacement had compiled the photos into a sort of face smash. They showed Patricia's descent into the void. It looked like one of those Scared Straight campaigns.

The arrest records stopped a few years ago. Replacement thought she might have died. It was as if she fell off the planet. Then she came across an address scribbled in the margins of the paperwork.

Replacement looked back at Jack and bit her lower lip.

How do I tell him?

He suddenly groaned and turned over.

She got up and walked to the window. As she stared out into the darkness, her resolve started to fade.

How do I tell him? Jack, your mom is alive but…she's institutionalized…

She exhaled.

And I think there's more…

Here's a preview of the next book in the Jack Stratton Collection:

JACK KNIFED

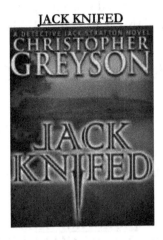

"Why do I keep doing this…thinking about her? It was so long ago, but I can't get what happened out of my head. I shouldn't let any of that junk define me, but I still do. I'm driving in circles, caught in some loop that I can't break out of. I want to know why she abandoned me…but some things, I guess, I'll never know…"

Constant nightmares have forced Jack to seek answers about his rough childhood and the dark secrets hidden there. With Replacement by his side, Jack travels to Hope Falls to solve a murder that occurred before he was born. Everyone in the small town remembers the unsolved murder of Steven Ritter, but after twenty-seven years, no one thought that someone would look into it. They don't know Jack.

A heartrending mystery-thriller about lost love, betrayal, and murder, Jack Knifed will keep you on the edge of your seat.

Available at **ChristopherGreyson.Com**

Acknowledgments

I would like to personally THANK YOU for taking the time to read this story. It was my goal to tell the story of Jack and Replacement and to take you along for the ride. I am so grateful for all the words of encouragement I have received. Thank you for spreading the word via social media on <u>Facebook</u> or <u>Twitter</u> and taking the time to go back and write a great review. Word-of-mouth is crucial for any author to succeed. If you enjoyed Girl Jacked, please consider letting others know; it would make all the difference and I would appreciate it very much. Your efforts give me the encouragement and time to keep writing. I can't thank YOU enough.

I would also like to thank my wife. She's the best wife, mother, and partner in crime any man could have. She is an invaluable content editor and I could not do this without her!

My thanks also go out to; My two awesome kids, my dear mother, my family, my fantastic editors: Faith Williams of The Atwater Group and Karen Lawson and Janet Hitchcock of The Proof is in the Reading, the unbelievably helpful Beta-Readers, and Stuart and Rachel.

About the Author

Since I was a little boy, I dreamt of what mystery was around the next corner, or quest lay over the hill. If I couldn't find an adventure, one usually found me, and now I weave those tales into my stories. I am blessed to have written the best-selling Jack Stratton mystery series. The collection includes "Girl Jacked," "Jack Knifed," "Jacks Are Wild," "Jack and the Giant Killer," and "Data Jack."

My background is an eclectic mix of degrees in theatre, communications, and computer science. Currently I reside in Massachusetts with my lovely wife and two fantastic children. My wife, <u>Katherine Greyson</u>, who is my chief content editor, is an author of her own romance series, "<u>Everyone Keeps Secrets</u>."

I love to hear from my readers. Please go to <u>ChristopherGreyson.com</u>. I plan in the next coming months to add free content, including side stories and vignettes involving the characters from the series. Please sign up for my mailing list and receive periodic updates on this and new book releases, plus be entered for prizes and free giveaways.

Thank you for reading my novels and I hope my stories have brightened your day.

Sincerely,

Christopher Greyson